ABOUT THE AUTHOR

Mandy Magro lives in Cairns, Far North Queensland, with her fiancé, Des, their daughter, Chloe Rose, and their two adorable pooches, Sophie and Sherlock. With pristine aqua-blue coastline in one direction and sweeping rural landscapes in the other, she describes her home as heaven on earth. A passionate woman and a romantic at heart, Mandy loves writing about soul-deep love, the Australian rural way of life, and the wonderful characters who call the country home.

Also by Mandy Magro

Rosalee Station
Jacaranda
Flame Tree Hill
Driftwood
Country at Heart
The Wildwood Sisters
Bluegrass Bend
Walking the Line
Along Country Roads
Moment of Truth
A Country Mile
Return to Rosalee Station
Secrets of Silvergum
Riverstone Ridge
The Stockman's Secret
Home Sweet Home
Savannah's Secret
Road to Rosalee
Back to the Country
Jillaroo from Jacaranda
One More Time

MANDY MAGRO

Gum Tree Gully

First Published 2023
First Australian Paperback Edition 2023
ISBN 9781867264613

Gum Tree Gully
© 2023 by Mandy Magro
Australian Copyright 2023
New Zealand Copyright 2023

Except for use in any review, the reproduction or utilisation of this work in whole or in part in any form by any electronic, mechanical or other means, now known or hereafter invented, including xerography, photocopying and recording, or in any information storage or retrieval system, is forbidden without the permission of the publisher.

This book is sold subject to the condition that it shall not, by way of trade or otherwise, be lent, resold, hired out or otherwise circulated without the prior consent of the publisher in any form of binding or cover other than that in which it is published and without a similar condition including this condition being imposed on the subsequent purchaser.

All rights reserved including the right of reproduction in whole or in part in any form.

This is a work of fiction. Names, characters, places, and incidents are either the product of the author's imagination or are used fictitiously, and any resemblance to actual persons, living or dead, business establishments, events, or locales is entirely coincidental.

Published by
HQ Fiction
An imprint of Harlequin Enterprises (Australia) Pty Limited (ABN 47 001 180 918),
a subsidiary of HarperCollins Publishers Australia Pty Limited (ABN 36 009 913 517)
Level 19, 201 Elizabeth St
SYDNEY NSW 2000
AUSTRALIA

® and TM (apart from those relating to FSC®) are trademarks of Harlequin Enterprises (Australia) Pty Limited or its corporate affiliates. Trademarks indicated with ® are registered in Australia, New Zealand and in other countries.

A catalogue record for this book is available from the National Library of Australia www.librariesaustralia.nla.gov.au

Printed and bound in Australia by McPherson's Printing Group

*For my beautiful forever friend, Rebecca Magro,
for lighting up my life, always, even in the
darkest of times. I treasure your friendship,
loyalty, and goddess spirit with all my heart.
Love you mate! Xx*

The glow of true love never dies, no matter how hard you try to extinguish the flame ...

There comes a point in everyone's life, when you're forced to stop and ask yourself the hard questions, and it's then you really start to wonder, if you'd done things differently: would your life have turned out any better? When it comes to the ways of love, there's not a single living person who could say they didn't have regrets, or harboured scars caused by bad judgment, hasty decisions or times of selfishness. Occasionally, it's all three – played out in the most cataclysmic of ways towards those you love most. And once you pull the trigger on the very person you'd take a bullet for, well ... losing your one true love is crushing, but what's worse is knowing you've gone and shattered their heart in the process. It's in these poignant moments we wish we could turn back the clock, and get one more time, one more chance, to make things right ...

CHAPTER 1

Gum Tree Gully, North Queensland, Australia

Midnight had come and gone. The new day was closing in. Way too quickly. Sitting on the lid of Connor Gunn's esky, Samantha Evans felt excitement rush through her as she thought about opening Gum Tree Gully's very first health-food shop and juice bar with her mum in just a month's time.

Sejuiced. That was the business name they'd registered and been approved to use. They'd been dreaming about it for years, and thanks to her dad taking on more shifts at the mine to fund the project, it was going to become their reality. Plan was, she and her mum were going to make a killing so her dad could eventually retire. Imagining how wonderful it was going to be to have her role model, hero and best mate home permanently, instead of away two weeks out of every month like he had been for most of her life, she threw back the last of her cheap bubbly, then plonked the empty bottle on the grass beside her. She was determined to work super hard and make her parents proud. This weekend was going to be her last hurrah of adolescent freedom. Monday would be her first day of becoming a responsible adult.

Looking to the star-studded sky, she wondered where her boyfriend had disappeared to. Maybe he'd crashed in his swag; it felt like hours since he'd said he was ducking off for a ciggie. She wished he'd give up. Even though it bugged the heck out of him, she kept on telling him smoking would kill him. Besides that, it stank and made his breath smell, and when she kissed him she could taste it. But telling Angus Gunn to do anything he didn't want to do was like pulling teeth. Wilfulness was an inherent trait of the Gunn bloodline, as was the country blood that ran through his veins. A fourth-generation stockman, he was still in his teens but already knew his calling. Samantha loved a man in jeans, boots and an Akubra, and Angus wore each one like they were custom made for him, with the swagger of a guy who lived in the saddle too. It was one of the many things that had attracted her to him in the first place, almost three years ago.

Squeezing her eyes closed, she sighed. If only they could move past the fact that she wasn't going to jump into bed with him until they were married, maybe they could happily move forward. He just seemed so preoccupied with sex, it was making her more and more uncomfortable – to the point where she was pulling back a little. And that was causing arguments. Heated ones that left her feeling empty and upset. Just thinking about it all now, about how his insistence on taking her virginity made her feel so pressured, the sheer emotional weight of it threatened to pop her happy bubble. If only Angus could be a little kinder, a little more considerate and a lot more selfless, like his twin brother Connor was. Like her father was. Then he'd come very close to being the whole package. Argh, a girl couldn't have everything though … could she? There'd always be something to cause waves and rifts when it came to a relationship. It was how two people dealt with such instances that made all the difference. Or at least that's what her wonderful mum had taught her.

She rolled her eyes at her ability to overthink everything lately – becoming a responsible adult was already exhausting. She didn't want to get trapped in that same old oppressive train of thought. Not tonight. So, rising to her feet, she took a moment to adjust to the slightly spinning earth before walking back towards her lifelong friends. Gum Tree Gully High's graduation afterparty had been a party to end all parties. The one they'd all been waiting for. Talking about since mid-year. Planning for since August. And she wanted to immerse herself back into the electric energy of it. Longneck bottles of beer had been clinked together countless times. The tower of empty rum and cola cans was growing. Their mobile phones had captured all the memorable moments so far. There had been many. And there'd be more to come. She was sure of it.

Raucous laughter echoing across the paddock caught her attention, as did the distant low of cattle and whinny of horses. Nearing where Connor, Shea and Jack were dancing their booties off, she chuckled as a bunch of larrikins raced past her, all five of them stark naked, their hands covering their dangly bits and the silvery moonlight igniting their lily-white butts. Man, how she wished she could stay within this night forever. Smiling to herself, she moseyed on, a little unsteady on her feet, but upwards and onwards all the same. Cheery faces shimmered and disappeared in the glow of the bonfires dotted around the paddock, and the bass of the subwoofers perched on the tray of Connor's LandCruiser sent Garth Brooks' 'Ain't Going Down ('Til the Sun Comes Up)' echoing through the cool night air, and rhythmic vibrations through the ground beneath her bare feet. Where her boots had ended up, she had no idea. Most likely in the same place as her hat. Pfft. She'd find everything in the morning, when she crawled from her swag to make her way home. That was if she ever got to sleep in the first place.

The song changed to the unmistakable voice of an Aussie legend. Skipping in beside her greatest friend in the whole wide world, Shea Davis, Samantha sang the lyrics to 'Rising Sun' by Cold Chisel at the top of her lungs. Grinning, Shea tossed an arm over her shoulder, while her other remained wrapped around her date, Jack Farley. The tall, lanky red-headed larrikin couldn't stop smiling like a lovesick fool – falling in love suited him, and Shea. After almost a year of flirting with each other, the pair had finally acknowledged they liked one another. Samantha couldn't be happier for them. She loved all there was to do with falling, and being, in love as much as she loved living in the country.

Spinning in dizzying circles, her hands clasped tightly in the reassuring grip of a guy that could possibly, one day in the future, become her brother-in-law, she tipped her head to the vast star-studded sky and squealed with delight as east, west, north and south became a kaleidoscope of sparkling colours. Conner chuckled beside her, his wholehearted laughter infectious. Never had she felt so alive, so free and so happy. This was what life was all about. Living in the moment. Being herself. Spending time with those she loved. The simple things. That's what mattered most. Lost in her blissful bubble with her dearest of friends, she was stopped dead in her tracks by a firm hand to her arm.

'What in the hell are you doing, Samantha.' Heated slurred words swirled, the speaker reeking of rum.

'Samantha, huh, sounds like I'm in trouble.' Chuckling, it took her a few moments to focus her blurry gaze on Angus. 'I wondered where you'd gotten to.' She prodded him playfully in the chest. 'I thought you might've fallen asleep, so your lovely brother here …' She thumbed over her shoulder. 'Has been taking very good care of me.' She hiccupped, and her stomach swirled the wrong way – maybe she shouldn't have drunk the entire bottle of bubbly.

'Yeah, of course he has.' Angus turned his steely gaze to his twin, now standing protectively at her side 'It's time to get out of here, Sam, right now,' he ordered, grabbing her wrist then half dragging her in the direction of his car.

'Sammie, no, he's had way too much to drink.' Shea raced after her and pushed her way in front of Angus, placing firm hands upon Samantha's shoulders. 'Please, stay here like we have planned, and Jack will drive us all home later in the morning, after the barbecue brekkie and a swim in the dam to sober us all up.'

Conner stepped in. 'Yeah, bro, Shea's right, you shouldn't be driving in your state.' Racing past Angus, and then reaching through the window of the hotted-up Commodore, Connor plucked the keys from where they dangled in the ignition.

'Just watch me,' Angus growled.

'You're not going anywhere if I've got anything to do with it.' Connor swung the keys in the air before shoving them deep into his jeans pocket. 'And neither are you, Samsung.'

Samantha smothered a chortle at Connor's use of her new nickname, all because she had a Samsung phone, and …

Raising a clenched fist, Angus fired an entire sentence of expletives at Conner.

Oh Lord, here they go again …

'Now come on you two, stop it.' She frowned and her hands went to her hips. 'You used to be best mates when you were kids, but all you seem to do lately is argue.'

Angus's stern gaze shot to her. 'Shut up, would you, and stay the hell out of this.' Folding his arms as tightly as his furrowed brows, he looked back to Connor and chuckled sarcastically. 'It's over my dead body that you're telling me, or her for that matter, what to do, little brother.' He held his hand out. 'Now give me my damn keys.'

Connor half-smirked. 'Or what?'

Angus grunted. 'Smug bastard, aren't ya.' Diving for his seventeen-minute-younger brother, he shoved Connor to the ground.

It was on for young and old as the two boys wrestled, rolling this way and that. Grunts and swear words echoed, and fists were brandished, then there was a full-on tussle, and a tug of war with the keys before Angus leapt triumphantly to his feet with the keys back in his possession.

'Samantha, get in the car, now, we're getting the hell out of here.' Angus's fierce tone made it clear he wasn't in the mood for any mucking about.

Not wanting the boys to end up in another punching match, Samantha remained as quiet as a mouse as she did as she was told and quickly climbed into the passenger seat of the car. She didn't want to be the one to upset the apple cart – there'd been too much of that lately, with Angus growing increasingly jealous of her friendship with his brother. It was odd, given the fact they'd all been mates since kindergarten. Her nerves now on tenterhooks, she jumped with fright when Shea rushed to the passenger side and knocked on her window.

Without the keys in the ignition, she couldn't wind it down. She held her hands up and made an 'I'm sorry' face. Shea placed both hands up against the window and begged her not to go.

'I have to,' Samantha replied.

'No, you don't,' Shea retorted.

Angus leapt behind the wheel and three willing passengers piled into the back seat. Unable to hold Shea's worried gaze any longer, Samantha looked away. Revving the muscle car to growling life, Angus spun the wheels in showcase fashion, to the cheers of some, but not all, of the partygoers. As they fishtailed away, Samantha turned in her seat, wishing she'd had the guts to tell Angus to get stuffed, and instead stayed with her friends. But it was too late now. As Shea, Jack and Connor's worried faces quickly faded in the taillights, she accepted her stupid decision and settled back with a suddenly heavy heart.

Tugging her seatbelt on, she made sure it was locked into place. This night wasn't fun at all anymore. In fact, it suddenly felt very *very* bad. Her gut reaction in that moment of clarity was to tell Angus to pull over so she could get out, but then she shoved the spine-chilling sensation off. She didn't want to upset him any more than he already was. She didn't want another argument – tonight was all about celebrating. She'd been working towards this moment for twelve long years and talking about their high-school graduation party for what felt like forever. And now, in the blink of an eye, it was almost over. But not just yet; there were still a few more hours before the sun would rise on the first day of the rest of her life. And she was going to do her best to relish every second until then. So, twisting in her seat so she could keep one eye on the road and the other on Angus, she tried to be her usual carefree self. After all, with almost every girl at Gum Tree Gully High vying for his attention this past year, she felt lucky he'd remained true to their relationship.

Raucous, drunken laughter of familiar yet unacquainted fellow teenagers filled the back seat and carried into the front, as did a joint. Taking a decent draw, Angus passed it clockwise. Shocked, Samantha declined – drugs weren't her thing at all, and neither had they been Angus's, until now. Or not that she had known of. It would be a conversation for tomorrow, when he'd sobered up. When *they'd* sobered up. Their breaths lingered in a cannabis cloud that twirled in lazy circles, and she tried her best not to breathe it in, but it was hard with all the windows up. She hoped she didn't reek of it when she arrived home – her dad would be livid, and she wouldn't blame him. Outside, the world spun in a phantasmagoria of colours and images, too many drinks now making her feel woozy. Or maybe it was the second-hand marijuana? Nausea abruptly gripped her. Tight. Her stomach cramped and swirled. Oh god. Was she about to throw up? Angus would kill her if she heaved her dinner all over the interior of his beloved car. Momentarily squeezing her eyes shut, she breathed through the queasiness as Angus tore around the snug curves of the outskirts of the small North Queensland township, sending the back end of the car sideways. One too many times.

Terrified for her life, she gripped the sides of her seat. She couldn't keep her mouth shut any longer. 'Angus, slow down, please.' Her plea fell on deaf ears. 'Angus!' But he wasn't listening to her.

He floored the accelerator as they hit the straight, and the rickety old bridge above the creek they all swam in during the scorching summer months rumbled beneath the hot rod. The inky darkness, broken only by the beam of the headlights, suddenly became suffocating. She breathed faster, shallower, then almost forgot to. Waylon and Johnny's honky-tonk voices boomed from the speakers, and the three travellers in the back sung the lyrics way out of tune, cans of rum and cola raised.

She was about to demand that Angus pull over so she could get out when her breath caught as a kangaroo shot out from the scrub and bounded across the road in front of them. She watched with wide eyes as it narrowly defied death. Swerving to miss the springing mass of muscle, Angus fought to stay between the white lines, all to congratulatory cheers from the back seat when he eventually regained control. But then headlights suddenly appeared over the hill and a male voice enthusiastically proclaimed a dare from the back seat. To Samantha's horror, Angus eagerly accepted the game of chicken with the oncoming car. Petrified, she begged him not to be so stupid, but he still wouldn't listen to her.

Then it all happened within a matter of seconds.

Time suspended.

She held her breath.

Her terrified gaze met the approaching, familiar-looking sedan.

It couldn't be?

Please god, no.

'Anguuuuus ...' Her cry resonated. 'Noooooooooo!'

The car swerved to the opposite side of the road, the V8 engine roaring like a wild beast when the accelerator was once again slammed to the floor. The oncoming car flashed its headlights to high beam. Once. Twice. The approaching driver pushed the horn intermittently, and then strongarmed it to an incessant blast that echoed through the night. The oncoming headlights grew bigger, brighter. Fast, way too fast. The jovial atmosphere cracked and crumbled. Fear sliced through the air. Sharp. Intense. Headlights met. Blinded. People cried out, screamed. Angus lost control and in a moment of grace that defied the imminent tragedy, the tyres no longer gripped the road and the hot-rod spun in dizzying circles. Samantha clung to what she could, preparing herself for the inescapable as Angus fought with the steering wheel.

Seconds felt like hours.

With nowhere else to go, the oncoming car veered onto the gravel bank. Connecting with the guardrail, it trailed sparks before catapulting through the air, flipping three times and coming to rest in an open paddock on its roof, tyres still spinning. A millisecond later the hot-rod slammed into one of the towering paperbark trees with a horrendous grinding crunch, wrapping itself around the trunk as if moulded for it, the twisted metal ripping the bark open like flesh. A body flew through the windscreen and landed in a mass of blood and shattered limbs. A vast empty space now sat where the star-studded sky used to be.

And other than Waylon and Johnny's voices, there was spine-chilling silence.

CHAPTER 2

London – 11 years later

Once upon a time, in another time, another place, Samantha Evans had believed in happily-ever-afters. Untroubled by what might lie ahead of her, she'd roamed and ridden the endless stretches of sun-baked land beneath a wide Aussie outback sky, her soul as wild as her chaotic hair, and her spirit as free as the wind. But in the blink of an eye, her entire world had been flipped on its head. She'd been left behind by almost everyone she held dear, and been left questioning her threadbare existence to the point of collapse. Her very right to walk the earth felt immoral. Everything changed, everyone looked at her differently. Every moment, every breath, hurt. In a matter of days, she lost the will to eat, to laugh, to live, and she all but gave up on ever feeling joy or peace or hopefulness again.

But then, in that impulsive, breathless moment, beneath the star-studded sky, *he'd* gone and sparked something inside of her. Like a match meeting red phosphorus, the volatility of his touch had ignited a part of herself where she hadn't felt ready to feel such vivacious life. And she wasn't sure she ever would again because she truly believed she didn't have the right to. That, him, the thought of there being a *them*, had terrified her. So she did all she was capable of at that point in her life and ran as fast and as far as she could, and never dared look back. For damn good reason. *He* was someone she could never go to that special place with. Not again. No matter how much she had wanted to remain there for the reprieve his kisses and caresses gave from her heartbreak. Because it was wrong of her. And of him. So wrong she hadn't told another soul. Not even Shea knew she had lost her virginity that night, to Angus's brother. She'd been too ashamed to speak of it at the time. And as time passed, she'd allowed herself to pretend it had never happened in the first place, so telling Shea would just bring it all flooding back. In the grand scheme of things, her escape strategy had worked, had in some way numbed the pain by hiding it way down deep, beneath the fractured pieces of herself so she could function in a somewhat normal way, so she could move on. Or at least pretend to. Fake it till you make it, and all that.

But now, finding herself frozen to the spot, with her heart beating in her throat and her reading glasses perched on her freckle-dusted nose, Samantha stared at the text message until the words went blurry with tears. What was Shea thinking? Did her dear friend really believe she had the strength to be able to go back to the very place she'd run from? Her shaky hand instinctively went to the beginning of the scar that snaked its way from her collarbone, down her chest and beneath her left breast as the ground almost gave way beneath her stilettoes. Slowly shaking her head, she only stopped her knees from buckling by resting her hip against her desk. Looking out at the cityscape view, she reminded herself to breathe in. Hold for the count of four. Then breathe out. Slowly. Measuredly. Methodically. It gave her back a sense of control and calm. Then, and only then, having gathered what bits of herself she could, she blinked faster and brought Shea's words back into focus.

Hey Sammie, I've tried calling you a couple of times this week and left a few voice messages for you to get back to me, too. What's going on girlfriend? I hope you're okay? I didn't want to do this in a text, but, seeing as I can't get a hold of you, and I'm running out of time, here goes! ☺ Jack and I have decided to have a shotgun wedding, in four weeks' time, and I want you to be my maid of honour! I know it will be a huge step for you, coming back here, but maybe it's time to take that leap of faith? I know you're ready, you just have to believe it yourself, my beautiful friend. We can do this together. I promise. Love you heaps. Xx

Realising she was holding her breath, again, Samantha inhaled sharply. As selfish as she knew it was, she'd been dreading this day since Shea and Jack had announced their engagement, but hadn't expected it to be so, for lack of a better word, *impulsive*. She'd hoped – since the pair had been together since they were teenagers, and engaged for the past seven years, with a five-year-old to contend with – they might have decided to elope. Just like she and Benjamin had. Or at the very least, go to the local registry office. Anything but have a big shindig. In Gum Tree Gully of all places. Oh. My. Goodness. Breathe in. Hold. Breath out.

Get a hold of yourself, Evans …

She hated herself for feeling like this, when her soul ached to be beside her best friend on her special day. Because she loved and missed Shea like crazy. Being asked to be an integral part of the bridal party was such an honour, and any normal human being would be excited, but for Samantha, she wasn't *normal*, and it wasn't that simple. Nothing in her life had ever been. Saying yes would mean returning to the one place she'd avoided for over a decade. Hence the reason Shea and Jack had taken four trips to London and then any holidays they could all swing anywhere in the world but Australia. She knew Shea had done her fair share of keeping in touch, of showing how much she cared. Samantha also knew that saying no would hurt her best friend beyond belief. Of that, she was certain. And she couldn't, wouldn't, blame her.

She was a few months shy of turning thirty, and she'd learnt the hard way that leaving her heartbreaking past behind was an impossible task. No matter how fast she ran, or how far, no matter what or who she tried to barricade herself behind, the shadows were always there, lurking at the next obscure corner to taunt her all over again, ready to drag her under to that deep dark place she might one day never be able to climb out of. That frightened her. And now, on top of having to think about possibly returning to Gum Tree Gully, it made matters worse that her present situation right here was slapping her hard and sharp in the face and heart, too. Nothing was going to plan. Maybe she deserved it. Was this her comeuppance? Why should she be able to live her life to the full, when so many had theirs taken away that horrific night?

The memories of the crash came at her. Full force. She sunk to her office chair before she crumpled to the floor. The screams, the crunching of metal, it was like it had happened yesterday. Her aching heart slipped further with the grim recollections. If only she could call on her parents. They'd love the hurt right out of her and guide her in the right direction. Just like they always had when she was a child. God rest their souls.

Fighting off a fresh batch of grief, she fiercely wiped the tears from her cheeks. She'd had enough of crying. She'd wept oceans since the accident. But now Shea needed her. Therefore, she had to find a way to be there for her best friend. Big girl pants and boots were in order.

Not that she'd worn a pair of boots for over ten years. She'd actually made a conscious effort not to. The country girl was long gone, left in the dust of Gum Tree Gully, only to be replaced with a stylish citified version of herself. One she'd tirelessly pretended had a clean slate, a fresh start, a second chance. But now, as she dealt with her husband and his sordid affair, along with his hard-hearted approach to their separation, it felt as if her concerted efforts to make a happy life for herself were going up in smoke. What a fool she'd been to believe that living in another part of the world would give her the miracle of becoming a brand-new person with a brand-new life. As a haunted eighteen-year-old girl, she'd told everyone who'd listen that coming here had been all about a journey of self-discovery and healing. Who'd she been trying to fool? It was plain as day that it was, in fact, herself. Nothing, and nobody, was ever going to be able to heal this kind of engrained hurt out of her. She knew that now.

Hindsight could be a real pain in the … heart.

Sucking in another short, sharp breath, she stood, squared her shoulders and firmly told herself for the umpteenth time this past six months that she was a successful, independent, in-control, and, in her firm opinion, very-low maintenance woman, even though her soon-to-officially-be-ex-husband liked to tell her otherwise. Just because she like to be loved with passion didn't make her high maintenance, or did it? Man oh man, she was sick of second-guessing herself. As a highly sought-after risk analyst, she should know better than to do so. But as with most things in life, it was easier said than done. She could hand out logical advice to her clients, but to heed it was another thing altogether.

Closing her eyes, she began to pace back and forth as she silently lectured herself …

Don't sit in idle thought for too long. Work hard. Then work harder still. Carbs are evil. Keep moving forward. Get some decent sleep. A bottle of wine won't fix the problem. Focus on the future. Let go of the past … yadda yadda yadda

When the blaring of a car horn rudely interrupted her thoughts, she slumped back into her leather office chair and with one high-heeled foot propelling her, began slowly spinning in circles. Resting her head back, she stared at the ornate ceiling that was older than any building in Australia, as the hollow ache in her chest reminded her just how much she'd lost. How was she ever going to discover the true core of the woman she was when, beneath her cool, calm, collected exterior, she was still a lost, broken, anxious teenage girl? Feeling as if she were tumbleweed – or hairy panic grass, to speak her native Aussie lingo – at the mercy of the ever-changing winds of life, she'd found herself asking this confronting question frequently of late. Not long ago, she'd thought she'd found everything she needed in her life to feel somewhat happy, somewhat content, somewhat fulfilled. She'd even begun to humour the thought of giving up her career to have the children she so longed for. The children she'd believed Benjamin had longed for. She anticipated that a baby would fill the void that lingered within their marriage.

Pfft.

Yeah right.

And pigs flew too.

There was no way anything she did would've made their marriage complete.

Not with Benjamin's lies rotting the core of their nuptial vows – to love and to cherish.

What-the-hell-ever!

With her track record she might as well give up on love entirely.

As much as she wanted to find *her* person, the one she could live to a ripe old age with, she now had so much baggage packed into her tortured heart it would be almost impossible to unload it all, let alone have room within it to harbour love for another. So maybe she needed to give up the hope of ever having a family to call her own. Or perhaps she should give up on the notion of meeting a man who truly loved her, and instead go down the route of a donor father? Why not? So many women did it. Then again, perhaps she needed to stop pondering all of this, before she drove herself nuts.

But with her maternal clock ticking, it was terribly hard not to …

Groaning, she heaved a weary sigh as she spun her office chair faster. As a teenager, all she'd ever wanted was to eventually settle down, buy a chocolate-box house, name some pets and start a family. Then, with the snap of fate's ill-omened fingers, that childhood dream was snatched away from her, as were her parents, in tragic circumstances. Now, with only a few months until her thirtieth birthday, alone, childless and about to officially become a divorcee, she no longer believed in destiny, or cosmic plans, or fate, or soulmates, or wishes coming true, even if she'd once believed in the magic of wishing upon a star. She'd once been a dreamer, in another life lived far away from here, but not anymore. The accident, the catalyst that had forced her to shed her skin and move across the oceans, to become someone her past self would barely recognise, had also set her on the career path to becoming a successful risk analyst. And now she was a realist, a woman who believed that magical thinking was just the way people tried to make sense of what was, most of the time, a chaotic and ever-changing world.

Beginning to feel dizzy, she skidded the spinning chair to a stop, then once the room stopping twirling, kicked off her heels and rose to her feet. She may have become a realist, but never in a million years would she have thought she'd be on this treacherous trail of heartbreak again. It was like some cruel joke. After all the self-searching, all the counselling, she'd finally found the courage to allow her heart to be vulnerable to another again. And Benjamin had been so steady, so reliable, so sweet, so sure. She'd sincerely believed her heart had found its forever home in his. But now, she felt as if she were a character in what had once been her favourite sitcom, *Grace and Frankie*. Having trained herself to become prim and proper, with a fondness for dry martinis, she'd once likened herself to Grace's respectable character, although, beneath her façade, she knew she was a lot more like the wild and free Frankie. And now she knew the truth, she understood why Benjamin had insisted on watching the show religiously. It was as if he'd been trying to tell her via the television that just like Grace's husband, he was in love with, and loved by, a man: her friend Jane's husband, Harry Holland. And had been for just over half their married life.

Never would she have believed it if someone had told her. She'd had to see it for herself.

And now, as much as she wanted to, she couldn't unsee it.

The images of the two men, wrapped up in each other's arms, sleeping soundly in *her* marital bed after exhausting one another, were on continuous loop every single time her head hit the pillow at night. It was no wonder she barely slept. The fact that Benjamin had kept it secret from her had hurt her way more than the truth about his feelings. Lying was the epitome of disrespect, the root of all evil. Recalling how devastated, overwhelmed and raw she'd felt in that confounding moment, when she'd returned home for a very rare lunch break and walked in on Benjamin making use of their bed without her, she shook her head sadly. Up until that pivotal point in time, she'd been blind to her husband's ways. But from that second on, at the very least, she'd learnt the cold hard truth of her failing marriage in blinding clarity. No longer did she need to blame herself. No longer did she need to try so hard to bring happiness into their days. They were done. Dusted. Finished. Ruined. Just like the version of herself she'd left behind in Gum Tree Gully. Thank goodness she'd chosen to keep her last name out of respect for her father – she was the only one left living in their family – so she didn't have to go through the rigmarole of having to change it back.

Losing herself once again in hurtful thoughts, she mentally slapped herself. She needed to get a grip. She needed to focus on what she had control over. She might have lost so much, but the one thing she did still have was the ability to make a choice – although making one was far easier said than done. Shea. Maid of honour. Could she pluck up the courage to go back to the very place that had sent her running eleven years ago? Could she handle seeing Connor again? There wasn't a doubt in her mind that he'd be Jack's best man, because from what Shea told her, he and Jack were the closest of mates. Did she really have a choice, given the circumstances?

And there it was: even her power to make *that* choice was limited.

She did her best to think logically. In the risk analysis world, timing was everything, and now wasn't the time to be traipsing halfway across the world. But would it ever be the right time to go back to the place that had changed her forever? A place where she'd have to gather the courage to stand at the graves a second time round, and finally admit to herself they were long gone. She had to find a way. Because how could she even consider not packing her bags, getting on that sardine can for two long hauls across the oceans and being the maid of honour at Shea and Jack's wedding? What kind of friend would that make her, if she made the self-centred decision to stay put? It would one hundred percent make her the worst friend ever. After all her losses, she didn't want to risk losing Shea, too.

Not only would making the trip mean paying a long overdue visit her parents' final resting place.

She would also have to face the subject of Connor Gunn.

Could they ever move past what they'd done to try and ease the anguish?

Shadows began to stretch across the office and sirens echoed in the growing twilight, as the sounds of the high-street traffic travelled up to her office. After slipping her reading glasses off, she rubbed the ache in her temples, heaved what felt like the hundredth weighty sigh for the day and then wandered over to the window. Gazing out into the dark afternoon, she watched drifting snowflakes highlighted by the streetlights. And for that tiny moment, lost in a trance, she almost allowed herself to believe in that same old magic. Nearly said hi to her old self. But then she firmly reminded herself she was being ridiculous. As her last client for the day had cancelled, five minutes after they were meant to arrive – tardiness was a pet peeve of hers – she decided to take a rare early Friday knock-off. As cold as it was out there, a jog would be just what the doctor ordered to help blow out some of her internal cobwebs.

So, before she changed her mind and opted for her usual Friday night with Netflix, a takeaway, chocolates, a blanket and a bottle of red, or two, to keep her company, she grabbed her runners from where she'd tossed them into her storeroom two weeks earlier. From her closet in the staff-only bathroom, she retrieved the set of thermal gym clothes she always kept there, for such random moments, and after slithering out of her tailored suit, slipped the gym gear on. Pausing to look in the mirror, she grimaced at the dark rings beneath her green eyes. Good grief, she really needed to try and get some rest; if only the sleeping tablets her doctor prescribed her did the trick. Tugging her long dark hair up and into a ponytail, she tried to force a smile she was far from feeling, but instead looked like she was constipated. And that enticed a genuine chuckle. At least she could still laugh at herself – that had to count for something.

She slapped her laptop closed, flicked the lights off, then strode from the office with a click of the door behind her, down the hallway and to the elevator. Jabbing the button, she impatiently waited for it to arrive. Ding! She stepped in, and to her frustration, just as the doors were about to close, they slid open again, and in stepped the one person in the world she wouldn't want to share a lift with.

Benjamin caught her eye, and grimaced. 'I'll catch the next one.'

'No, you don't have to do that, Benjamin.' Stepping aside, she forced herself to be the bigger person and made way for him. 'There's plenty of room for both of us.'

The lift doors closed and as it descended, so did an uncomfortable silence. There was so much Samantha wanted to say to him, but as he was refusing to be fair about the separation of their assets and bank accounts, none of it was overly nice, so she clamped her lips firmly shut. They'd handpicked office spaces on the same floor as a newly married couple, and while sharing the same office tower was now not ideal, neither of them was going to move their business elsewhere – and nor should they need to, she thought. They were both professional adults. Well, he was. Right this second, she wanted to stomp her feet and scream at him like an insubordinate child.

Turning to her, Benjamin didn't bother covering up that he was studying her.

Her hackles rose. 'What?'

'You look tired, Samantha.'

She crossed her arms and lifting her chin, levelled her gaze with his. 'That's because I am tired, Benjamin.' She wanted to add, *because you're being an arse*, but didn't.

'Well then, why don't you take some time off?' His gym-buff shoulders lifted in a casual shrug. 'It's not like you have to ask a boss for holidays.'

'Thanks for the advice, but I don't need it from the likes of you.' Her tone was icy cold.

He pulled a 'whatever' face and shrugged again.

It made her blood boil. 'I'm planning to head back to Australia for a little holiday soon.' She'd spoken before thinking, and instantly regretted doing so. Benjamin knew more than anyone just how much she didn't want to go back there. Ever.

'Is that so?' He eyed her dubiously.

'Yes, it is.' She mimicked the shrug he'd just given her. 'Shea and Jack are getting married, and she's asked me to be her maid of honour, so it's the perfect time to go back.'

He took a long moment to reply. 'As long as you're sure, I'm glad to hear it, because finally crossing that bridge will do you the world of good.'

'I know it will, which is why I'm going.' She couldn't help the sharpness of her reply. 'Not that I need you to remind me of the fact.'

The strained look on Benjamin's face conveyed that he clearly knew he was treading dangerous waters. He offered her a tight smile, and said 'You're right, Samantha, I shouldn't have offered my opinion when it wasn't asked for.' Then he looked back towards the doors as if counting down the seconds until they opened.

Samantha bit her trembling bottom lip as they both fell silent once more. It felt so strange, standing beside him but worlds apart, like meeting in the lift was the extent of their relationship. Her ten-year relationship with him flashed through her mind, as if on fast forward. Long story short: she'd fallen for him as a nineteen-year-old, hook line and sinker, had married him a year later and had dreamt of one day having his babies ever since they'd tied the knot. But he'd gone and proved to her that dreams were overrated. So too was love, and marriage, and everything that went with it.

Ding! Destination reached. The door slid open.

'Enjoy your run,' he said, stepping away.

'Will do,' she replied. 'Say hi to Harold, won't you.' Even though the husband-stealer was known as Harry, she simply couldn't help using his formal name.

'Will do,' he called back before disappearing out the revolving doorway and into the busy London high street.

Samantha followed his familiar aftershave-laden trail, the scent of it bittersweet. Stepping outside was like a slap to her face with an icy hand. Knowing she needed to run the chill off before it seeped into her bones, she started jogging at an easy pace along the crowded pathway, past rows of cafés and restaurants. At first, the frigid air stung her lungs, but a block and a half later and she was attuned to the wintry evening. Inhaling the fresh air deeper and deeper, she gradually felt it invigorating her stagnant insides. This had been exactly what she'd needed. And it was something she needed to do more often.

Slowing her pace as she come to an intersection, she jogged on the spot as she waited for the lights to change. Controlled chaos was all around her: bumper-to-bumper traffic, honking horns, hordes of people making their way with determined strides, their eyes directed downwards and brows creased. It was rare to see people acknowledge another, rarer still to catch another person's gaze. Unlike the place she'd once called home, if she dared say hello to a passer-by in the street here, they'd most likely think she'd lost her marbles.

Turning to her left as she jogged in place, she spotted a familiar face in the crowd. Her heart stammered then galloped wildly. Their gazes clashed, darted and then clashed again, for just a breath. Samantha almost waved, and a big part of her wanted to go on over and wrap the woman in a hug, but then she stopped herself.

Jane Holland had slipped off the face of the earth when the news of their husbands' affair had become common knowledge. After myriad one-sided texts, unanswered calls and ignored voice messages, Samantha had gotten the gist, loudly, that Jane didn't want anything to do with her. It was as if she blamed Samantha for her husband cheating with Benjamin. Samantha was saddened by the fact. Deeply. A woman she'd once thought of as her closest friend in London was now looking anywhere other than in her direction. And when the pedestrian chime sounded, and the crowd pressed forward, Jane took off like a bull at a gate, clearly flustered and in one hell of a rush to get as far away from her as possible.

Well, Samantha thought with a stiff upper lip, *stuff her, and the horse she rode in on. I'm done playing nice with people that don't give two hoots about how I'm coping.*

It made her miss Shea even more. Her best friend had always cared. Immensely.

And that's when it really hit her. She had to go back for the wedding. She owed it to the only true friend she'd ever had. She wouldn't be able to live with herself if she didn't. And she couldn't deny how much she needed a break, especially one taken back in the far-reaching countryside, with so much room to breathe, to be, and hopefully to set herself free. But she hadn't told Shea about her marriage breakdown. Hadn't known how to without her friend jumping on the first plane to comfort her, and she didn't want to put that on her. Shea had a life to live. A wonderful man to love. A child to dote on and raise. She had all Samantha had ever wanted, and more. And she couldn't be any happier for her.

If only she could say the same of herself.

After jogging for another forty-five minutes, then returning to the office to collect her things, she left Piccadilly Circus behind her and skilfully navigated the London Tube. It was close to eight when she slipped her key into her apartment lock, and wearily stepped within the darkness. Flicking the light switch, she tossed her bag to the lounge chair and padded towards the kitchen, hoping to goodness there was something edible in her fridge, and a bottle of wine she was yet to miraculously discover. Half an hour later, showered and in her pyjamas, she was opening the door to her usual Japanese food delivery guy.

'Thanks, Haru.' She gave him a ten-pound tip.

'You're very welcome, Samantha.' He stepped back and gave her a wave. 'See you next week …' He paused, grinning. '… Or maybe tomorrow night for some teriyaki chicken?'

'Ha, maybe. Have a good evening,' she said, closing the door.

The fact that her deliveryman knew her weekend menu picks was dismal.

That's when she decided. From this moment on, all that was going to change. It was time for her to gather the courage to face the ghosts of her past, so she could step forward, into a fresh start, a new kind of life, one where she wrote the story, and turned the pages when she was good and ready, and certainly one where she controlled the ending. So she picked up the phone, dialled Shea's number, and in a conversation that took two and a half hours, told her bestie everything – except what had happened between her and Connor all those years ago.

Two weeks later, strapped into her first-class seat, Samantha drew in a big breath as the whine of the jet engines increased, and the Boeing 787 charged down the Heathrow airport runway. Her stomach lifted with the plane as it catapulted towards the sky. It was only once they were thousands of feet in the air that she pondered whether she might have just made the biggest mistake of her life in going back to Far North Queensland – or was it going to be for the better?

CHAPTER 3

Gunn Station, Gum Tree Gully

His headlights caught an incoming kangaroo just in the nick of time, and Connor Gunn swerved to miss it. Fast asleep in the passenger seat, his mother stirred but didn't wake. Another near miss to add to his repertoire.

Early on, life had taught Connor that nothing was guaranteed. He'd learnt the hard way that if the hands of fate wanted to take you out, nothing would stop the inevitable. Under the cruellest of circumstances, he'd been forced to understand that no matter what, his days were numbered. Of this, he was certain. Just like anything with a heartbeat, he had a predestined end date. He had no say in the matter. So, armed with this knowledge as a nineteen-year-old with a who-gives-an-F attitude – and a chip on his shoulder so heavy he couldn't see past it – he'd done everything in his power to test fate, at the same time trying to somehow shake the haunting memories of losing his twin brother. Then, way too soon after that, he'd lost the love of his life – the beautiful, mesmerising, incredible Samantha Evans. And even though they'd shared the most intimate, the sweetest, of nights together, she hadn't even bothered to say goodbye. Just vanished into thin air, like he hadn't mattered to her at all. Still to this day, he longed for an answer as to why. Was it because she felt nothing for him? Or was it because she'd felt too much?

Maybe, possibly, he was about to get the answer he longed for.

A broken young man, after Samantha left he'd joined the rodeo circuit and ridden the meanest bulls, daring every one-tonne beast to end his insufferable life. When that hadn't worked, he'd partied hard, then harder still; he'd taken risks where most wouldn't; he'd picked bar fights, and been locked up for a month because of it; hell, he'd even tried the no-ties one-night hook-ups, which had only left him feeling emptier and emptier. Then, when his father suddenly died from prostate cancer, Connor found himself landing the position of the only Gunn male left on earth, and he'd pulled himself into line, for his mother's sake – she'd already lost a son, and her husband. He'd had to step up to the plate and work hard, play none. Seven days a week. Three hundred and sixty-five days a year.

After that he'd tried the whole relationship malarkey, had even thought about asking the girl to marry him, but before he'd gotten the chance, that had gone belly up too. Good thing it had, because looking back he could see she didn't love him, and even though he'd cared for her immensely, he hadn't loved her either. Turning all his focus to running the family property had been his saving grace. And just when he thought he had a tight grip on the reins of his life, just when he wanted to live it to the fullest, the hands of fate had decided to throw him another curveball in the form of Samantha Evans. And the outcome was totally out of his hands.

God only knew what it was going to be.

Literally.

For now, he was hell-bent on taking his best man duties seriously, but it was going to be tough, given the fact he'd be partnered with the one woman he'd never been able to get out of his system. He still couldn't believe she'd agreed to come back here, after avoiding the place for so long. It had stung, the way she'd left so suddenly. But then what had he expected after everything they, and she, had gone through? How could they have ever gotten married, had kids and lived happily ever after? The problem wasn't only that Samantha had been his brother's girlfriend.

It was also that he'd kept something hidden from her.

Deep in his heart of hearts, he knew he'd never be able to spend a lifetime with her without revealing the part he'd so innocently played in that horrific night. It was a cross he bore silently, but the guilt over his decision sometimes threatened to crush him. Therein lay the problem. A relationship built on a foundation of lies would never work – if he kept it from her, he wouldn't be able to live with himself, but if he told her the truth, she would likely never be able to forgive him. A vicious circle. Catch-22. He'd chosen to keep it from her, and he had to live with the repercussions of that. There was no use feeling sorry for himself.

Slowing as he approached the first set of traffic lights he'd seen in hours, he heaved a weighty sigh as he pulled to a stop. Frustratingly, he once again found himself wondering what it was going to be like laying eyes on her after all this time. Would they leave what they'd done behind? Could they? He knew she'd have an easier time with it than he would. He'd been invested emotionally. She very clearly hadn't. But how could he hold that against her? They'd both lost loved ones in the car accident. His brother had been the lawbreaker, and her parents had been Angus's unsuspecting victims in his reckless game of chicken. How Samantha had moved past losing not only her boyfriend, but both her mother and father in an accident that could have quite easily been avoided, had his brother not been so careless, was beyond his comprehension. Yes, he'd lost a piece of himself that night too, but not as much as Samantha had.

He and Angus may not have seen eye to eye, but that didn't mean Connor didn't love his brother. Being measured up, challenged and judged by Angus in absolutely everything they did as children had worn extremely thin by their teenage years. Then throw in the fact that Angus had deliberately gone after Samantha because he'd learnt Connor had developed deep feelings for her – well, that had been the final straw. Not that Samantha had known – just another secret to add to his closet of skeletons. If only he could rewind time, he'd have fought harder to keep the set of keys that had led to the death of six people. Hindsight, hey, what a bitch it could prove to be. The accident had been a tragedy that had changed the town, and its people, forever. He just thanked god Samantha hadn't been among the fatalities. Although as the only survivor, her grief and guilt had almost killed her.

When the traffic lights turned green he heaved another sigh as he thought about how long and hard he'd battled with his own grief and guilt. Although he'd eventually climbed over that treacherous mountain of culpability, the battle scars remained on his heart. And would be there forever. Every single day, he had to push through the dark clouds of his past, because he wasn't about to allow his mother to lose the only home she'd ever known. Keeping Gunn Station afloat, and profitable, was his objective. So far, he was succeeding. But for how long?

For the irony was that just as he'd made strides in dealing with his past and mental health, his physical health had begun to fail him.

The welcome sign for Gum Tree Gully shone like a beacon in his headlights. Whipping past it, he smiled. Not long now, and they'd be home. Thank god. Stifling a yawn, he stretched his aching neck from side to side. He couldn't wait for his head to hit the pillow tonight. It had been a long day spent chasing the white lines of the highways. Having left Rockhampton just before dawn, he'd watched the sun rise gloriously into the bright blue sky, hold its own for almost twelve hours amid a listless sea of cloud, then descend into bewitching indigo-blue, trailing streaks of dusky pink and fiery reds in its wake. Then the black velvet drape of night had cascaded, providing the perfect backdrop for the plethora of glimmering stars. This was paradise right here.

Laying off the accelerator then taking a turn at the t-intersection, he felt his tyres leave the bitumen and meet with gravel. Winding his window down to allow the cool country breeze in, he sighed in pleasure as it whipped his shaggy blonde hair against his cheeks. He breathed in the scent of cow dung and lychee blooms as if it was the greatest smell in the world. After a week of inhaling hospital disinfectant and staring at four walls, this was heaven sent. Even the thought of being able to saddle up his stockhorse in the morning and go for a decent gallop gave rise to a flood of goosebumps. Country blood ran though his veins, and the wide-open stretches of Gunn Station were his drug. He could never imagine living anywhere else.

He pushed the clutch to the floor, and a growing restlessness gripped him as he went down a couple of gears. After steering his four-wheel drive up the hilly slope and then reaching the summit – with what were jaw-dropping, never-ending views in daylight – he pulled his LandCruiser to a stop at the gates of his family property. He didn't need to see the wide expanses to know the mesmerising landscape – he knew intimately every curve, every bend and every crevice of Gunn earth that had soaked up the blood, sweat and tears of his forefathers over the years.

Dimming his spotlights from high beam, he watched the glow of headlights bounce off the gleaming sign stating they'd arrived at *Gunn Station, Prime Angus Stud and Horse Agistment.* He'd added the last three words after his father's death, to get him and his mum by in the lean times, and even though it had been one hell of a big job, fencing all the paddocks off, and plugging like heck to catch the attention of horse owners, it was now paying off nicely. Every paddock was occupied. The horses were content. The owners were more than happy with the level of care and attention he showed their four-legged friends. And rain, hail or shine, he loved what he did.

'Hey there.' Stirring to life, Joyce Gunn stretched wearily in the passenger seat. 'Oh, hallelujah, we're finally home sweet home.' Her usual warm-as-sunshine smile spread as she turned to Connor. 'Sorry I fell asleep, love, I'm not a very good passenger, am I?'

'Don't be silly, Mum, I would have done the same.' He offered her a loving smile. 'You haven't slept much these past two weeks, worrying and fussing over me, it's no wonder you crashed.'

She casually waved off his mention of her caring nature. 'That's a mother's job.'

Connor knew better than to argue with that – his mum had always put him, and Angus, first. 'It feels so good to be back, hey.' Unclipping his seatbelt, he stretched his back out.

'It sure does, give me these wide-open spaces over those ghastly skyscrapers of the city any day.' Brushing her long salt-and-pepper hair back from her face, she undid her seatbelt too.

They sure had plenty of space, almost four thousand acres of it. 'Tell me about it, I don't know how people cope in the big smoke, with all that noise and rushing about.'

'Uh-huh, life might get stressful here at times, but at least we're closer to Mother Nature's heartbeat.' Sighing thoughtfully, she grabbed her door handle. 'I'll jump out and get the gate.'

'No, you wait right there, Mum, I'll grab it.' Wincing as his boots hit the ground, Connor did his best not to let his mother see he was still in a bit of pain.

'Now remember what the doctor said about taking it easier, Connor, won't you.' Her concerned voice followed him. 'We don't want you back in hospital because you're pushing yourself too hard.'

'I know, and I promise I'll do my best to,' he replied over his shoulder.

After jumping back behind the wheel, then rolling over a cattle grid, he got out a little more carefully this time and latched the gate shut. Half a kilometre down the driveway, and he was pulling up at the main homestead.

'You head inside, Mum. I'll grab your bag from the back and bring it in for you.'

'No, don't worry, I'll get it tomorrow. I'll just end up wanting to unpack tonight if I bring it in with me, and to be honest, I just want a nice warm bath, a hot chocolate and then bed.'

'Sounds good, enjoy.'

'Oh, I will.' Leaning in, she pecked his cheek. 'Nighty night, my amazingly strong, and at times very stubborn, son.' Her blue eyes twinkled spiritedly. 'Not that I'd want you any different.'

'Thanks, but I think you meant …' He couldn't help his grin. '… determined?'

'Nope, I meant stubborn.' She gave his arm a playful shove. 'Just like your father, God rest his beautiful soul.'

'Hmm, more a bit like you.' And he meant it. His father was a hard worker, but his mother was the one who loved fiercely and fought for what she believed in, tooth and nail.

'Okay, I'll give you that.' She smiled softly now. 'I hope you have a good sleep.'

'Yeah, you too, Mum.' He watched her step out and close the door.

She tapped the window. 'See you tomorrow.'

'Will do.' He made sure she was safe and sound inside before he drove on, another couple of hundred metres down the road.

Pulling up in his carport, he killed the engine. He decided to do the same as his mum and leave his bag for the morning. At least, for now, there was always tomorrow. A quick glance across the house paddock confirmed their hired help, an old stockman who went by the name of Oyster because his last name was Kilpatrick, was home and awake; the gas lantern hung beneath the awning of his caravan was still flickering. He'd catch up with him tomorrow – if he headed over there now, Oyster would rope him into drinking a whisky, or three, and he didn't want the haze of it come morning. As he climbed the four steps, his footfalls clomped rhythmically across the timber verandah. Reaching the back door of his modest farmhouse, he slipped the key into the lock as he kicked off his boots, relishing the squeak of the wooden door as he opened it, and the slap of the flyscreen door behind him as he stepped into the heart of his home, the kitchen. Being a cattleman was his true calling; good food and the cooking of it was his passion. He flicked on the overhead lights, and it took his eyes a few moments to adjust. Ahh, it was so good to be home. He needed a shower, and an icy-cold beer, in that order. Striding down the hallway, he headed towards his bedroom where the creak of the timber floorboards beneath his socked feet was music to his ears. Tomorrow was going to be his first day back here after almost two weeks away and he couldn't wait to welcome it with a steaming cuppa on the back verandah before immersing himself back into this glorious countryside as slowly-does-it as he could.

* * *

Forty-eight hours of taking it easy almost drove Connor to the brink. And that's when he had to put down his foot, or boot in his case. Gently, but confidently. He may have had a run-in with testicular cancer, but he wasn't dead yet, and with a good outcome he could quite possibly have another sixty-odd years left in him, so he had to do the only thing he knew and get on with life. His mum's concerned counsel came from a good place, and he loved her for it, but he just couldn't help himself when it came to the running of Gunn Station. If anything, he believed the work would help him heal faster, better, stronger. Just as long as he didn't overdo it.

Squinting into the mid-afternoon sunshine from beneath his weatherworn wide-brimmed hat, he eased the lowing mixed mob of yearlings, heifers, steers, a couple of their prime breeder bulls and their trusty leader cattle along the earthen trail. Off to his left, Oyster moseyed along on his sixteen-year-old bomb-proof stockhorse, Ol' Mate, man and horse doing a good job of making sure the cattle stuck together. Dust hung in a shimmering cloud over the mustered herd, and the sun-baked landscape surrounding them glistened with heat. The sweet scent of golden wattles drifted from the myriad trees swathed in bright yellow flowers. It was mindboggling how such vivid trees could survive, and flourish, without a drop of rain. They'd had a couple of weeks without even a sprinkle from the heavens, uncommon around these parts, but, fortunately, the weatherman had announced on the radio at five this morning that the monsoon season was finally on its way. As Connor's father would have said, it was better late than never.

Feeling as parched as this part of the station was, Connor took a swig from his Camelbak. After a couple of hour's droving, they were now only five hundred metres from the holding-yard gates. But if his previous experiences were anything to go by, he wasn't about to relax just yet. When it came to livestock, everything could turn south in an instant. Especially when they were so close to their destination; it was as if the rebellious cattle could smell it.

And just as suspected, being so tuned into his surrounds, he sensed the anarchy mere seconds before the rogue bull broke ranks, for the second time that day, and made a final dash for freedom. Warning him, Oyster hollered from the wayside. Fastening himself to the saddle, Connor spun his stockhorse in an impressive pirouette and rode hell for leather across the flats, toward the rocky ridges. Veering out wide, he cut in just in the nick of time and, with his horse's skilful footwork, drove the bull back toward the scattered mob. Oyster met him at the edges, and worked alongside him, both men pushing the cattle back into order. They shared a nodding glance from the shade of their hats – a stockman's way of thanks – and got back to it. A ripple of unrest had settled over the herd but with a crack of his whip, Connor quickly urged the loiterers and breakaways back into line.

Allowing his dependable horse, Banjo, to take the lead while he sat easily in the saddle, his thoughts went back to his role as best man for Jack and Shea's big day. With his mate's wedding now only a couple of weeks away, Connor tried not to think about the fact that he was going to be the last man left standing in what had once been the handful of eligible bachelors of Gum Tree Gully, nor did he want to consider that the woman to be paired with him was the one and only Samantha Evans. God only knew what was going to transpire once they met up. Hopefully, they could leave the past where it was, and move on as mates. That would be a great start. But after all this time, he honestly had no idea what to expect.

By the time they reached the holding yards and had sorted the cattle, sending some lucky ones back out to pasture, it was nearing the end of another day as twilight began to descend upon Gunn Station. His saddle creaking beneath him, Connor smoothly reined Banjo in and stole a few moments to breathe in his surroundings. Tomorrow, the road train would arrive to ship his cattle off to the abattoir, and he felt the same way every time he watched his branded cattle being loaded onto a truck – both proud and downhearted. It was all part of being a stockman. Closing the rustic timber gate of the yard, he was happy his efforts were proving lucrative and knew his father would be proud, but he also felt the pinch of knowing his latest herd was about to be led to the slaughter.

Oyster and Ol' Mate met him. 'Are we done and dusted for the day, boss?' A half-smoked rollie hung from his bottom lip.

Connor lifted his hat and wiped the sweat from his brow. 'Yeah, thanks Oyster.'

'Good.' Oyster's gap-toothed smile was lopsided. 'Bright and early on the morrow?'

'Yup.' Oyster being a man of few words, Connor gave his old mate a nod. 'Catch you at six.'

Without wasting any more breath, Oyster turned his horse around, gave Connor a wave over his shoulder and headed towards home.

Connor chuckled to himself as he watched the eccentric old-timer clip-clop away. His father had hired Oyster on the spot when he'd turned up after the town's publican had mentioned Gunn Station was looking for a 'jack of all trades, master of one' – in other words, an experienced stockman. After a firm rap to the front door, and a genuine handshake in greeting, Oyster had announced in his gravelly voice that he wanted a job where cattle outnumbered people, reiterated that he wasn't afraid of hard yakka, and said instead of the going pay rate he just wanted a place he could live out his days in his caravan with enough money to get by.

That was eighteen years ago now, and Connor was thankful for Oyster's hard work and even-tempered company. And in his own unique way, Oyster had been there for him when he'd lost his father, offering a reassuring slap to the back, taking on more of the workload when Connor was at his lowest, and giving him short, sharp, wise advice whenever the time was right. In more ways than one he was like the uncle Connor never had. Not that he'd say it to Oyster's face, for fear of copping a swift clip to the chin, but he loved the old bloke with all his heart.

He heaved a breath, then made sure everything was in order at the holding yards before heading towards the stables. After a hard day's work, he was going to treat his horsey mate to some molasses. Alighting from the saddle, and with his boots now on solid ground, he felt his belly grumble in protest at his having skipped lunch. A mammoth T-bone steak with a mound of garden salad and crispy air-fryer chips was on the menu. Washed down with a couple of icy-cold mid-strength beers. The very thought of it made him work faster, and by the time he kicked off his boots beside the welcome mat and stepped inside his farmhouse he was beyond starving. As the front door slapped shut behind him he paused to hang his hat on the hook beside his father's weatherbeaten Akubra, then headed in the general direction of the kitchen, making a pit stop in the laundry to strip down to his jocks and wash his hands at the sink.

Half an hour later, showered and dressed in his Peter Alexander boxer shorts – a Christmas gift from his Mum – he heard a knock at the back door and wandered towards it. 'Hey, Mum, I keep telling you that you don't have to knock, just waltz on in whenever.'

'Yeah, I know you do, but you need to know you have your privacy.' Reaching up on her tippy toes, she pecked him on the cheek as she brushed past him. 'Gee whizz, something smells good.'

'Uh-huh.' His gaze flashed over the myriad pans and kitchen utensils now dotting the timber benches. 'I'm cooking up a storm.'

'Hmmm, so I can see.' She grinned as she surveyed the chaos.

'I've got steak, salad and chips for dinner, and I've whacked up a golden syrup pudding for dessert. Oh, and I'm making mushroom sauce to drench it all in, not the pudding, though, that'd taste a bit weird.' He flashed her a cheeky grin. 'Moral of the story is I shouldn't let loose in here when I'm starving.'

'You've always loved to cook, son.' She pulled up a stool at the breakfast bench. 'One lucky woman will benefit from that, and your big, beautiful heart, one of these days.'

'We'll see.' He got back to manning the T-bone in his cast iron frypan, using a spoon to splash bubbling garlic butter over the top of it.

'So, are you going to the bucks party?' His mum's voice carried above the beeping of the microwave.

'Of course I'm going, what kind of best man would I be if I didn't?'

'Yes, true, and good, I'm glad you're getting out and about, you don't do it nearly enough these days.'

'I'm always too bloody tired to even think about heading out at night.' Grabbing the tea towel from where it was tossed over his shoulder, Connor used it to pick up the handle of the pan and carry it over to the sink. 'If I'm being honest, I'm not really looking forward to it, though, but them's the breaks.'

'Why the heck not? I'm sure it'll be fun.'

'I'm not into being around all those people.' He plonked his steak on his dinner plate, then got to dishing up the rest of the feast. 'You would have already eaten, hey Mum?'

'Yes, thanks, love, but if I'm still here when you're dishing up dessert, I'll have some, pretty please.'

'No bloody way, what do you think this is, a restaurant?' He chuckled as he placed his plate and a knife and fork on the bench. 'You'll be here, I'm not letting you leave until you have some.'

'Deal.' She clapped her hands together. 'I love your golden syrup pudding.'

'You would say that even if you didn't.' He poured his mushroom gravy into a jug, and plonked it near his plate. 'Would you like a beer?'

'Are you having one?'

He pulled an are-you-kidding face. 'Is the Pope Catholic? Does a duck waddle? Does a bear …'

'Okay, alright, I get it.' She laughed. 'In that case, yes please.'

Connor grabbed two of the coldest longnecks from the back of the fridge, twisted the tops off, stuffed each into a stubbie cooler, then passed one over to his mum.

His mouth watered as he sat on the stool beside her, then, silently thanking all the farmers for what he was about to eat, he tucked in.

'Seeing as there are quite a few people coming from out of town, do you reckon you might meet a lovely girl at the wedding?' His mother's blatant question came out of nowhere, momentarily stumping him.

Connor was thankful for his mouthful of food, so he had time to think rationally about his reply. 'Not sure, Mum, I haven't really thought about it.' Little did she know he'd thought about running into the lovely Samantha Evans ever since Jack told him she was coming.

'Well, you should be thinking about it.' She sighed impatiently. 'Because I'd love it to be you being the one getting married sooner rather than later.'

'Mum …' he said with caution. 'You do fully understand what the doctor told us, don't you?'

'Yes, of course I do, I'm not senile yet.' She sighed again, but this time it was done in a loving way. 'I know in my heart of hearts that you're going to live a long, happy life, Connor.' She tapped his arm. 'You're not going anywhere.'

'Yeah, well, if me getting married is meant to happen one day, it will, and if it's not, then, it won't.' He half shrugged, trying his best to play it all down. 'I'm not too concerned either way because if you look at the divorce rates, marriage is quite often a bad decision.'

'Stop it, Connor.' She gave him a little shove. 'I'll have you know that marrying and being married to your father was the best part of my life, and I want that kind of love, and life, for you, too.'

He feigned shock-horror. 'I thought having me was the best part of your life.'

'Nuh-uh.' She waggled a finger at him, just like she had whenever she'd scolded him as a young boy. 'Don't try and weave your way out of this conversation with humour, Connor Gunn.'

'Righto, then, spoilsport, I'll try and be serious, for a minute or so.' He huffed playfully. 'Yours and dad's marriage was one in a million, Mum.'

'And you could have that too, Connor.'

'Maybe, maybe not.'

'Definitely.' She wrapped an arm around him and gave him a squeeze. 'You're too much of a catch to be living the single life. There's your special someone out there somewhere, looking for you, I just know it.'

'I'll take your word for it.'

'You do that.' She grinned and nodded. 'I'll be proving myself right, you'll see.'

'Thanks for loving me like you do.' He didn't know what he'd done in his past life to deserve a mother as good as his, and he thanked his lucky stars every day.

'You're an easy one to love, my boy.'

Before they got too deep and meaningful – they'd done enough of that in the hospital – he grabbed his now empty plate, stood and offered dessert. 'Would you like cream, or ice-cream, or both?'

She rubbed her hands together. 'Oooh, I think I'll be naughty and have both.'

'Ha, yeah, me too.'

The next hour floated along in an easy manner, and then, once the dishes were cleaned up and they'd chatted over a cup of tea, Connor waved goodnight to his mum as she hopped into her four-wheel drive and drove back towards the homestead. After flicking off the kitchen lights, he headed down the hall, cleaned his teeth, then climbed into bed. The last thing he thought of, as his eyes drifted closed and he met with sleep, was the freckle-faced girl of his long-ago past, her fiery red hair wild and free like flames, and her laughter sweetly addictive as they galloped across the paddocks of Gunn Station.

CHAPTER 4

Huffing and then cursing an entire sentence beneath her breath, Samantha applied the brakes, and backed off the accelerator until she was a couple of car lengths back. 'Just bloody great.'

Sitting up the back end of the beat-up four-wheel drive that had rudely pulled out in front of her in a cloud of gravel and dust wasn't making whoever was behind the wheel go any faster. If anything, they'd infuriatingly slowed down even more, as if to teach her a lesson in country road rules. The bigger the vehicle, the more right of way they had. That was usually how it went. Time very clearly hadn't changed a thing. Where were the police when needed? The driver was doing thirty kilometres under the hundred k an hour speed limit and had been for the last couple of kilometres. She could already imagine an old farmer with nowhere pressing to be, just cruising from one moment to the next, with total disregard for people who had things to do, places to be, people to see.

On the verge of overtaking him, she decided not to. Why rush towards her ghosts? They weren't going anywhere. With nothing to do but get lost in her thoughts, she pondered how choices were a funny thing. Making one could catapult a person from one life into another, backwards, forwards, around and around. From one side of the world to the other. The velocity of it made her head spin.

An indicator flicked to life.

'Hurrah.' She cheered loudly while fist pumping the air.

A glimpse of the driver in his side mirror as he turned off the highway confirmed her imaginings – he was as silver as a fox, with skin the texture of a prune after many, *many* years beneath the scorching Aussie sunshine. The English didn't get leathery skin like this; there wasn't enough sunshine to go around, let alone burn you to a crisp. Whereas here, under the tropical north Queensland scorching sunshine, it was a whole other story.

A story she'd been forcibly reminded of this morning.

Having taken advantage of her late check-out, she'd gone for a mid-morning jog along the timber boardwalk of the picturesque Cairns Esplanade in a bid to try and shake off her jetlag and pent-up nerves. Arriving in Gum Tree Gully wound tighter than a three-bob watch was going to do her no favours. She wanted to start the visit off on the right foot. Beginning her five-kilometre run at the skate park right beside the popular Muddies playground, she'd admired the sparkling trinity inlet and surrounding lush green mountains while passing meandering tourists and enthusiastic runners, people walking their dogs and riding their pushbikes, or lazing beneath the many banyan trees. As time had ticked by, and her runners had swallowed up the distance, she'd found herself lost in the entrancing beauty of it all until she'd met with the lagoon filled with swimmers cooling off and the odd backpacker having their morning rinse-off. As she came to a halt, the stillness of the air made her feel as though she'd just stepped into an oven. Swept up in the Far North Queensland splendour, she'd all but forgotten just how scorching even a spring day could be. She'd almost jumped into the sparkling coolness of the swimming lagoon out of sheer desperation, but the thought of retracing her steps in wet activewear stopped her, as did the contemplation of how many kids, and adults for that matter, that had opted to pee in the pool rather than make the lengthy trek to the public toilets. While she took her much-needed breather, the familiar smell of Aussie snags and onion sizzling on one of the public barbecues had made her stomach growl.

The entire way back to her swanky hotel the warmth of the pathway had felt as if it were seeping into her runners as the bright orb of the sun glistened in a sky so blue it was iridescent. Returning to her room for a cooling shower, she'd enjoyed a room-service brunch of eggs Benedict and the outlook from her ocean-view room for as long as possible before checking out and jumping behind the wheel of her hire car. It had taken her quite a few deep breaths before she'd centred herself and then turned towards the direction of Gum Tree Gully. Mile after mile, the further she'd gotten from the coast, and the deeper into the charred countryside, the lonelier the road had become, leaving her with nothing but her idle thoughts. Not the best thing. But she'd tried her best to focus on the journey, and not the destination, pleased that she hadn't needed a map – she still knew the way like the back of her hand.

Now, almost four hours into her trip westward, she was starting to feel as though she was as far off the beaten track as she could get, although she knew this was a figment of her imagination – thousands of miles still separated her from the tip of Australia. Barely avoiding a lone kangaroo that seemed to appear out of nowhere, she released a few more hearty swearwords as she fought to steady her erratic breathing. Returning to Australia had her potty-mouth returning, too. *Ha, go figure.* The near miss made her ease off the accelerator as she remembered that livestock quite often used this road as a fairway. She didn't want be responsible for hurting an animal, or god forbid, losing control of her car. Long-gone memories of that fateful night tried to grip her heart tight, but she fought the sensation off. Crossing over the first of three bridges, she spotted the beady eyes of the resident crocodile eyeing her off from the banks. The four-metre beast, nicknamed Chompers, had become a legend round these parts – drawing many a tourist from their car to take photos from the safe viewpoint of the purpose-built platform. He'd been close to thirty-five years old when she'd lived here, making him well into his naughty forties now.

Staring past the dangling pine-tree air freshener, she saw the familiar line of telegraph poles that guided her in the direction of Gum Tree Gully. Stifling a yawn, she glanced at her watch – just under twenty minutes to go before she arrived in the main part of the little township. Her belly backflipped and her pulse quickened. How was she going to feel, seeing her old stomping grounds again? After the days and months had become years, and the years had become over a decade, she'd truly believed she would never set a foot back here ever again, but here she was, defying the odds.

Look at me go!

And then, in the blink of an eye, she was almost at *that* horrid place. Although she was doing her utmost best to stay upbeat, long-buried grief threatened to rise to the surface and drag her under. Her soul swirled with a mixture of memories, both blissful and wretched. She'd lost three loves of her life among the six dead, in one breath, one last heartbeat. Her boyfriend and her parents –as well as Angus's three friends – had been here one minute, then bam, they were gone. Just like that. Her trauma counsellor's advice had been that she needed to try and let the anger go. Yeah, right. It wasn't that easy. In fact, it was damn near impossible. So, instead, she'd ignored the evil beast of resentment and blame scratching at her soul and tried to get on with life as best she could.

And once again, just look at me go … what a mess I've made of it all.

Her heart began to race, and her palms grew sweaty. She tried to swallow down the fear, but her mouth was drier than the Simpson Desert. Pulling to a stop at the T-junction that had changed all their lives forever, she took a moment to realise how tightly she was gripping the steering wheel. Haunting images came at her, for her, sickening her. The sounds of the screeching tyres, the bloodcurdling screams, the last, conclusive, lethal crunch of metal echoed in her head. She heard her whimpers as she'd come to, felt her panic as she'd tried to move and couldn't. Her desperation for any sound of life in a dark, sinking, silent world. Her breath caught. Her nerves fired to life. Her resolve began to unravel. The terrible crushing grief, the deep sense of loss, and the guilt that came with that, threatened to return full force, so it could engulf her as it once had.

'Damn it.' She bent forward and rested her head against the steering wheel, taking deep breaths. 'You got this, Samantha, you got this.' She repeated this, silently, another two times, or was it three, before she straightened and stared at her reflection in the rear-vision mirror. 'You've come too far to turn back now. Keep going. You can, and will, get through this. You must, for Shea.'

She couldn't, wouldn't, let her past sink its fangs in deep. The beast had almost destroyed her once – she wasn't about to let the feral creature have a second chance. The familiar cold sinking feeling pressed down upon her, but she used every bit of resolve to shake it off. It did her no good, going back to the past. Her haunting memories might chase her, when she was tired, or lacking willpower, but she was tougher, faster … she could hide behind the life she'd built, if she had to, for these next few weeks. No matter the cost to her heart. It was already broken anyway, so what harm would a few more cracks do? She couldn't change what had happened, no matter how much she wanted to. Bearing this in mind, she firmly told herself she hadn't been the one at the wheel. It wasn't her fault that she'd been the only one to survive.

If only she could wholeheartedly believe it.

Remembering what her many therapists had taught her over the years about being present in the moment, she consciously made a choice to think about anything other than that horrific night. She took a swig from her water bottle. Screwed her face up as the lukewarm water rolled down her throat. She wound her window down. Turned the radio up. Sang the lyrics of the INXS song 'New Sensation' out loud. Anything to keep a firm grasp on her deliberations as she turned left and went from first, to second, to third, to fourth gear. Doing eighty k, she briefly noted the old sign announcing she'd arrived at the outskirts of Gum Tree Gully, broadcasting that the township had a whopping population of three and a half thousand – it now had a few more people and a few more bullet holes in it. Some things never changed. In a town as small as this one, things stayed stuck as they were. It was how the locals liked it. She'd been like them once.

It was time to pull herself together. Turning the radio back down, she sat up straighter. Just up ahead, the township appeared like a mirage on a heated road. The very first building she came across made her cringe. It would have been the health-food business she was going to run with her parents, but was now a lolly shop, The Sweet Emporium. Talk about a slap to the face. Remaining resolute, she stuck to the forty k an hour limit down the main street. As she slowed to a halt at a pedestrian crossing, an older bloke tipped the brim of his hat in a good-natured salute to her stopping. She flashed him a smile in response to his show of country hospitality. Such a small gesture, yet it lifted her spirits tenfold.

Cruising past a row of shops, she noted the number of four-wheel drives parked out the front of the pub she used to frequent for a game of pool or a delicious counter meal. Just on five, it was beer o'clock. Picturing the old blokes sitting around the bar inside, nursing cold beers and exchanging stories of days gone by, the weather or how the world was being tugged out by its roots, she smiled softly – there was something to be said for the casualness of a true-blue Aussie pub. She bet nothing much had changed inside – not that she was planning on finding out.

She couldn't help but wonder if one of the dusty trucks was *his*. Her stomach pitched with the thought of seeing him in the busy beer garden, drink in hand and his easygoing smile on his face. She fought the urge to gawk to confirm his presence, or lack thereof. The crazy sensation in her stomach told her it was going to take more guts than she'd first thought to see Connor Gunn again. At least at the wedding there would be loads of people around, which hopefully meant the conversation wouldn't be going anywhere near what they'd done. And as for the preparations leading up to the big day, she would keep any encounter with Connor businesslike, cordial and to the point.

Get in, enjoy Shea and Jack's special day, then get out – that was her plan of action.

But first up, a growing onslaught of cramps meant an unwanted pit stop at the local IGA. She hadn't thought to pack any feminine hygiene products, given the fact she'd only had use for them ten days ago. Her period was seriously out of whack lately. Stress, her doctor had told her. No kidding, she'd replied dryly. Parking next to a Holden ute that had more tailgate stickers than metal, and enough aerials to contact outer space, she killed the engine. Like a private investigator scoping the area out, she sunk down in her seat and scanned the footpath, making sure no faces were familiar, before stepping out and dashing towards the sliding front doors. The late-afternoon heat pressed down upon her back and the air-conditioning slapped her in the face the minute she stepped within the hustle and bustle. As it was the only grocery store for miles, it was understandably busy. Keeping her gaze downwards, she hustled along then headed down the health and beauty aisle. Supplies in hand, she made a beeline for the tills. Almost out without being noticed, she froze to the spot when a voice came from behind her.

'Samantha Evans, is that really you?'

Oh crap ... She could pick that sweet singsong voice anywhere.

Spinning around, she came face to face with Janet Vine. 'Oh, hey.' Crow's-feet and salt-and-pepper hair had replaced the youthful vigour and jet-black locks of her much-loved high school music teacher.

'Oh, my goodness, it really *is* you.' Her hand pressing upon her chest, Janet turned and looked over her shoulder. 'Jonathon, darling, look, it's Samantha.' She pointed to her.

His glasses perched on the tip of his nose, her old woodwork teacher and the man who'd been her father's best friend longer than she'd been alive came for her, his arms wide open. 'Sammie, oh my.' He pulled her to him and hugged her like a boa constrictor. 'It's so wonderful to see you.'

Feeling like a deer in headlights, Samantha caught her breath when he stepped back. 'It's good to see you both too,' she said, her smile a little trembly.

Reaching out, Janet placed a gentle hand on her arm. 'We had no idea you were in town.'

Samantha instantly felt bad for not telling the people who mattered. There weren't many – but Janet and Jonathon were certainly two of the few. 'Oh, yes, well, I only just got here.'

'Lovely.' Janet smiled warmly. 'How long are you here for?'

'A couple of weeks.' Realising she had a packet of heavy flow pads in her hands, she tried to place them in a more private position, behind her back. 'I flew over for Shea's wedding,' she added, hastily.

Janet nodded, her smile widening. 'Oh yes, isn't it fabulous that the pair have finally decided to make it official.'

Spotting an elderly woman staring from the vegetable section, her brows furrowed and arms folded tightly, Samantha took only a few more seconds to realise who she was – the town's biggest gossip, and her mother's archenemy because of it. Hillary Stern hadn't aged well.

'It sure is fabulous they're getting married, finally.' Her reply was distant, and her face must have conveyed her discomfort because Jonathon's concerned gaze quickly followed hers.

'Oh, here we go.' Jonathon said with an almighty huff. 'The two tittle-tattles of the town.'

Samantha remained silent as she fought to breathe, watching wide-eyed as Gum Tree Gully's aptly nicknamed Mrs Gossipmonger leant into the notorious Mrs Blabbermouth standing beside her, both women's hard-hitting, judgmental gazes honed in on their topic of conversation. Samantha.

Well, I never … Samantha didn't need to be a lip-reader to understand what the gossipmonger had just whispered. *Yes, I never thought I'd see the likes of her again either …* the blabbermouth replied.

'Sam, are you okay?' Janet turned to catch the two women still whispering. 'Oh, for goodness sake, you two busybodies, don't you have anything better to do than gossip all the time.'

Two sets of brows shot to matching tightly permed purple-hued hair. 'Well, I never.' Mrs Gossipmonger tutted again. 'It's a free world, Janet, I'll have you know.'

'Yes, I know, Hillary, but how about keeping whatever it is you have to say to yourself,' Janet said calmly. 'And as for you, Gertrude, it's like the blind leading the blind.'

'You need to control your wife, Jonathon,' Mrs Blabbermouth spat before trotting off with Mrs Gossipmonger hot on her heels.

Shaking his head, Johnathon guffawed cynically. 'There's always one, or two, in a country town, hey.'

Turning back to Samantha, Janet placed a hand back on her arm. 'Don't let people like that upset you, darling.' Her soft voice and gentle touch were reassuring. 'Their lives are so pathetically boring that gossiping is, woefully, all they find pleasure in.'

Blinking faster, Samantha pressed her trembling lips together as Janet's kind, wise words hung heavily in the air. Then, fighting the urge to run for the safety of her car, she forced a wobbly smile. 'Well, I best get going, it was so nice to run into you both.'

'Okay then.' Regarding her with concerned kindness, Jonathon nodded. 'Enjoy your stay, won't you.'

'Yes, I'll certainly try to,' Samantha said with one last wobbly smile, before vanishing out the sliding doors.

Stifling air and bright sunshine met her when she strode back outside, over to her car and basically threw herself into the haven of it. Gripping the steering wheel, she took a few deep breaths. Her shock and fear quickly morphed into anger. How dare those two fuddy-duddies make her the topic of their conversation. She wasn't behind the wheel. She hadn't forced Angus to do what he did. She was the one who'd lost so much that night. Where did they get off? She almost stormed back into the shop to tell them just as much but stopped herself. It wasn't worth her wasted breath. The only thing she had control over was her reactions to actions. And she wasn't about to give them more to talk about. So, after revving the car to life, she turned the radio up, backed out of her parking spot and sung her heart out to the old-school country songs as she headed towards her home for the next couple of weeks.

Ten minutes later she was turning down a comfortingly familiar dirt road. So much had happened along here. Good, and bad. She had come off her pushbike countless times and nursed gravel rash for weeks, she'd learnt how to drive, had experienced her first kiss with Angus, had foolishly given all of herself to Connor beneath the starry sky. What had they been thinking? Or was it more the case that they hadn't been thinking at all?

CHAPTER
5

Arriving at the front gates of Shea and Jack's free-range egg farm, Lotsa-Love-Layers, she pulled to a stop, and got out to open the gate. It swung open in a sweeping arc, as if inviting her into the lush green landscape beyond. Rolling the rental car forward in neutral, she tugged the handbrake on, then made sure to latch the gate closed behind her. Gravel crunched beneath the tyres as she slowly made her way towards the homestead that had become her haven in the weeks after her parents had died. Without a second's hesitation, Shea's mother had taken her under her wing, and patiently gotten her through the worst, god bless her loving soul. Mavis Davis was yet another soul taken way too soon. Damn cancer. She drew in a breath in a bid to fight off the swirling of guilt in her stomach – she should have come back for Mavis's funeral. And when Shea's father had left with a woman from Tasmania two years later, to start another family, she should have come back to console her friend. Regrets were futile – she had to try and make up for it all now.

The land dipped, then rose again as she drove through the heart of the mini mango orchard, past the huge chicken shed, then towards the stables. It was so lush, so green here, it was if the countryside was begging her to climb aboard a magnificent horse and gallop through it. If only she could remember how to ride a horse like she'd stolen it. Only one way to find out, she supposed. Lost in the beauty surrounding her, she caught her breath when she spotted the sprawling white house with its wide hugging verandahs, perfect to kick back on with a cuppa, surrounded by a plethora of colourful flowers – clambering bougainvillea, Bangkok rose bushes, scented frangipanis and rambling roses, and the huge water tank they used to drink from as kids towering on one side. Ever since she'd become best friends with Shea in Grade 1, this majestic place had been like her second home. And it felt good to be back. Too good, almost.

Parking beneath the canopy of the booming jacaranda tree she and Shea had climbed as children while pretending they were Indians on the lookout for cowboys, she stepped out, leaving her luggage for later, a little wobbly in her low heels. The old tyre swing still dangled from a reliable branch, albeit much higher than she recalled. Taking a moment to breathe it all in deeply, she smelt the hints of the plump mangoes hanging heavily upon weary branches, horse manure – a smell she'd always liked – and the sun-baked North Queensland earth. A wistful smile tugged at her lips. There was a sense of hope in the air, of life promising to burst forward. Being in the country was like moving closer to Mother Nature's heart; the rhythm she felt here was unlike the pulse of the city, frantic with human activity, but instead was the strong steady beat of the living, breathing countryside she now stood upon.

Her mobile chimed from the depth of her handbag, startling her. The noise was like a smoke alarm going off at three in the morning, instantly ruining the peace and quiet she was immersed in. Uncharacteristically, she decided to ignore it. For now. That's what message bank was for. If it were important, they'd leave a voice mail. Wouldn't they? Or would they? She almost, *almost*, grabbed it and stabbed the answer button. *Oh, stuff it.* Feeling a little naughty, she shook her head at her impulsive rashness. Good god, where was the meticulous woman who'd stepped on the plane three days ago? It was as if the country air was already getting rid of the rigid parts of her. She climbed the front steps, her heels clomping over the timber boards as she headed towards the front door. From inside the house, she could hear footsteps racing down the hallway towards her.

The screen door squeaked open and welcoming arms shot towards her. 'Oh, my goodness, Sammie, I can't believe you're actually here.' Shea squealed and jiggled on the spot.

'Hey, Shea.' As she was crushed within her childhood friend's hug, a smile Samantha hadn't felt for ages spread spontaneously across her face. 'It's so nice to see you.' And it really, truly was.

'Nice?' Shea stepped back and her hands went to her hips. 'Nice?' She repeated herself jestingly. 'How about amazing, or awesome, or how about bloody fantastic!'

Laughing, Samantha nodded. 'A big fat yes, to all of that, and more.'

'Far out, Sammie, I've missed you.' The thick glasses perched on her petite nose made Shea's brown eyes appear as big as saucers.

Reaching out, Samantha squeezed Shea's arm. 'I've missed you, too, bestie, so much.'

'Come in and let me and Jack fuss over you.' Hooking her arm into the crook of Samantha's, Shea tugged her inside. 'Thank goodness for Facebook and Instagram, huh, otherwise we'd never know what was going on with each other's lives.'

Guilt pinched Samantha, mighty hard. 'So sad, but also so true.' The scent of what she could only describe as coming home greeted her, instantly taking her back eleven years. 'Oh, my goodness, I feel like I've never left,' she said, glancing down the hallway then up to the open-beamed ceilings.

'Yeah.' Shea glanced around, too, as if viewing the homestead through new eyes. 'I've tried to keep it the same, you know, since mum passed.'

Samantha fought to blink the image of Shea's mum, apron on and smile wide, from her mind – she didn't want to cry as soon as she'd arrived. 'I'm so sorry I didn't make it back for the funeral.'

'Don't apologise, I totally get it.' Shea offered a compassionate glance, filled with so much understanding. 'The fact that matters the most is that you're here now, though, my darling friend.' She tugged her forward. 'Now, come with me to the heart of the house, because have I got a surprise for you.'

Oh, crap, Samantha silently thought, *please don't let it be Connor…*

She wasn't ready to face everything in one day.

As she wandered through the lounge room, past the formal dining room and into the kitchen, the smell of garlicky roast lamb had her mouth watering. 'Oh my gosh, Shea, you've made my favourite.' She put her nose into the air, sniffing madly. 'It seriously smells like I've died and gone to heaven.'

'That's my infamous roast, along with all the trimmings, including my super-duper thick minty gravy, made from the rich lamb juices of course.' She gave Samantha the once-over with a very concerted gaze. 'And by the looks of you, Samantha Evans, you need to have two helpings of everything. My gosh, woman, don't they feed you good hearty food over in the UK?'

'Ha, not really.' Samantha knew she looked a little on the lean side, so she chose to ignore Shea's innocent comment completely – her friend meant well, as she always did. 'Come to think of it, I haven't had roast lamb for ages,' she added, by means of steering the conversation anywhere other than her thinness. 'Probably since you came for a visit last year.'

'Well then, tonight shall be an epic feast.' Grabbing the oven mitts from the bench, Shea slipped both on. 'Followed by copious amounts of yummy vino and great conversation.'

'Sounds like the perfect night to me.' Samantha pulled up a chair at the breakfast bench, and watched Shea manoeuvre a roasting tray from the oven, and onto the sink just as the pitter-patter of tiny feet sounded, as did the clicking of dog paws.

Shea looked over her shoulder. 'Uh-oh, look out, trouble is inbound.'

Amaya came skidding around the doorway, her chocolate-coloured labrador, Fudge, hot on her heals. 'Aunty Sammie.' Her face a picture of delight, she ran towards her. 'You're here!'

Shooting to her feet, Samantha caught her, and lifting the wild-haired mini replica of Shea into her arms, she spun her in circles and kissed her cheek repeatedly.

'That tickles.' Giggling, Amaya wriggled free. 'You're a funny one, Aunty Sammie.'

Samantha's hands went to her hips. 'Am I, now?'

'Uh-huh. That's what Daddy says sometimes …' Amaya nodded exaggeratedly and looked to Shea, who was wide-eyed with whisk in hand. '… hey Mummy, Daddy reckons that Aunty Sammie is a real funny one.'

'Does he now?' Smirking, Samantha looked to Shea, who was now stirring her pot of gravy into oblivion. 'And what does Daddy Jack mean by that, I wonder, hmm?'

'Oh, you know.' Shea overtly shrugged but didn't meet Samantha's eye. 'That you're witty and comical, and sometimes a little weird, which is why we love you so much.'

'Good save, my friend.' Samantha knew Jack meant it kindly, as did Shea, so she wasn't offended, and instead found it endearing that they still saw that quirky side of her, instead of the straight-laced side that had been nurtured by her day-to-day life in London for over a decade. Ps and Qs were important in her career, especially with her clientele.

'Speaking of your father,' Shea glanced at the clock above the stove, 'I hope he's not too much longer putting the chickens to bed, or dinner is going to go cold.'

Right on cue, the back door flew open and Jack stepped in, along with the scent of the earth he provided from. 'Howdy doody family.' Fudge ran to his master's socked feet, wagging his tail madly as he received a warm hello from Jack.

'Speaking of the devil himself.' Shea's smile as she looked towards him was filled with so much love.

Jack caught Amaya as she leapt up and into his arms. 'I thought my ears were burning.' Father and daughter shared a tight hug. Pausing briefly to brush a kiss on Shea's cheek, he then took long strides towards Samantha and popped Amaya back to the floor. 'Welcome home, stranger.' He pulled her into the tightest of hugs, filled with brotherly love. 'We've all missed you.'

Samantha relished the feeling of being part of such a tight-knit, loving family. 'Hey, soon-to-be-brother-in-law, it's good to see you.' She watched as a giggling Amaya dragged Fudge around the kitchen, a ball tied to a rope clenched tightly in his mouth.

'Of course it's good to see me, I rock.' Jack's larrikin side shone through immediately. 'We're stoked you made it. I wasn't sure you'd be able to, although wifey-to-be here was positive you would.' He made his way to the stylish Smeg fridge, grabbed a beer from the depths, and then held it up. 'Want one, Sammie?'

'Not for me, but thanks.' There were way too many carbs in a beer for her, not that she was about to say such a thing out loud in an Aussie country kitchen where the gold liquid was often referred to as a gift from the gods.

Leaning against the bench, Jack took a decent glug. 'Ahhh, that hit the spot nicely.' He grinned. 'Would you like a cuppa, or maybe a glass of…' He seemed to be trying to look posh. '… pinot noir?' It was said with a hilarious accent that was a total British failure.

'You're a dag, Jack Farley.' Laughing, Shea tossed the tea towel in his direction.

Catching it, Jack mocked offence. 'I'll have you know that I'm not the little bit of pooh that hangs off the end of a sheep's butt.'

'Hmm,' Shea replied playfully. 'You sure about that?'

'Ha, very funny.' His face a picture of mirth, Jack gave her the middle finger. 'Now, about that wine, Sammie?'

Samantha chuckled at the pair's playful antics. 'A glass of pinot noir would be perfect, thank you.'

'Yes please, and make it a big one, it's been a long day,' Shea said, before Jack got the chance to ask her. 'The wedding planning is doing my head in, given it's all so last minute.' She looked to Samantha. 'Thank god you're here to help me now.'

'We could have given ourselves a little more time, sweet.' Grabbing a bottle from the wine rack, Jack got to pouring two glasses. 'We've waited this long. We could have waited a bit more.'

'Yes, we could have, but I'm done with waiting, and you know what I'm like when I get an idea into my head, I like to put as much pressure on myself as I can to get it done.'

'Ha, too true,' Samantha said to a playful dirty look from Shea.

His eyes widening to saucers, Jack made the motion of zipping his lips shut.

After popping a glass in front of Shea, he then passed an equally full glass to Samantha, grimacing when a little bit sloshed onto the countertop. 'Oops, I'll go grab the cloth.' Quicker than he was, Shea tossed it to him. 'So, what's been going on over your side of the world?' he said casually, as he wiped up the puddle of wine.

Mid-sip, Samantha shrugged. 'You know, whole lot of nothing, and a little bit of everything.' She was sure he knew everything, seeing as she'd filled Shea in, but she liked the fact he was showing he cared.

'That's a bit cryptic, Evans.'

'Yeah, I guess it is, Farley.' She grinned.

'Shea told me a snipped-down version of the past six months or so.' His kind smile gave way to sympathy. 'I'm so sorry you've been having a rough time. You deserve better, Sammie.'

'I'm all good.' She wasn't, but what else was she meant to say – she didn't want the focus to be on her problems. She'd done enough of that.

'Righto, if you say so.' Jack regarded her through knowing eyes. 'I know Shea and you talk, *a lot,* but if there's anything I can do to help …'

'Thanks, Jack, I really appreciate it.' Fiddling with the stem of her wine glass, she blinked faster to ward off tears, then forced a wide smile as she looked back to him. 'There is one thing you can do, please keep it between us three. I don't want to give the townsfolk more to talk about.'

'Yeah, of course I will.'

He nodded and she smiled.

'I want the focus of my visit to be on all the great things happening here over the next few weeks, because apart from the huge fact I'm so happy to be a part of your special day, it's going to help me heaps, being around all of you.'

'I'm glad to hear it.' Shea arrived at Jack's side and gave Samantha's arm a loving squeeze. 'Now, let's get this dinner underway, before we blink and it's breakfast time, shall we?'

Two hours later, with bellies filled to the brim, and all conversationed out, Shea and Samantha retired to the swing chair on the verandah, third glass of wine in hand, while Jack took over clean-up duties.

'I'm so glad you're here, Sammie,' Shea said, over the squeak of the support chains as they swung the chair to and fro. 'It's so hard, living so far apart.'

'It is, hey.' Offering her forever friend a tender smile, Samantha then rested her head back. 'And FYI, I'm so glad I'm here, too,

Shea.' A few lengthy moments passed, before she sighed softly. 'I'd almost forgotten just how peaceful it is, especially at night.'

'Yeah, so true, Sammie.' Shea sighed. 'I think I take it for granted a lot of the time, which is bad of me, given I call this piece of paradise home.'

Samantha offered a kind sideways glance. 'I think we all take stuff for granted, especially when we're around it all the time.'

'Mmm, I think that can go for people too.' It was Shea's turn to offer a kind glance. 'I'm so lucky, having a man like Jack to love me, and to love in return, and Amaya, oh, that darling girl brings me so much joy I could burst sometimes, yet some days fly past me and I haven't even stopped long enough to let both of them know just how much they mean to me.'

With Samantha's heart overflowing for adoration for Shea, she turned her head to the side, catching tears in her friend's eyes. 'Oh, lovely, you've only got to see how you look at both of them, and I'm telling you, Jack and Amaya can see very clearly just how much you love them.' She gave Shea's leg a pat. 'Don't be so hard on yourself.'

Wiping her cheeks, Shea snorted. 'Ha, you can talk.'

Samantha snorted too. 'Yeah, well, that's a subject for another time.'

The flyscreen squeaked open, and Amaya stepped out in her pink polka-dot jammies.

Shea leant forward, almost tipping both herself and Samantha out of the swing chair. 'Oh, hey sweetheart, what's up?'

'I can't sleep, Mummy.' Padding towards them, Amaya wiped at her eyes with clenched hands. Shea placed her empty wine glass on the side table and opened her arms wide. 'Come here, my little munchkin.' Lifting Amaya from the ground, she plonked

Amaya into her lap. 'You have to try and get some sleep seeing as you have day care tomorrow.'

'I know.' Amaya snuggled in. 'Can you come and read me a story please, Mummy.'

Shea looked to Samantha. 'Do you mind if I duck off?'

'Of course not, go.' Samantha waved her inside. 'I should probably try and get some sleep, too.'

Shea seemed hesitant to leave her. 'Okay, but only if you're sure.'

'Yes, I'm positive, now be gone, the pair of you.'

Easing to her feet with Amaya now wrapped around her, she smiled softly. 'See you in the morning, my darling friend.'

'You will, nighty night Amaya.' Samantha gave her a wave.

'Sleep tight, Aunty Sammie,' Amaya replied sleepily.

Samantha watched mother and daughter disappear inside the house. Looking back towards the sparkling sky, she swallowed the last of her wine in one big gulp. Somewhere in the garden, just below where she was swinging, the loud scuffle of nocturnal animals had her rising to her feet and quickly making her way inside. Good god, she thought, as she retreated to safety and wearily climbed the staircase, she'd really become soft after living away for so long. Maybe it was time to pull on those big country girl boots and toughen up a little, and Gum Tree Gully was the best place to do that.

CHAPTER
6

'Mornin', boss,' Oyster said as he shuffled past Connor's swag, loo roll in hand.

'Morning, mate,' Connor garbled amid a yawn.

With the fog lifting, dawn began to stretch to life before Connor, the landscape untouched, untainted by human hands. It was the gift of a brand-new day, a chance to start afresh, to let go of yesterday, to grab a bull by the horns, so to speak – although some days he literally did just that – and yet, as stunning a spectacle as a sunrise was, most of the glowing orb's audience still slept in their beds, pining for that extra few minutes of shut-eye, totally ignorant to the magic of Mother Nature's heartbeat and the power it had to heal one's soul. He felt himself a lucky man to be witnessing such beauty unwrapping before his very eyes. There was something ethereal about it. From his vantage point, he gazed in awe as the warm glow emerging from behind the distant mountain ranges stretched its pink, yellow and indigo arms across the lightening sky. Briefly closing his eyes while breathing in cool air drenched with the sweet frangipani flowers and the earthy cow dung and horse manure dotting the surrounding paddocks, he sighed in pleasure. Unlike most, he loved the deep, earthy scent. Good job, given that he was a cattleman to his very core.

Watching the few listless clouds changing from crimson red to yellow, he enjoyed the comfort of his swag for a few moments longer as he breathed the crisp morning air in deeply. Give it another hour, and he'd be sweltering. If only he'd gotten to share all of this with Angus, but the cruel twist of fate had put a stop to that. Would they have worked through their brotherly teenage fights? He liked to think so. But they'd never have the chance to find that out now. Neither would he get to see the pride on his father's face as he went about his daily jobs, making the station the very best it could be. It made him even more eager to live, for the memory of both his brother and father. If only he had a son, or daughter for that matter, to pass all of this on to. But that was never, ever going to be possible. The cancer had stolen his fertility, as well as leaving the possibility of a premature death hanging over him. And he'd gone and done a really stupid thing, by asking for his frozen samples to be destroyed for fear of dying and leaving a child without a father. If only he'd slept on it, he would have woken with a different mindset. But it was too late for 'ifs' now – he just had to live with the consequences of his hasty decision, made under the influence of painkillers and hopelessness.

Rolling onto his side, he looked in the direction of the plot of land he'd picked out to build his forever home. He knew exactly what he'd wanted, before his shattering prognosis: four bedrooms, two and a half bathrooms, a big kitchen, a games room, and sweeping wraparound verandahs to take in the far-reaching views. Hell, he'd even had the plans drawn up – but what use would a big house be to him if he was faced with the worst-case scenario? He'd live with his sentence, for as long as he possibly could, because if he'd learnt anything in this short, hard life he'd lived, it was that every second of life was worth living. His longing for a home, and his very own family to share it with, wasn't because he felt lonely, but because he wanted to be able to share this wonderful life with another, and then have children to pass it on to, just as his father, and his father, and his father, had passed it down the generations. But, given what he'd lost, and the fact that he could never have a child of his own, would any country-hearted woman want to fall in love with him? And if push came to shove, would he allow her to?

His heart sinking, he rolled over to where a view of the rolling hills met him and brought his thoughts back to the present. What good was it going to do him to pine over something he never had the capacity to change? Absolutely sweet F all. And he wasn't about to let his mother in on his regret over signing the paperwork that rid him of his ability to ever have a child. She'd had enough on her plate of late; she didn't need more with his revelation.

His campfire smouldering, he climbed from his swag, stretched his body to life, tugged his boots on and then made a move to put more wood on the pile, fanning the new flickering of flames with his hat to bring it back to crackling life. Then, grabbing his billy can, he strolled down to the trickling creek and filled it with water. A strong sweet pannikin of tea would be just what the doctor ordered, along with one of the corned beef and mustard sandwiches he'd premade for the muster. Then it was time he and Oyster hit the dusty trail once more.

Three hours later, the sun was gaining momentum and getting higher in the sky as Connor edged the livestock along at a nice easy pace. Up ahead, Oyster and his horse were doing the same. They wanted to get the cattle into their new paddock before the heat of the day had them begrudging the move, and judging by their dwindling pace and the force of the sunshine upon his back, that pivotal moment wasn't too far away. There was some good feed once they got there, though, a reward for their early morning walk. And for an early afternoon smoko, he had a couple of cans of Coke on ice, and a packet of Arnott's Butternut Snap biscuits. His absolute favourite, and Oyster's too.

With nothing but his thoughts to keep him company, his mind drifted aimlessly until he found himself right back in the same contemplations as yesterday. He couldn't help but wonder what it was going to feel like for Sammie, coming back here after so long. By the grace of God, he hoped she had somehow found a way to get over her past, so she could enjoy her time here. Back in her true home. Around the people who loved her the most.

Bearing witness to how that night had damn near destroyed her and had damn near destroyed him, too, he'd felt like a helpless bystander, watching as the dark shadows had pulled her apart, piece by piece, until there were only broken parts of her left. Oh, he'd tried to put her back together, but she hadn't been ready, and in hindsight, neither had he. They'd been two lost souls, trying to find comfort in the familiarity of one another. The moment her lips had met with his was the very moment all his feelings for her had been confirmed, tenfold. In some strange way he couldn't blame her for running far away from here. And from him. Hell, at the time, he would've liked to have the guts to have done the same. But then again, running never solved a thing. Facing things head on, now that's what worked, at least that had been the case for him.

'Cooee, Connor.' Oyster's bellow from the front of the mob alerted Connor to the fact they'd reached the new paddock. 'We good to go?'

'Right you are,' he hollered back, giving Oyster the thumbs up, which was the go-ahead to open the gates.

Bloody hell, talk about being lost in my thoughts.

As he was surrounded by a persistent cloud of dust and the bellows of the cattle, the day stretched into an absolute scorcher – even by five-thirty the air still shimmered with heat. With the cattle all tucked away in the hundred-odd acres of their new abode by two o'clock, Connor had gotten to his list of chores that had to get done by the day's end. He tugged the brim of his hat down to ward off the late afternoon glare, and finally downed tools, stepped over a steaming pile of horse manure, then rested against the railings of the agistment paddock to admire his handiwork. He'd achieved so much in the past twenty-four hours that he mentally patted himself on the back. He'd even found time to mend the fence his stud bull had decided to have a fight with, collect the weekly supplies from the local feed store and mow the lawns around the homestead and his farmhouse. Next up, before he headed home for the night, he wanted to call in on his mum.

Kicking his boots off and wandering down the hallway, he found her in the kitchen, tidying up. 'Man oh man, Mum, something smells bloody good.' Taking centre stage on her butcher's block, her coconut and pineapple frangipani pie was a picture of absolute perfection. 'Ahh, that's what it is.' He reached out to pick a piece of the sweet crumbly pastry from the corner.

'Oi, you.' She slapped his hand away, her stern look also playful. 'Go sit down, and I'll cut you a piece.'

'Righto, seeing as you've twisted my arm.' Pulling a chair up at the breakfast bar, he did as he was told.

'You're a cheeky bugger, Connor Gunn.'

'I wonder where I got that trait from, hmm?' The squeeze of his heart contradicted his grin.

'Hands down, your father, God love him.' Her smile was a little sad. Taking two plates from the overhead cupboard, she plonked them down, grabbed a knife and then served them up a hefty piece each. 'So, tell me, have you got everything sorted for the bucks night?'

'I think so, I've just got to confirm numbers with the publican, and we're pretty much good to go.' He took the offering of delectable delicacies from her outstretched hand. 'Thanks, Mum, you're the best.'

'I know.' She licked sweet pineapple goodness from her fingertip. 'When are you going to catch up with Sammie, seeing as you two are in charge of organising the finer details before, and on the big day?'

'This week sometime, I guess.' He hoped his answer would satisfy her curiosity, because he didn't want to go into it any further – she'd be able to read right through his blasé facade.

'That's a bit lackadaisical for a man who likes everything in order.' She paused, regarding him through motherly eyes – all-knowing, all-seeing. 'Don't you think you should touch base with her sooner rather than later, seeing as she arrived two days ago?' She very clearly wasn't about to give up her subtle interrogation.

'Yeah.' He half-shrugged. 'I reckon she might need a few days to get over the jet lag before I start talking wedding business with her, though.'

'I see.' Remaining standing on the other side of the bench, she scooped some pie onto her spoon, then raised it to her lips as if in slow motion, her astute gaze pinned to Connor.

'What?' he said, garbling through his mouthful.

She failed at stifling a little grin. 'Nothing.'

He pointed his empty spoon at her. 'Exactly.'

She pointed hers back at him. 'As I told you all those years ago, you're allowed to like her, you know.'

'Am I now?' He should have guessed she wasn't finished with the conversation – his mother was always like a bull at a gate when she had a point to get across. 'Thanks for the heads up, Mum, I'll make sure I keep it in mind.'

'Good.' She nodded affirmatively. 'Because you always get that special sparkle in your eye when it comes to Samantha Evans.'

'Sparkle, schmarkle, you're talking gobbledegook.' Connor cringed at his overuse of silly words – a dead giveaway that he was playing cool when he wasn't. 'FYI, too, Mum, you know she's married, right?'

'Oh, is she?' Joyce pulled a cat-who-got-the-cream face. 'I heard they'd broken up.'

Stunned, Connor had to take a moment before replying. 'Where did you hear that from?'

'Oh, you know, around.' She motioned her spoon in little circles.

'Far out, she only got here two days ago.' He shook his head at the speed news travelled around Gum Tree Gully – like a ball fired from a cannon. 'Besides, you know better than to listen to gossip.'

'Yes, in most cases I do.'

'What's different about this case?'

She shrugged melodramatically. 'Nothing.'

'Exactly,' he replied, trying not to laugh at her look of earnestness. 'Thanks for the pie, it was bloody delicious, as always.' The change of subject was deliberate. 'Can I have a piece for the road?'

'Of course you can, help yourself.'

Standing, he used the same plate and did just that. 'You want a hand with the dishes before I go home and get me a well-needed shower?'

'Nope, I'll clean this up.' She waved him in the direction of the hallway. 'No, shoo, be gone with you.'

'Love you, too.' Chuckling, he then pecked her cheek. 'Catch you tomorrow,' he called over his shoulder as he disappeared out the kitchen doorway to her reply of how much she loved him too.

* * *

Rising from her sleep and drifting into the waking day just as disorientated as she had the morning before, Samantha took a few moments to recall where she was. Buried beneath a soft doona, with the air conditioner set at twenty degrees, she stretched her relaxed body to life. She plucked her earplugs out, and the sounds of the countryside instantly filled her ears – the distant hum of a tractor, the growl of a four-wheeler motorbike flying past the homestead, horses whickering, cattle lowing. After taking a few more moments to wake, then sliding from the bed, she wandered over to the window and tugged the curtains open. Squinting into the bright sunshine, her gaze was instantly drawn to where the sky appeared so big, so blue, so perfect, it almost felt forged. Over to her left, wire fencing stretched on for as far as her eye could see. The closest section cornered off the paddocks that housed Shea's beloved horses. With yesterday spent unpacking, shopping for her odds and sods, and helping Shea with a few wedding plans, it had flown by before she had a chance to wander about the property. She couldn't wait to greet the magnificent creatures and inhale their equine scent. Bottled as men's aftershave, it would sell like hot cakes, she was sure. Off to her right, vivid-coloured bougainvillea climbed up the side of the water tank, and beside it was a fruit, herb and vegetable patch to be proud of. Shea had always had a green thumb, just like her mother. As for herself, she killed anything plant-like. Even her cactus had died because she'd overwatered it. Smack bang in the middle of the backyard was the big old mulberry tree that promptly reminded her of the days she and Shea would return home with pink-stained fingers, T-shirts and lips from the delicious berries. Those were the days.

Yawning, she stretched her arms high and considered having a shower before heading downstairs to face the day head on. Half an hour later, dressed in a free-flowing yellow sundress, with her long hair tamed into a ponytail, and a dusting of make-up on, she made her way to where Shea was hard at work in the kitchen.

'Hey, lovely.' Shea's bright smile took up most of her face. 'You sleep well?'

'Morning, bestie, I sure did, better than I have in ages, actually.'

'Excellent.' Her hand going to the lid, Shea fired the blender to life. 'What would you like for breakfast?' she called over the racket. 'I can whip you up some bacon and eggs, or an omelette.'

'Thanks, but all good.' Samantha tugged the fridge open. 'I'll just have a tub of yoghurt.'

'Yuck,' was Shea's hollered reply right before the blender was silenced.

Retrieving a strawberry low-fat Yoplait from the second shelf, Samantha turned to a grimacing Shea. 'What's so wrong with it?'

'What's right with it?' She plucked it from Samantha's hand and read the label. 'Fat free, no added sugar … it should just say taste-free and horrid.' She handed it back. 'Yuck.'

Samantha peeled the lid back and dug her spoon in. 'Well then, what do you suggest I have instead?'

'Other than good old bacon and eggs …' Shea wriggled her brows. 'A cinnamon bun.'

'Oh my gosh, I'd forgotten all about those.' She swallowed her second spoonful. 'We used to basically inhale them.'

'I still religiously have one every Friday, when I go into town to grab the weekly grocery shop, but seeing as you're here, I reckon I should make an exception and take you to get one this morning.' She slipped her apron off. 'Let me turn this dishwasher on, and we'll head into town.'

Just the thought of all the calories, and how much exercise it would take to burn said calories off, had Samantha squirming. 'I'll be full after this, so let's leave it until Friday.'

'Oh, come on, Sammie.' Shea looked at her as if reading her mind. 'I know you like to stay fit and healthy, but how about you live a little seeing as you're on holidays, for goodness sake.'

It was the shove Samantha needed. Dumping her teaspoon into the sink, and the tub of yoghurt into the bin, she wiped her hands together. 'Right, my friend, let's go commit carboside.'

'Now there's the wild, free, reckless Sammie I remember.' Shea grabbed a bunch of car keys from the bowl. 'Let's head, before you go and analyse everything and change your mind.'

'Oh, stop it.' Samantha gave Shea's arm a playful slap as they headed down the hallway. 'You stirrer.'

'Never ever will I stop stirring you …' Shea's face was a picture of brazenness, '…because I know how much you love me keeping you on your toes.'

'Ha, yes, too true,' Samantha replied with a wide smile.

Between the light conversation and the picturesque scenery, the trip into town didn't take long. After pulling into a park right out front of the bakery, the pair of them climbed out and made their way to the front door. A bell tinkled their arrival as they stepped inside. The mouth-watering buttery scents instantaneously made Samantha want to bury her face in the display cabinet. Shea ordered them one glorious cinnamon bun each, and after fighting over who was going to pay, with Samantha winning when Shea was tapped on the shoulder, Samantha stepped aside while Shea chit-chatted with the unfamiliar older woman. Unable to wait any longer and with the enchanting smell wafting from the paper bag, she plucked the still-warm cinnamon bun out and sunk her teeth into the mound of delicious, sticky carbs, groaning in absolute pleasure.

Shea finally came back to her side, and she passed hers over. 'Oh my god, Shea, these little beauties are as yummy as I remember, if not more.'

Shea grinned. 'See, aren't you glad I told you to live a little?'

'Uh-huh,' Samantha garbled.

The tinkle of the bell drew her gaze past Shea, and to the six feet of hunky man stepping inside, his wide-brimmed hat shadowing his face. Her breath caught when she realised it was *him*. And like a bolt of lightning, she felt Connor Gunn's presence right down to her very core. She'd never been able to fully shake him since that night, especially in her dreams, which he'd unwelcomely popped into from time to time over the past decade; she knew it couldn't be his twin brother visiting her in slumber, because of that little scar on his right hand, the one from when he'd sliced it open on barbed wire while trying to let her between two railings of a paddock fence. A long time ago, he knew her truest self like the back of those hardworking hands that were now removing his hat and sliding through his unruly head of sandy-blonde hair. Hair that matched his wild personality. In faded jeans and timeworn boots, with the sleeves of his dark blue button-up shirt rolled to the elbows revealing the dark ink of tattoos spiralling upwards, and shoulders wide enough to carry the weight of the entire world, the air of trouble clung to his every inch. From head to toe, he was masculinity in its finest form. Rough and rugged, muscular and somewhat intimidating, Connor Gunn had matured from a lanky teenager into one hell of a man.

Shea gave her arm a squeeze, snapping her from her trance. 'Look away, Sammie, and for god's sake, take a breath woman.' She grinned cheekily. 'Told you he was a hottie now, didn't I?' she whispered with an elbow nudge.

'Mmm, it appears you are a woman of your word,' Samantha mumbled.

An armful of bags clutched to her, the woman who Shea had been talking to stopped at her side again and started another chinwag. Shea's stealth eyeroll conveyed annoyance, but Samantha was glad for the distraction — she needed a moment to catch her breath. She was dead right in saying he was hot.

Smoking, in fact. So much so Samantha found herself forgetting to breathe. Again. Tall, fair-haired, tanned and with striking blue eyes, he was an arresting cross between a strong rugged stockman and a tattooed, axe-wielding Viking warrior.

Lifting his gaze from the row of pies and sausage rolls, then turning as if sensing eyes upon him, Connor's thoughtful expression gave way to a fleeting look of shock then a heart-stopping smile. 'Oh my god, Sammie, it's really you.'

Struck by the sensation of travelling back in time, Samantha grasped for her inner cool. 'It sure is, me, here, in the flesh,' she garbled, hoping to god there wasn't flaky pastry all over her lips.

'Wow.' He closed the short distance between them.

'Hey there.' It was all she could muster as their gazes locked tightly, just like they had once before, and as his blue eyes pierced hers, she was reminded of Angus. She shook the image of her teenage boyfriend's mahogany casket away. She wasn't going back to that awful place.

'Jack mentioned you were coming home for the wedding, but I needed to see you to believe it.' His easygoing Australian accent was pronounced. 'It's been forever.'

'It has been, forever.' Caught in his gaze a little longer than was socially acceptable, she blinked and tore her eyes from his. 'So, how have you been?' To her frustration, and embarrassment, her eyes snagged on his chiselled biceps that were straining the material of his button-up shirt.

'Yeah, can't complain I suppose.' He shifted from boot to boot, then rocked back a little on his heels. 'You?'

'Yeah, same.' As firecrackers exploded inside her, she fought to remain cool, calm and collected as she blew a stray lock of hair out her face.

Seconds ticked by before he broke what was becoming an uncomfortable silence. 'So, how long are you home for?'

'Three weeks.' Far out, his five-o'clock shadow gave him a rugged edge she wasn't used to.

His smile pinched. 'Gee whizz, you're not mucking about with getting back to London, hey.'

'I have to get back for work.' Her reply was a little defensive.

'Fair enough.' He glanced over her shoulder, then back at her. 'Did your other half come too?'

She shook her head. 'Oh, no, he couldn't, he's super busy.'

You liar liar pants on fire, Samantha Evans, what's wrong with you?

She watched this lips twitch at one corner, as if that information possibly pleased him, and the fact that it might have pleased her, and it shouldn't. Couldn't.

No, Samantha, don't you dare go back there.

But my god, he smelt so delicious, like leather and horse and earth and so much man. She had to stop herself from leaning in closer and breathing him in deeper because there was something about that scent, *his* scent, that hit her sweet spot.

As if privy to her thoughts, his lips curled into a charming smile. 'You should swing on over while you're here, check out how much my place has changed since you last saw it, and we can maybe go for a fair-dinkum gallop and a dip in the dam afterwards, like the old days, if you want.'

She recalled all the times he'd been there for her, when she and his brother had lovers' tiffs, or when she was struggling with her maths homework, and especially when … 'That sounds, nice, I might just do that.'

'Good, I look forward to it.' Fire danced in his electric-blue eyes. 'I hope you remember how to ride a horse like you stole it, because I don't reckon you'd get much of a chance to gallop through the streets of London like you used to hurtle across the paddocks here.' There was a slight tremor in his voice, as if he were holding pent-up feelings at bay, and something unfathomable momentarily crashed his steady gaze. 'Those days were the best, weren't they?' he added, after clearing his throat, a dreamy look then crossing his face as though he was right back there, riding his horse alongside her as they laughed into the wind.

Bam, there it was again. *That* feeling. And right then and there, with the way he looked at her with such intensity, as briefly as it was, she knew he felt the same magnetic pull that she did. And that terrified her. Beyond words. As it seemed to do to him, too. The moment stretched on a little uncomfortably as that faintly familiar longing rose up inside of her. She'd felt the power of it once before, had acted upon it in the heat of the moment, and in doing so had experienced the deepest connection she'd ever felt. And it had scared her enough to run as far and as fast as she could.

Clearing unwanted emotions from her throat, she blinked away the memories of she and Connor and Angus galloping through the paddocks, bareback and free, as the sensation from Connor's tender touches and lingering caresses, from so long ago, echoed inside her.

'Well, I should let you get back to whatever you were doing,' she said, a little hastily.

'Yup, the day's getting away from me.' He glanced to where a watch would usually be. 'I'll catch you soon, Sammie, and we can touch base on the maid of honour and best man wedding duties while we're at it.' He flashed her a wicked smile before turning his attention to Shea, who had at some point arrived back at her side. 'Hey, Shea, tell that fiancé of yours to give me a call when he gets a minute.'

Shea's smile was filled with warmth. 'Will do, buddy.'

Somehow, Samantha refrained from buckling at the knees as he put a safe distance between them and turned his focus back on the warm rows of hot pastry delights. A quick sideways glance was met with Shea's all-seeing one.

'What?' She felt like she'd just been caught with her hand in the cookie jar.

'You know what,' Shea replied casually, as they headed back outside, and over to where they'd parked.

The chiming of Shea's mobile thankfully saved her from a reply.

Samantha used the time it took to get into the passenger seat, drag her seatbelt over and clip it in to try and ground herself from the clouds Connor had just lifted her up to and gently placed her upon. She'd forgotten how his smile had always put her at ease, and how his mischievous side had enticed hers. It would be so easy to fall for his charisma and chivalry in the coming weeks. Lord knew it had been an age since she'd been skin on skin with a man. Benjamin had been her last, and even then, it hadn't felt like it should. But she didn't have the time, nor the heart, to fall, especially for a man that she had tumbled into bed with before. It had only been the once. But *oh my god*, she'd never forgotten how he'd made her feel that night, when she'd reached for him to help rid her from the crushing guilt and hurt. But then all she'd been left with the following day, when she'd stood at his twin brother's funeral and watched the coffin disappear into the fire of the crematorium, was utter shame with her actions.

Her phone call having ended, Shea then dialled Jack's number through the hands-free connection and filled him in on the details of the caterer's call as she backed out and headed towards home. Staring out the window, at the stretches of countryside broken up by the occasional farmhouse and outbuildings, Samantha heard Connor's final words after their night together replaying in her head like an old tape.

I love you, Sammie Evans, I always have and always will.

At the time, so torn and tortured, the L word had been the last thing she'd wanted to hear, especially from Angus's brother. What would the township think of her getting into a relationship with Connor so soon after the accident? It would have been grounds for painful gossip, gossip her deceased parents were no longer able to remedy, gossip she hadn't had the courage to face. So she'd filed his declaration away, and had eventually put it down to words said by a caring friend in their mutual time of need. But in those fleeting moments, the ones when she would dare to bring it back out when she felt alone in her marriage – which had been often of late – she'd begun to wonder if he'd really meant it. And if he had, would she have wanted him to?

Maybe she'd fallen for the wrong brother, but it was a little late to remedy that.

Way too much life had passed between then and now.

CHAPTER 7

For the rest of the day, and into the next, Connor had to keep pinching himself and slapping his face to stay conscious. Just like that, with a click of fate's fingers, Samantha Evans had stepped out of his dreams and contemplations, and was standing there, right in front of him, in the flesh, her striking green eyes wide and filled with nervousness the second he'd spotted her tucking into her cinnamon bun like there was no tomorrow. It had been over eleven years since he'd laid his eyes on her, and time had most certainly been kind to her. She was even more beautiful than he recalled. Her chaotic curls had been tamed into mild waves, her wild red hair had been dyed the darkest of browns, and her freckles had faded, but that sparkle in those tiny golden flecks of her green eyes, the ones he only got to witness when looking long enough, closely enough, were still there. And the way her lashes had fluttered as her captivating eyes had landed on his, man oh man, he'd almost lost his footing on solid ground.

Bam! He hadn't expected to feel so much. And just by being near him, she'd taken his breath, and then stolen it some more, effortlessly, until he was desperate to step out of the bakery for air. What he would've given to have reached out and wiped away those few crumbs stuck to her glossy lips, or better still, kissed them away. He didn't know how it was possible, but she was even more of everything he'd envisioned her to be since he last laid his eyes on her that final time, at his brother's funeral, almost eleven years ago. She was more woman, more stunning, more alluring, all the more captivating, just … *more*. In that flicker of a moment, when their eyes had caught and locked on one another's, all the longing and connection and depth that he'd pushed to the wayside the moment he'd learnt from Jack that she'd left town, without even a goodbye, returned full force and punched him hard in the chest. It had been hard to keep that hidden as they'd chatted like old friends. Hell, he was still trying to decipher the powerful sensation twenty-four hours later. Over the years, he'd talked himself out of feeling anything other than a past with her, but now, knowing she was back in Gum Tree Gully, just a few kilometres down the road from Gunn Station, so close, so within his reach, there was that same blazing fire rushing through his blood. But she'd gone and lost her strong Australian accent in her time away, and it made him wonder what other parts of her were gone after so long. He still couldn't believe he'd invited her over within minutes of talking to her. Here. To visit. Him. What the F was he thinking? He was treading on dangerous ground.

For all he knew she was still married.

Yes, his mum had explained last night that Amaya had innocently told a little friend at day care that Benjamin had been mean to her Aunty Sammie, so Sammie had left him, all said while the day-care mum had been in earshot, who'd then told her friend, who then told their friend, and so the Gum Tree Gully whispers had started.

But gossip was gossip.

And he was no wife-stealer.

A safe distance needed to be kept.

Otherwise, he risked falling head over boots for her again, only for her to leave a second time.

It was going to take every bit of resolve for him to keep himself in check.

Three weeks. Exactly twenty-one days. Then she'd be gone. Again. He could do this.

That had been his train of thought for what had felt like the entire night. With only a few hours of sleep, if that, he'd of course stirred before the birds, risen from his tousled sheets, tugged on his work clothes and slipped his mismatched socked feet into his boots while he'd sculled the last of his extra-strong coffee. His body clock was set to a five am awakening, rain, hail or shine, sleep or not, Monday through to Sunday. Usually, he was good with that, but unlike almost every other day, today he just couldn't seem to find his centre of gravity. Utterly exhausted, he didn't know how he was going to make it through the day, let alone well into the night for Jack's bucks party.

It was nearing ten, yet the ferocity of the sunshine beating down upon Connor's back made it feel like the middle of the day. He took a glug from his water bottle, then slipped it back into the saddlebag and wiped the sweat from his brow with the sleeve of his R.M. Williams shirt. With the vibrant clear blue sky stretching into the distant horizon as far as his eye could see, he tried to focus on all the little things that brought him joy daily.

Just over yonder, in the agistment paddocks, magnificent horses languidly swished their tails, their elegant necks bent towards the lush feed at their feet. All around him, the vast stretches of untainted land, his land, a lot of it untouched by human hands, was breathtaking. This unhindered view from his saddle was everything he loved in this world, and yet there was something scratching at his soul, irritating him beyond words. And it had nothing to do with his health scare. Of that, he was certain.

Moving at a slow and steady pace, it had taken a good couple of hours to move the mob from the ridge, down the steady slope of the hill, and towards the holding yards – tomorrow the mustered cattle would be drenched. He knew all too well that besides skill, moving thirty head took patience and focus, and although it was very unlike him, today he was lacking in focus. The relentless voice in his head, chinwagging about the same subject like a broken record, was getting on his tethered nerves. Samantha Evans didn't have the right to take up so much of his attention. He needed to find another distraction. A growl from his empty stomach gave him one.

For now.

An hour and a half later, with the cattle holed up in the holding paddock, Connor made sure their troughs were filled to the brim with water and each and every head was settled in before thinking about heading back to the farmhouse so he could throw back some fodder and have a rare afternoon nap before heading into the pub for the bucks party. He wasn't going to be good company if he didn't get an hour or so of shuteye, and then, hopefully, get his head straight.

Directing Banjo over to Oyster and Ol' Mate, he stopped in the shade of a massive old gum tree. 'I've got to knock off for the arvo, mate.' He watched the old bloke take the makings of a cigarette from his top pocket, devoting all his attention to rolling, lighting, then inhaling enough smoke to blow rings skywards. 'So how about you enjoy an early knock-off, too, and we can meet first thing in the morning to drench this lot.'

'What do I need an early knock-off for, boss?' Oyster's wiry shoulders rose slowly. 'I'd rather be useful, than sitting around twiddling me thumbs.'

'Righto.' Connor gritted his jaw against a grumble; Oyster was just trying to be helpful. 'If you want to keep going after your lunch break, then you can service the tractor if you like.'

'Yup, will do.'

'Right then, I'll catch you tomorrow.'

Oyster tugged the brim of his hat in a silent cheerio.

Cantering back to the stables, Connor reprimanded himself for his bad mood. Lack of sleep and whirling thoughts weren't doing him any favours. Nor was the chemistry he'd experienced between himself and Sammie yesterday. Although her eyes had been everywhere but on him towards the end of the conversation. Had it been because she didn't want a bar of him, or was it the opposite? Was she still married? Or was his mother's second-hand, or very possibly fifth-hand, information right? It wasn't like he was going to outright ask Jack. It would be a dead giveaway that he was keen on her. And that, *them*, was in the past. It wasn't going to happen again. He wasn't about to lay his heart on the line, only to have it shattered by her leaving. Again. Besides, why in the hell was he even going down this track? Just because, as a teenage boy, he'd daydreamed about one day making her his, but then his brother had nabbed her first, none of it gave him an excuse to act like some immature teenage boy now. He was a fully grown man, with self-control, experience and forethought. He and Sammie were old friends. End of story.

And with that assertion, he slipped through the back door of his farmhouse, his stomach now growling fiercely. Plucking a can of baked beans from the cupboard, he peeled the lid back, grabbed a spoon and dug in. Delicious. Thank goodness for the staple, because he didn't have the energy to make something more substantial to eat. Next, a long shower to ease out his aching muscles, then he planned on faceplanting in his bed for an hour or so before facing the night. Not that he expected to sleep, but at the very least shutting his eyes would grant him a bit of a recharge.

Three hours later, his mobile phone dragged him from the depths of deep sleep. Blinking into the dimness of his room, he grappled for the phone on his bedside table, and answered the private number just before it went to message bank. 'Connor speaking.' He sat up while still trying to grab hold of his bearings.

'Hey bud,' Jack's voice bellowed over the echo of music and chatter. 'Isn't it about time you got your arse down to the pub and joined us for a couple of drinks?'

Jack. The bachelor party. Uh-oh. 'Sorry, mate, I um, got caught up.' He scrambled from his bed, tripped over the laundry basket, and barely saved himself from hitting the deck by grabbing hold of his tallboy drawers. 'What time is it?'

'Seven-thirty.'

'Oh mate, sorry hey, truth be told I fell asleep.' Connor rifled through his cupboard for his going-to-town jeans, and hopefully a shirt that was already ironed.

'You? Sleeping during the day?' Jack chuckled. 'Now that's a first.'

'I know, I must've needed it.' Gripping the phone between his ear and shoulder, he jumped on one leg, then another as he pulled his jeans up.

'Fair enough.' The phone muffled then Jack was back. 'I want my best man here to celebrate with, so hurry up, would ya!'

'On it.' He slipped his arm into the one and only ironed shirt. 'I'll be there as quick as I can.'

And he did just that. Striding into the packed Roundyard Pub less than thirty minutes later, Connor kept an eye out for Jack and his rowdy footy mates as he zigzagged through the noisy crowd, making sure to give a quick 'g'day' in passing to the faces he was familiar with. Knowing the group of blokes invited to the bucks party well enough, he knew they'd most likely be hunched over a pool table, and considering they'd been here since five, well on their way to being tanked up by now. A quick scan in that direction confirmed his thoughts when he spotted Jack being huddled into what looked like a footy scrum as his head was ruffled by the loudest larrikin of the bunch. Oh, Lord help him get through this – partying hard just wasn't his thing anymore. Making his way to the bar, he grabbed a beer for himself and one for Jack, then wandered towards where Jack was giving him a lopsided grin.

'Hey buddy.' He passed Jack the schooner and got a back slap in thanks. Raising his glass to Jack's outstretched one, he smiled. 'Cheers to being a kept man by a wonderful woman very soon.'

'Oh yeah, a big cheers to that.' Jack clinked his glass against Connor's, succeeding in sloshing almost half of his beer onto his jeans. 'Oh, bloody hell.' Gingerly, he tried to wipe it off, then realising it wasn't going to happen, shrugged, and took a glug. 'Not too sure how much longer I'll last, this mob are drinking me under the table.' He half snorted, half laughed. 'I've become a lightweight the past couple of years.'

Grinning at Jack's red cheeks, a byproduct of the alcohol, Connor nodded. 'Yeah, don't worry, me too, buddy.'

'Oi, Jackster, it's your shot.' The tallest of the lot tossed an arm around Jack's shoulder and dragged him towards the pool table. 'Hey, Gunn.' He called back over his shoulder.

Connor raised his beer in greeting, then pulled up a bar stool at the corner of the barrel-style table. With the rowdy group on a totally different wavelength to him, he enjoyed stepping out of the limelight and just watching the goings-on. As long as he was here for his best mate, that's all that mattered – thank goodness Jack had called and woken him up, otherwise he might have slept straight through to the morning. He never would've forgiven himself if he'd gone and missed Jack's bucks party.

Grabbing the pool cue and taking his shot, Jack somehow sunk two balls. A loud cheer erupted, and suddenly the groom-to-be was being lifted into the air before being dumped unceremoniously back to the floor. Chuckling, Connor shook his head. Poor Jack was going to have one whopper of a hangover tomorrow. As for himself, he was glad he'd be driving home and waking up fresh as a daisy.

There was a lull between songs coming from the jukebox, and the boisterous cackle of women caught Connor's attention, drawing his gaze from the pool table and over to the other side of the pub. His heart skipped a beat. And then another. He knew the sound of that honey-sweet laughter anywhere. From his dark corner, he spotted Sammie, and the ache she'd left in his chest the day she left, the one he'd felt beneath his armour at the bakery two days ago, returned. But he couldn't pay it any attention, because not long after the wedding day she'd be long gone, just like she'd gone after his brother's funeral. Leaving him to mourn the losses of both his twin sibling, and his one true love, with one painful punch.

'Well, well, well, bugger me dead, if it isn't Gunn himself.'

The hairs on the back of Connor's neck bristled, and he turned to see the only face on this planet he longed to never see again – the man who'd cheated with his then girlfriend of almost two years. 'Lumley.'

Lumley smirked. 'I didn't think I'd ever see you in here again.'

The smug look on the bloke's face made Connor want to sock him one. 'And why's that?'

'Just after everything that went down the last time you were here, is all.'

'I don't know what you're on about.' Even though he recalled every second of knocking Lumley to the ground, then being dragged off to the cop station, Connor pretended to be baffled. 'So, how's things going with Jasmine?' Even though Connor knew she'd cheated on Lumley, too, he couldn't help but ask.

Lumley's smug smile all but disappeared. 'She ran off to Cairns with some bloke from her work, but you know what, I say c'est la vie.'

'Go figure, a leopard never changes its spots, hey.' Connor gave Lumley a hard slap on the back, causing him to shuffle a little to the side. 'And while I got you, I never got to thank you for saving me from the likes of her.' He raised his almost empty glass. 'So, cheers to you.'

Eyes narrowing, Lumley remained speechless for a few lengthy moments, and then said. 'You're a smart-arse bastard, Gunn.'

'Cheers to that, too,' Connor added right before Lumley was dragged off by one of his quick-thinking, sober mates.

His jaw clenching, Connor watched the cheating son of a bitch trudge begrudgingly towards the front doors, then disappear outside. This was why he didn't like being here. But for this one night, he'd grit his teeth and bear it. For Jack's sake. At least, from where he was sitting, he had a bird's-eye view of the most stunning woman in the room. Now that was something.

CHAPTER 8

Having escaped performing the methodical moves of Ike and Tina Turner's 'Nutbush City Limits' dance by the skin of her teeth, Samantha took a quick glance back at the dancefloor and smiled. With Shea having the time of her life, she allowed herself to bask in the glow of a maid of honour's job well done as the barman hustled to and fro, filling her order. Pressing the side button of her smart watch, she squinted into the glow of the screen. It took her a few moments to work out it was already a quarter past ten, and she'd clocked up over twenty thousand steps for the day. Good god, it was no wonder her feet and lower back were aching. Climbing into bed tonight was going to feel mighty good. With her at the helm of the get-together, the hens' party had been in full swing for the past four and a half hours. It had evolved from a dignified dinner of Shea's all-time favourite of garlicky chicken Kiev, beer-battered chips and dressing-drenched garden salad, to a few hilarious party games that had proved a hit, to a now bedraggled-looking bunch of women – Samantha somewhat included – trying their best to appear sober when they very clearly weren't.

As the Nutbush ended, gleeful female voices began to sing way out of tune to Cold Chisel's 'Khe Sanh', while Samantha paid the hefty dinner and drinks bar tab before Shea got a chance to – a pre-wedding gift from her. From here on in, the ladies could pay for their own drinks. With the laden drinks tray now in hand, she carefully made her way from the bar and back to the makeshift VIP area, her credit card clenched between her teeth. Placing the tray down and onto the table, she felt a sudden stampede of boots, their owners all wearing matching pink sashes that read *Shea's Biaches* – a tasteless addition by one of Shea's friends who Samantha wasn't familiar with, and didn't want to be. Only two of the attendees were girls she'd gone to high school with and, as the night had stretched on, with the topics of conversation mainly about Country Women's Association gatherings and lamington drives to raise money for the hall, along with the highs and lows of raising children, she'd felt increasingly like a fish out of water. She wasn't about to let Shea cotton on to this, though, or so she hoped – tonight was all about her lifelong bestie. She was doing her upmost best to fit in with the crowd.

'One, two three, annnnd, bombs away.' The announcement came from a short middle-aged lady Samantha couldn't for the life of her remember the name of.

The ten women tossed their heads back. Samantha jiggled on the spot as the tequila warmed her belly and the corners of her eyes twitched as she sucked on the piece of lime. She and Shea saluted their successful shots with a high five as some of the group dashed back towards the dance floor, and a few to the opposite direction where the toilets were. Right then 'Macarena' blared from the massive speakers at the sides of the dance floor. Clearly keen for another choregraphed boogie, Shea grabbed Samantha's hands and tried to drag her towards the flashing lights, but by literally digging the heels of her stilettos in, Samantha avoided another sweaty bout of dancing.

Feeling a little wobbly on her feet, she flopped into one of the three lounge chairs that had been cornered off for the hens' party and grabbed a handful of Bombay mix from the bowl at the centre of the table. She was usually a red wine kind of gal, and the sparkling wine was going straight to her head, as were the three shooters she'd now had over the course of the evening. While munching on a couple of curry-flavoured dried peas, she thought about how the night was going to end – women without shoes, lots of hollering in the street as they hailed the one and only taxi, maybe even a pit stop on the way home for someone to heave their dinner into the scrub. Her stomach backflipped at the thought. Oh lordy, she hoped it wasn't going to be her. She also hoped the couple of more wayward women attending had listened when she'd asked them not to organise a stripper, because Shea's one firm request had been that she didn't want one.

Sacrilege! had been one of their replies. *A hens' night without a stripper will be like a cake without the icing* had been another. Samantha was in agreement with Shea; yuck to some stranger rubbing themselves all over you.

Glancing around the rowdy pub, she felt a sense of country camaraderie. She had initially questioned Shea's choice of location for her hens' party, seeing as the bride and groom should never be caught dead at the same place, but then, where else would her friend celebrate in a town as small as Gum Tree Gully? The publican and his staff had done their best to try and separate the bucks and hens, and so far, so good. Every seat was taken, and there was a boisterous crowd milling around every corner of the horseshoe shaped bar, so there was enough degree of separation to allow no unwanted run-ins with the blokes.

Grabbing the water jug, Samantha poured herself a glass. The music lulled and up on the stage the lone singer and his guitar returned from his break. She gave thanks to the powers that be, because she couldn't cope with hearing another retro pub classic that involved a series of coordinated dance moves. Taking his place at the microphone, the musician began to play a familiar Clearance Clearwater Revival song. Taking sips from her water, she couldn't help but hum along to 'Lookin' Out My Back Door' as her foot tapped in time to the catchy rhythm that took her back to the few B&S balls she'd gone to as a teenager. The partygoers were loving it, too, their combined voices hollering every word. When the song finished, the crowd exploded in whistles, claps and cheering. Clearly chuffed with the applause, the singer took a bow before strumming his guitar to a Guns N' Roses classic, 'Paradise City'. By the chorus, there was headbanging galore.

A red-faced, sweaty Shea reappeared and leant into her ear. 'Passionate mob, aren't they.'

'They sure are,' Samantha called over the crooning of the crowd.

'Oops, looks like I'm empty again.' Shea held up her champagne glass. 'You want another?'

Feeling as though she was tipping over the edge of tipsiness, and into drunkenness, Samantha shook her head. 'I think I might stick to my glass of water for now.'

Shea pulled a pouty face as she flopped down beside her on the couch. 'Boo to that, water is so yesterday.' Hooking an arm around Samantha's, she rested her head on her shoulder and swallowed a hiccup. 'Come on, bestie, have another drink with me because we never get to go out and party together anymore, seeing as you live hundreds of thousands of miles away from me.'

That old familiar guilt pounded Samantha's heart, and her resolution caved – it wasn't often that Shea could rope her workaholic aunt into babysitting, and it was never that Samantha was back here, in her hometown. 'Oh, okay then, but this will be my last, otherwise you might be holding my hair back while I throw up.'

'Of course I would do that for you.' Shea's easygoing smile was skewed. 'Because that's what friends are for, right?'

'Ditto, lovely.' Grabbing the bottle of bubbles from the ice bucket, she poured them their fifth glass – or hang on, was it their sixth? She went to ask Shea, but her friend was now resting back with her eyes closed. 'You know, it might do you good to have a water, too, Shea.' She rested a hand on her leg.

'Hmmm.' Her eyes flicking open, Shea offered Samantha a weary sideways glance. 'Yeah, the room's spinning a little bit so maybe you're right.' She pointed to the jug. 'I'll have a double.'

All Samantha could do was laugh.

Swapping the glass of bubbles for a big glass of water, she passed it to Shea, who downed it in a couple of gulps. 'Aah, thanks Sammie, always looking after me, you are.'

The lady with the forgotten name returned and playfully smacked her hands to her hips. 'I'm afraid I have to take Shea back to the dance floor for one last boogie because my hubby will be here in twenty to pick me and a couple of the gals up.'

Yay, the night's coming to an end… Thinking of what it was going to feel like to kick her shoes off, wash her face and then fall into bed, Samantha flashed a smile. 'Be my guest.'

Watching Shea disappear into the gyrating throng, Samantha blocked out the conversations around her as she searched the sea of faces. She didn't recognise anyone, but after so long away, and with many locals having left since the mine closed, what did she expect? But then, just as she was about to turn her focus back to the dance floor, her attention hooked on every country girl's dream. Dressed in nice-fitting jeans and a button-up plaid shirt, Connor Gunn stood almost a head above the rest. Unable to tear her eyes from him, Samantha could feel the potency of his presence, as if he had climbed inside of her. As Connor turned from the bar with two glasses of water in hand, their eyes briefly met, and they shared a moment of mutual understanding. Evidently, Jack was likely in the same state as his wife-to-be, and Connor was looking out for his mate. With a dimple-clad smile created only for her, he gave her a nod before disappearing back into the thick of the crowd.

'Oh my God, Samantha Evans, is that really you?'

Samantha swore beneath her breath. There was no mistaking that nasal voice, and she wasn't up for small talk with the girl who had taken great pleasure in antagonising her at high school, the granddaughter of the gossiping woman who'd death-stared her at the supermarket her first day back in town.

'Hi, Claire.'

'Oh my god, it is you.' A much older-looking Claire sank down on the couch, eyes wide. 'Grandma mentioned you were back, but I told her I had to see it to believe it.'

'Yeah …' A tight smile formed on Samantha's lips. 'I'm back for Shea's wedding.'

'I didn't think you'd bother coming all this way for some last-minute shotgun wedding.' She smiled a little smugly. 'Especially seeing as you haven't set foot here since you ran away.'

'I wouldn't dream of missing it.' Samantha ignored the dig – it wasn't worth wasting her breath on a person who thrived on upsetting people. 'But I understand you're not invited.'

Claire pulled an 'I don't care' face. 'I wouldn't have gone anyway.'

Samantha couldn't help her look of disbelief. 'If you say so.'

The air was suddenly thick, suffocatingly so, as they just sat and stared at one another.

'Okay, well, I better get back to my big group of friends.' Claire shot to her feet.

'Yup.' Samantha breathed a sigh of relief. 'See you round.'

Alone again, and beyond busting, she decided to make the trek past the bar, and the area the blokes were restricted to, so she could take another much-needed trip to the loo. Her eyes darted left and right as she passed the bar, the desire to lay her gaze on Connor again so irresistible she took the long way around. Standing over by the pool table with pool cue in hand, his gaze was fixed on her. They shared a smile, a moment in time that somehow fluttered into her heart and landed there, before she watched him get slapped on the back, then bend over the table and line the cue up, sinking three balls in quick succession. Hot damn, that man was good at everything. Snapping back to reality, she joined the line of women winding out of the toilets, her view of Connor now partial, but not blocked.

As if appearing out of thin air, Shea was suddenly at her side. 'Look at that, Connor is checking you out,' she said, gazing towards the blokes.

'No, he's not.' As the line moved forward, Samantha feigned indifference while her heart did otherwise.

'Oh yes, he is.' Shea nudged her with her elbow. 'Look, he can't take his eyes off you.' Caught in the act, Connor swiftly turned his attention elsewhere. 'Maybe you should go and hang out with him for a bit, reminisce about the old times and all that.'

'Nope.' Samantha felt giddy at the thought, but quickly blamed it on the alcohol. 'I don't want to reminisce with him in the slightest.'

'Wow.' Folding her arms, Shea eyed her sceptically.

Samantha eyed her back. 'What?'

'Bit defensive, don't you think?'

'Sorry.' She waved a hand through the air dismissively. 'I'm just getting tired.'

Once the toilet duties were done, she found herself being dragged towards the stage for a begrudging bout of karaoke. 'I don't want to sing in front of everyone, Shea.' She tried to yank herself free of Shea's deathlike grip. 'Get one of the other women to do it with you.'

'They've all left.' Shea wasn't giving up. 'And therefore, you soooo want to sing in front of everyone so I don't have to do it on my own, like a good friend would.'

'Noooo.' She fought to dig her heels in again. 'I don't.'

'Oh, come on, spoilsport.' Shea finally let go of her wrists. 'What's happened to the Sammie that used to be up for almost anything? Did you go and lose her in London?'

She had, but wasn't about to admit it. 'Right, come on then.' She stomped past Shea. 'Let's do this before I go and chicken out.'

'Yay!' Shea shrieked her reply as she clapped her hands madly.

The throng of people staring straight at her, or so it felt, cheered as she and Shea climbed the four steps and walked into the blinding stage light. Nervously, she leant into the mic and, at first quietly, sang the lyrics of the Cold Chisel song she knew all too well. 'Rising Sun' was a typical party song, one that would always fill the dance floor. And it didn't fail to this time around either. One chorus in, and the crowd was so pumped, and the beat was so snappy, and Shea was giving it her absolute all, that she couldn't help but throw her whole heart and soul into it too. The enthusiasm of the pub, and Shea, was contagious. Her courage quickly gathering momentum, she lifted the mic from the stand and leant back, bellowing the chorus, not giving two hoots if she was out of tune. She and Shea belted the final chorus out together, along with the crowd, and when it ended, she surprisingly found herself keen to stay up on stage so they could sing another song. But the next duo was already beside them, ready to grab the microphone. Flushed with exhilaration, she bowed to the adoring throng of partygoers, as did Shea. Passing the mic over to a tall ginger-haired lad who looked all of eighteen, she realised too late that she'd gone and taken things a step too far. Literally. Time seemed to stall. All sound ceased, as if people were holding their breaths. As she flailed through the air, the stage disappeared, and she tumbled forward with her arms flapping as if she could fly to save herself.

All she could think in that suspended moment was, *oh god, I'm about to fall flat on my face, and probably break some bones. On ya, Evans!*

But strong arms caught her, held her, helped her find her equilibrium and then placed her back on solid ground. 'You right?' Leaving his hands on her arms, Connor stared at her, his blue eyes searched hers.

Thank goodness for the shadows they were standing in because her face would've been the brightest of reds. 'Uh-huh.' With her trembling bottom lip between her teeth, she nodded. 'Other than a bruised ego, I think so.' Legs still trembling, she leant into the wall because leaning into him would spell a whole world of danger. 'Thank you for saving me from landing flat on my face.'

'Hey, anytime.' Pushing his shirtsleeves up, Connor offered her his trademark brazen smile.

A rush of heat scorched her insides. 'And just when I thought I was one of the cool kids.' She laughed, a little too forcibly, in a bid to ease her awkwardness, because if she blushed any harder from embarrassment, she swore she'd spontaneously combust.

'You're still hip as, Sammie.' His lips quirking at the corners, he shrugged casually. 'Just tell everyone you did it on purpose.'

Her forehead wrinkled in confusion. 'I did what?'

'You know, crowd surfing, like all the cool kids do.'

'Oh, yeah.' She loved the idea, and she also loved that just like in the old days, he still had her back in any given situation, even one as embarrassing as this. 'Great idea.'

'Don't worry, Sammie Samsung, I got you.' His words were playful, but his expression spoke otherwise.

'Mm-hmm.' It was all she could get past her pulse beating wildly in her throat. Oh, how she wanted him to *get her* right this very second.

Then something between them shifted and gave way. She could feel her emotional armour beginning to lose its solidity as his electric blue regard of her, so knowing, so pervading, added a kindling to the fire he'd already re-ignited deep down inside of her, and the sudden flare made the flames jump high enough to brand the edges of her heart. The feeling was so intense she now fought to breathe naturally.

He stepped a little closer.

Dangerously close.

The impact of what he could do to her, without laying a finger on her skin, burst in her chest.

She was falling for him again.

No, she couldn't be.

This was purely physical, with the added benefit of a long friendship.

Get a damn grip, Samantha, before you go and do something stupid, again …

'You want to get some fresh air?' she blurted, desperate to make some distance between them.

Watching her dash past him, he said 'Yeah, righto, sounds good' to her back as he took long strides to follow her.

Samantha couldn't get out of the pub, and out of dangerous territory, quick enough. Connor was right beside her as the door slapped shut behind them, and as they made their way over to the parking lot, the music faded away, as did the flashing lights from the front facade. She could suddenly hear the gravel crunching beneath her shoes, and Connor's breath, given he was walking so closely beside her.

'Aah, that's better, I can hear myself think out here.' She glanced up at the perfect crescent of the silvery moon, backdropped by a canvas of glimmering stars and black velvet sky.

Tipping his head skyward, Connor joined in her all-embracing regard of the stunning sight. 'Yeah, there's something to be said for the sound of silence that only the vastness of the country can give you.'

'So true.' She sighed, smiling softly. 'I hadn't realised how much I'd missed such simple yet remarkable things, until arriving back here.' She dared a glance in his direction, liking the look of adoration written all over his handsome face. 'Why are you smiling like that?' she said, when he just kept gazing at her.

'I'm thinking, seeing as you've only got limited time to enjoy all of this, before heading back to London …' He waved wide arms towards the sky. 'How about we take a breather, and a sit on the back of my LandCruiser, so you can soak up the ambience a little longer before we head back into the madness that's waiting for us in there.' He thumbed over his shoulder, towards the pub.

As much as she knew she most probably should, Samantha couldn't say no. 'That sounds lovely.'

'Great,' he said, clapping his hands to his thighs. 'Let's do it.'

Do it? Oh god, the wayward images going through her mind right now.

Reaching his four-wheel drive, he held her hand and helped her up and onto the tray. His touch felt so good, so familiar, so overwhelmingly addictive, she almost said *please don't* when he unravelled his fingers from hers. Then in one swift movement, he was sat beside her, their legs swinging in unison and their gazes back towards the sky. Crickets chirped and leaves rustled, the gentle breeze stirred her hair. Tucking it behind her ears, she was just about to ask him how life had been the past decade when her name was bellowed from the shadows.

'Sammeeeeeee, where are yoooou?'

'Shea, is that you?' Samantha squinted into the darkness.

'Yessss, it's meeeeee.' Close now, Shea appeared and skipped towards her, smiling from ear to ear. 'Everyone is keen to come back to our place for a nightcap.' Catching her breath as she flopped against the back of the ute, she looked from Samantha to Connor, then back to Samantha, a cheeky grin replacing her gleeful one. 'Are you two good to go?'

Samantha wasn't up for a nightcap. She just wanted to go home and go to sleep. 'Who's everyone?' She held back a grimace – only just.

Shea waved an arm back in the general direction of the pub, just as Jack and a couple of his mates staggered into sight. 'This motley crew.'

'Hi.' Samantha gave the group a wave then flashed Connor an *oh help us* glance, which he returned. 'How is everyone getting back to your place?'

'We've called the cab. He'll be here in two shakes of a lamb's tail,' Shea said before hiccupping, giggling, then snorting. 'Oh lookie, there he is.' She spun, wobbled, then pointed down the road. 'Honey bunny, our ride's a-comin',' she called to Jack.

But Jack was too busy singing along with his three mates at the top of his lungs that he didn't even hear her.

'Jack Farley,' Shea called louder. This time, he heard her. 'Cab's here,' she said in a hilariously stern tone, hands going to her hips.

The incoming beam of headlights of the taxi lit up a pair of kangaroos. Momentarily pausing with curious faces, they bounded off behind a mound of spinifex bushes just as the taxi pulled up.

The old bloke leant on his windowsill and glanced from left to right. 'How many of you are there, Shea?'

'Um.' Shea looked around the group and counted on her fingers. 'Six.'

'Sorry, but that's two too many. I'll have to do two trips, I'm afraid.'

'Nah, it's all good, Johnno.' Connor jumped down from the back of the ute. 'I've only had a couple of beers, so I'm good to drive.' He glanced at Samantha. 'I'll give you a lift home, and this rowdy lot can grab the taxi, if you like?'

Samantha couldn't think of anything better right now. 'That'd be perfect, Connor, thank you.' She planned to make a quick exit when she got back to the homestead, leaving Shea, Jack and their drunk friends to their afterparty.

CHAPTER 9

But as per usual in her life, things didn't go to plan ...

And the following morning came around way too fast.

Stirring from a dream where she was running through a field of sunflowers, her fingertips brushing the soft yellow petals, her hair wild and her spirit free, Samantha rose to the surface of reality. Light-headed, she momentarily panicked as she tried to work out where in the heck she was. Blinking her heavy eyelids fully open was a task, but when she finally did, sunlight burned through a window, and she threw a hand up to shade her eyes. A soggy Twistie was stuck to the back of her hand. *Eww.* Flicking it off, she watched it make an arc through the air, then land on Shea's coffee table, among myriad empty chip packets, beer cans and chocolate wrappers. Wow, talk about going all out; she'd have to run ten miles to work all the junk food off. Scanning her surroundings to try and piece together what was now a hazy memory of the return home, she laid eyes on an empty bottle of bubbly laying on the floor, alongside her heels and a tub of Connoisseur cookies and cream ice-cream, spoon still inside but contents well and truly gone.

Good grief, it was no wonder she felt bloated.

Propping herself up a little further, she felt as if a freight train was racing through her head and a planation of cotton had grown in her mouth. She needed water, and Panadol, desperately. Thank goodness Connor had made a speedy getaway as soon as he'd dropped her off – she hated to think what might have happened if he'd stayed, with her self-control clearly having left the building. After he left, Shea had caught her tiptoeing down the hallway, en route to her bedroom, and had roped her into staying up. Flashes of dancing around the lounge room with the bottle of prosecco to her lips, the pair of them singing their hearts out to Frank Sinatra classics, had her groaning. She had to admit it'd been fun at the time, but today was going to be a slowly-does-it kind of day.

Easing back again to stop the room from revolving, she beheld a collection of bras spinning from the overhead fan. A quick peek down her top offered her relief – her bra was still where it ought to be. She couldn't help but chuckle. It looked like some feminist party had occurred while she'd been crashed out. Or had she been involved in the bra escapade? Goodness, she couldn't remember for the life of her if she had. Even though she had a hangover from hell and couldn't recall what had happened in the wee hours of the morning, she'd honestly had the time of her life. It made her realise just how much she missed the girl from the country, and to be completely candid with herself, she wanted more of her. The businesswoman she'd become in London could take a back seat, because she wanted to get her fill of her childlike self before heading back to the grindstone. This new, old her was going shotgun for the rest of her holiday if she could help it along.

Look out Gum Tree Gully, she thought, laughing at herself, then wincing when her head start hammering. It was hard to believe how quickly she could shed her skin when surrounded by her real friends, the ones who loved her, for her. One minute she was a meticulous risk analyst spiralling down the black hole of divorce, and the next, well, she could only imagine the malarky she and Shea had gotten up to and were yet to get up to.

A mumbled sentence of expletives caught her attention.

'Shea?' Rolling onto her side, she spotted her friend buried in a pile of pillows and a doona. 'Are you awake?'

'Hmmm,' Shea groaned sleepily. 'I think I am, but the banging in my head makes me think I don't want to be yet.'

'Ha ha, hangovers are the worst.'

'Oh yeah they are.' Shea sat up, unaware of the hilarious state of her face, her make-up smeared from one side to the other. 'What time is it?'

'A hair past a freckle going on to a mole,' Samantha replied cheerily.

'Oh, hardy ha ha, Miss Evans.' Shea rolled her eyes. 'There's always one in the group, hey.'

'Yes, and for once, that'd be me.' Samantha stabbed her chest and pointed at Shea. 'And, FYI, by the looks of you, I reckon you better find another make-up artist because the one that done all of that …' She made a circle in the air with her finger. '… should find another profession.'

'What the heck are you on about, Sammie?'

'You've got lipstick where blush should be, eyebrows drawn to your hairline, and…' She tipped her head to the side. 'I don't know what is in your hair, but I'm guessing it's food.' She grimaced. 'Or possibly regurgitated food?'

'Ew, I didn't throw up.' Shea pulled a similar grimacing face. 'Or did I?'

Samantha shrugged. 'Your guess is as good as mine, my darling mate.'

'Oh, deary me.' Shea rubbed her face, spreading the lipstick on her cheeks even further. 'I think we should both have some painkillers, then showers to make ourselves somewhat respectable before Amaya and my aunty get here, and then after cleaning this mess up,' she said, glancing around the shambolic room, 'devour some greasy bacon and eggs washed down with some extra-strong knock-your-socks-off caffeine.' She looked to the bra-ladened fan, her head moving in circles as she watched it. 'Good lord, how in the heck did my entire bra cabinet get up there?'

Samantha shrugged. 'Again, your guess is as good as mine?' She burst out laughing.

And so did Shea.

Several hours later, after basically inhaling her greasy brunch, then feeling like a frump, Samantha somehow found the energy for a bit of a gym session. Having gathered what items she could find in the machinery shed – a couple of old tyres, a few paint tins and a bag of chicken feed pellets, along with a rainbow-coloured skipping rope borrowed from the toy box – she turned on the industrial fan and got to it. After forty-five minutes of rolling the tyres around the concrete floor, lifting the paint tins like weights, squatting with the feed bag on her shoulders, and skipping in between sets, she was dripping in sweat and puffing as if she'd just run a half marathon. Thinking about doing one more round of lunges, begrudgingly, she jumped with fright when footsteps came up behind her.

'Oh my god, there you are.' As Shea looked at the makeshift gym, confusion creased between her brows. 'What in the heck are you doing, you crazy woman?'

'What's it look like?' Samantha grinned as she raised the paint cans to chest height, then repeated the movement. 'Working out.'

'There's easier ways than doing this.' Shea waved a hand around. 'Why don't you go for a walk through the countryside, or even better, ride a horse through it.' She winked. 'Or possibly ride a cowboy instead.'

'Oi, you, stop it.' Chuckling, Samantha placed the paint tins back on the ground. 'I'd love to go for a good gallop, but I haven't ridden a horse in years.'

'All good, Sammie, because you never forget how to.'

She tipped her head to the side. 'Hmm, I don't know about that.'

'Trust me.' Shea's glossy lips spread into the widest of smiles. 'Actually, seeing as Jack has taken Amaya for a drive into town to buy some ice-cream, after we ate it all, how about we go and test the theory out now?'

Samantha's already laboured breath hitched as she imagined falling from the saddle, and possibly breaking a bone, or three. 'Like, right now?'

'Uh-huh, why not?' Hands went to Shea's hips.

'Because …' Samantha tried to think of some rational excuse but was coming up blank.

'Come on, Miss Evans.' Shea grabbed her hand. 'Let's go on an adventure, just like we used to.'

Half an hour later, dressed in jeans and a button-up shirt, with a borrowed pair of Shea's boots, Samantha at least looked the part, but she didn't feel it as she tightened the girth strap and readied herself to get into the saddle. 'Now, you better take care of me, Garth.' The horse named after Shea's favourite country music artist neighed and tossed its head. 'Just slow and steady, you got that?' she said, resolutely. 'I don't want to go hell for leather straight away.'

'Are you saying that to me, or Garth, Sammie?'

'Both of you.' Samantha smiled, then inhaled again – she'd forgotten just how much she loved the smell of a tack room.

'You've let yourself become too citified, my dear friend.' Halfway through checking her horse's shoes, Shea looked over her shoulder. 'Go on then, up you pop.'

Samantha eyed the palomino horse sceptically. 'Yeah, okay, all right, just give me a minute, Little Miss Bossy Boots.' Through searching eyes, the horse stared back at her, giving her the impression that he was just as dubious as she was about this spur-of-the-moment ride.

A little hesitant, she watched Shea slip a boot into her stirrup, and then settle in the saddle as if she were born in it. 'Well, come on then, Garth is ready, so up you get.'

Carefully, Samantha put her weight into the stirrup and then tossed her other leg over. It was easier than she thought it would be. The saddle creaked beneath her as she gripped the reins tightly and found her seat.

'Righto, let's head.' Shea gave her horse the cue to head out of the round yard, and into the open paddock. 'You all good back there?' she called over her shoulder.

'Yup, right you are,' Samantha called back.

Bouncing at first, Samantha made a concerted effort to relax her body and flow with the horse's movements. Then she held her breath as she gave Garth the cue that he was clearly keen for. As if shifting gears, he surged forward. Taking long strides, Garth ate up the ground with rhythmic pounding hoofs. It felt like she'd just been shot from a cannon, in a good way. As goosebumps covered her skin she quickly glanced to where Shea was galloping beside her.

'This is amazing.' The wind snatched her words, and carried them away.

Shea was right, it didn't take her long to fall back into the horse-riding young woman she once was, and before she knew it, she and Shea were galloping side by side towards the top dam. They came to a stop by the glimmering water and stayed in the saddle as their horses took a drink from the water's edge.

'See, I told you that you never forget, Sammie.'

'You were right.' Samantha felt like her soul was singing. 'That was so much fun.' She breathed a contented sigh, then smiled dreamily.

'Well then, we need to get you some boots, Sammie, so you can make the most of the time here on horseback.'

'Nah, I'm not going to be here long enough to be spending money on boots.'

'My god, woman, you used to live in your R.M. Williams.'

'I know, but they're a rare commodity back in London, for good reason. You don't really need a pair of bush boots there.'

Shea shook her head and said nothing.

'What?'

'I wonder what you see in that place, given you were born and bred here.'

'Yeah, well, things change, I suppose.'

'They sure do.' Turning her horse, Shea took the next bit of the ride nice and slow.

With Garth on autopilot, Samantha turned her attention to the picturesque landscape around them. Cicadas echoed a chorus of incessant noise meant to attract a mate – it was crazy to think such a racket was attractive. A clear blue sky, void of clouds, stretched from one side of the lush green world to the other. She watched as a flock of noisy galahs flew overhead, then settled in the branches of a gum tree just up ahead. This was the quintessential Australian bush as she knew it, bursting with life, untainted, encompassing, liberating and so very peaceful. Hypnotised by it all, she and Shea didn't utter a word for the next little while.

She'd lost track of time, but was reminded of it as she moved side to side in a bid to ease out her lower back. 'Man, oh man, I'd forgotten how many muscles you use up here.'

'See, I told you that, too, riding a horse is much better exercise than those silly squats you were doing earlier.'

'Those silly squats give me a pert butt, my friend.'

Leaning back, Shea proceeded to check out Samantha's behind. 'Can't say if I agree, or not, because right now, you're sat on it.'

Samantha gave Shea a playful hand gesture, then instinctively leant forward as they started up a hill. As the trail faded away, their horses picked their way and took each step carefully as they manoeuvred over the unsteady terrain. Samantha rocked a little from side to side as the climb got steeper still. Feeling as if the summit were going on and into forever, she dug herself into the saddle, and held on near the peak. She knew she was going to find a whole new set of muscles tomorrow morning, when she stepped from her bed. Walking was most likely going to be more like waddling. Then, just as she thought she'd be able to reach out and touch the sky, the landscape flattened and rolled out from the most jaw-dropping of viewpoints.

'Holy moly, Shea.' Having never been to this part of the property, she slowly scanned from left to right. For as far as her eyes could see, there was beautiful nothingness that somehow made her feel as though she was being held by loving arms. 'This is just so …' Her hand went to her heart. 'Amazingly magnificent.'

'Ain't it ever.' Shea's smile was sad now. 'This is where we spread Mum's ashes.'

'I can see why, it's a very special spot,' Samantha replied softly.

Clearing her throat, Shea tugged the brim of her hat down a little, then turned to her left. 'See the glint of a roof over yonder?'

'Uh-huh.' Samantha nodded.

'That's Connor's place.'

'Wow, okay …' She took a moment to gain her bearings. 'So that means town is thatta way.' She thumbed over her shoulder to Shea's confirming nod.

Samantha looked back towards the glint of Connor's place, feeling a strange pull on her heart knowing he was likely out there, somewhere, tending to his livestock. 'It's so sad about his father passing away.'

'Yeah, apparently brain cancer is very aggressive. One minute he was walking through town, going about his business, and the next, he was gone.' She sniffled, then took a breath. 'Just like my mum, hey.' Shea's shoulders shook and she looped the reins over the saddle horn, then buried her face into her hands as she broke into sobs. 'I miss her so much, Sammie. Every, damn, day.'

'Oh, honey.' Samantha knew all too well what that gripping grief felt like. Close enough to reach out and give her friend a rub on the back, she did so. 'I'm so sorry. I wish there was something I could do to help with the pain of her loss.'

Nodding into her hands, Shea sniffled, then brought her teary gaze to Samantha's. 'I wish you'd move home because that would help.'

For a moment, and then another, Samantha didn't know what to say, so she said all she could in a moment like this. 'I'm so sorry, Shea, I wish I could be around more for you, I really, truly, do.'

'I know you do.' Shea wiped her face, then huffed. 'Come on, enough crying over things we can't change, let's head home so I can make a start on dinner.'

'Righto.' Samantha nodded. 'I'll help you.' They stayed side by side, their horses moseying casually. 'What are we having?'

'God only knows, I haven't thought that far.' Shea grinned through her puffy red cheeks. 'Hangovers really do suck, it's not like me to be so disorganised.'

'Yeah, they do, but you don't let your hair down much, so once in a while isn't anything to beat yourself up over.'

'Yes, fair point.' Shea offered a tender smile.

When they had gotten past the rocky part of the slope, Shea took the lead. Her ponytail swung at her back as she cantered just in front. With Samantha's confidence in her returned riding abilities building, they sailed down the mountainside, just two girls on their magnificent horses, the freedom and camaraderie of it making Samantha's heart swell with joy. For the first time since arriving here, she felt the pang of longing for the country life Shea was living. Getting away from it all took on a whole new meaning in Gum Tree Gully, and she missed being able to do that.

A few hours later, after a delicious dinner of lamb chops, mash and steamed veggies, Samantha settled into the swing chair on the verandah and folded her legs up beneath her. As time ticked by, she drank in the sunset-painted countryside while taking little sips from her cup of sweet Earl Grey tea. Pinks, apricots and oranges swirled into one another as the sun sank into the horizon. She was totally lost in the view until a silhouette atop a horse entered her vision. Was she seeing things? She shaded her eyes and honed her sight. Her heart flip-flopped, and her stomach somersaulted. From this distance, she couldn't see his face shaded beneath his hat, but there was no mistaking his broad shoulders and powerful frame.

'Connor Gunn.' His named quietly rolled from her lips. 'Well, hot damn, you're one sexy son of a gun,' she said beneath her breath.

Catching sight of her catching sight of him as he approached the homestead, he tipped his hat. Her pulse responded by picking up the pace, until it seemed to be in perfect union with the clomping of his horse's hoofs. Totally unprepared for his impromptu visit, she quickly tried to smooth her hair down and straighten her skew-whiff singlet and shorts while he pulled to a stop, dismounted effortlessly and, after hitching his horse to the picket fence, strode with swagger and confidence towards her. With his jeans slung low on his hips, and his shirt fitting snuggly to his burly torso, he lifted the brim of his hat and flashed her that same old smile, the one that had won her over all those years ago. She took a second to catch her breath, and firmly remind herself he was a no-go zone, before feeling safe enough to utter an intelligible sentence as he reached the bottom step, and, with one booted foot on it, stopped.

'Hey, Connor, how goes it?' Her voice was surprisingly cool and composed.

'Yeah, I've just had a nice dinner with my granny, so can't complain.' His gaze travelled fleetingly over her, but there was nothing un-gentlemanly, and then back to her face. 'You?'

'Same.' His V-neck revealed a hint of dark hair, and a part of her longed to see just how far down it went now that he was a grown man. 'Can't complain.' That was right about when she caught herself chewing her bottom lip.

Stop it, Samantha.

'Well, just so you know, I'm all ears if you ever feel the need to complain, Sammie Samsung.' He smiled and continued before she found a coherent reply to such an offer. 'Is Jack about?'

'Yup, he's in the man cave.' She pointed to the shed. 'Watching the footy.' Wrestling with memories of their lips and hands ravishing each other, she instinctively took a step back. They held each other's eyes. Time stretched a little. 'And Shea's inside, bathing Amaya,' she added, in a bid to break a slightly uncomfortable silence.

'I see.' Unmoving, he regarded her thoughtfully.

'So how is your granny?'

'She's great, living in a retirement village, but still as strong as an ox. I make sure I catch up with her every week for a cuppa, or some dinner.'

'Ha, yes, she was a tough nut, from what I can remember of her.' Samantha smiled at recollections of Granny sweeping the front porch of her little cottage until there wasn't a speck of dust in sight. 'It'd be nice to see her while I'm back, she was always so kind to me.'

'I'm sure she'd love to see you, so I'll try and arrange it.'

'Thanks, Connor.'

Another couple of breathless seconds passed.

'Righto.' His hardworking hand tapped the banister. 'I'll leave you to it then.'

'Yes, okay, right you are.' Folding her arms, she nodded.

'That was very regal sounding, Sammie.' He chuckled, and then turned on his heel. 'That British life is rubbing off on you way too much,' he called out without looking back at her.

And thank god for that because she could swear her face had just turned a bright shade of red. Silently chastising herself for sounding hoity toity, she watched him go back to his horse, give its long neck a tender rub as he said something too soft for her to hear, reach into his saddlebag, then head towards the shed, a six-pack of beer in hand. She couldn't tear her eyes off him until he'd disappeared through the doorway, and she almost choked on her shock when he paused ever so briefly to acknowledge her with one last Connor Gunn smile.

Retiring back to her swing chair, she passed a dreamy hour until the sun had sunk completely, the golden orb bowing out to the sparkling brilliance of night. Then the earth began to get sleepy, and the only sound now was the breeze stirring the leaves of the surrounding trees. The mesmerising pulse of it all drew her to her feet, and she padded down the steps and onto the lush green lawn. It felt cool and soft beneath her bare feet. Wrapping her arms around herself she felt the physical pull of the landscape, luring her deeper into its healing heartbeat. She'd all but forgotten just how magically alive her old hometown felt. Staring into blackness, she pondered the fact that she felt like the only person in the entire world right now. It was almost overwhelming to believe it was so. The big smoke of London didn't allow for such a poignant sensation – it was one she hadn't experienced for a very long time. So, closing her eyes, she drew in a long, slow breath, feeling as if it were the first decent one in years. Goosebumps rose and covered her entirely as she felt the land beneath her feet somehow lift her, so she felt lighter, less weighed down by her myriad problems.

* * *

The spellbinding sense of being looked after just by being among the nature of Gum Tree Gully carried through her deep peaceful sleep and into the next sunshine-filled day. Sitting at the breakfast bar after her morning shower, enjoying her first cuppa for the day, along with a piece of Shea's homemade sourdough thickly spread with Vegemite, Samantha watched her dear friend hustle about her happy place. Beside her, Amaya was drawing colourful pictures with her crayons, and Fudge sat loyally at her feet. There was a lot to be said for the family vibe of this loving household.

'Would you like some crispy skin teriyaki salmon and stir-fry sesame veggies for dinner tonight, Sammie?' Shea called over her shoulder as she prepared Jack's lunch for the day.

'Oh yum, would I ever.' Samantha smiled over the rim of her cup at her dearest friend in the whole wide world. 'We're very *very* lucky, having you take care of us all like you do, Shea.'

'Don't be silly.' Shea readjusted her glasses, then tossed a hand through the air. 'I love cooking for my loved ones, it makes me a happy little camper.'

'I see that, and it makes us happy little Vegemites.' Making sure she had the black stuff smeared on her lips and teeth, Samantha grinned. 'See, I'm absolute proof of that.'

Shea turned and buckled over with laughter. Her mirth drew a sideways glance from a very concerned Amaya. 'You're so silly, Aunty Sammie.' Eyes wide, she covered her mouth, laughing into her hand.

'Am I?' Samantha grinned wider. 'Why's that?'

Amaya pointed, giggling. 'Because you've got Vegemite all over yourself.'

'I have, have I?' She pulled a face, enticing louder laughter from Shea and Amaya. Licking it from her lips, she tipped her head. 'Better?'

Grinning from ear to ear, Amaya nodded.

Rising to her feet, Samantha sculled the last of her coffee, rinsed her cup and then popped it into the dishwasher. Miranda Lambert's 'The House That Built Me' began to play from the radio. A fitting song, she thought, given the fact she'd spent so much time here, and she felt a bubble of nostalgia rise and settle.

Shea regarded her over the top of her glasses. 'What are you up to today? Any plans?'

It was a perfect day outside, so outside she was going to be for a good part of the morning and early afternoon. 'I'm going for a wander out yonder.' She brushed a kiss on Shea's cheek. 'Jack is letting me use the four-wheeler, so I'll catch you a bit later on, when we head into town to finalise the flowers.'

Shea smiled. 'Okey dokey, enjoy, my lovely. And make sure to be careful on that bike, too.'

'Will do.' She sung the words of Miranda's emotional song to herself as she made her way out of the kitchen and down the hallway. 'See you at two-ish.'

The stained-glass panes of the front door sent a scattering of green, blue and red over the walls and polished timber floorboards of the hallway, and the intensely citrus scent of the lemon myrtle flowers in the vase on the entrance table lingered, filling her senses to bursting. The elegant foliage and bright perky blossoms Shea had hand-picked from her garden called to her, and she bent her head to breathe them in deeper. Worthy of housing a tiny gumnut baby, the blooms were a reminder of just how magnificent Australian natives were. Long ago, Shea's mum had taught her that not only did these beauties smell divine, they were antifungal and antibiotic too, and could be used in cooking as well. Bush tucker, and bush medicine, at its finest.

The grandfather clock chimed from the lounge room, reminding her that time was ticking. Tugging on her new boots she'd bought at the Western shop yesterday, she felt a shiver of excitement. It had been years since she'd slipped her feet into her very own pair of boots. It reminded her a little more of who she used to be, before she'd fallen in step in heels or ballerina flats, depending on the time of the day, along with almost all the women who called the city of London home. Standing in front of the full-length mirror, she struck a pose, liking what she saw – a glimpse of the young woman she used to be.

'You can take the girl out of the country, but not the country out of the girl,' she quietly said to herself, then nodded to affirm this before stepping out and into the warm sunshine.

It didn't take her long to be heading out on her adventure. Negotiating the four-wheeler motorbike over the rutted road that was spiralling uphill, she made sure to take it slow and steady; unlike when she'd been a teenager, and she'd tear around the property without a worry in the world about crashing. As she reached the summit, an approaching thumping sound had her pulling to a stop and spinning in her seat to catch sight of three kangaroos bounding past. Catching sight of her, they paused and eyed her up, and for a few seconds she felt as if she were in a Mexican stand-off. Then just like that, they were off and bounding again, disappearing very quickly into the surrounding scrublands. She spent the next little while cruising about, stopping, wandering, taking photos with her iPhone, then cruising about some more. At midday, she stopped by the dam and sat on the water's edge, mindful of not having her toes nibbled by a red claw. Lost in Shea's backyard, the hours flew by and before she knew it, she'd driven into town and was stepping into the shop that was like a full-blown sensory experience. Sweet, perfumed scents had her breathing a little more deeply, and the bright pops of colourful flowers had her eyes widening. Shea went straight toward the bucket of red roses, and inhaled the smell in deeply.

'I'll be with you in a sec, Shea,' a singsong voice carried from the back.

'No worries, Suzie,' Shea called back, before sighing in pleasure.

Samantha's gaze drifted over the shop. 'It's seriously like another world in here.'

'Isn't it ever?' Shea plucked a couple of bright yellow sunflowers from a blue vase. 'I think I might take a few of these beauties home with us. They'll look nice on the kitchen table.'

'They sure will.' Reaching to pick up a red rose, she winced when a thorn pricked her fingertip. 'Ouch.' She brought it to her mouth. 'The ferocious thing bit me.'

Shea grimaced, then grinned. 'Every rose has its thorn, Sammie, as Poison tells us.'

'Ha, yes, true that,' Samantha replied just as the florist appeared with a stunning bridal bouquet in her hands. 'I just had a practice run, Shea, what do you think?'

'Oh, my goodness.' Shea took the bouquet, her expression a picture of absolute wonder. 'I think this is the most beautiful bouquet I've ever seen.' She turned to Samantha. Her eyes glimmered with unshed tears. 'Do you like, Sammie?'

'I *love*, wow.' The dusky pink roses looked as if the petals had been crafted from the softest velvet, and when she brought her nose to it, the smell transported her to an English garden.

The florist clapped her hands. 'I'm so happy you're so happy, Shea.' Reaching out, she ran a hand down Shea's arm, and then gave her wrist a squeeze. 'You deserve to be overjoyed on your special day, especially seeing as you've waited so long for it.'

'Thank you, Suzie.' Shea wiped a finger beneath each eye, smiling through her happy tears.

The door jingled behind them and, leaving Shea to sort out the finer details, Samantha turned to see Connor waltzing through the door, his hat now in his hands. Man, she couldn't get away from him – not that she wanted to.

Connor's face lit up like a Christmas tree when he spotted her. 'Oh, hey, Sammie, fancy running into you two here, of all the places.'

She offered him a matching smile in greeting. 'We're finalising the wedding flowers.' Assuming he was buying one very lucky woman flowers, she felt a weird jealous sensation wash over her. 'What are you doing in here?'

Oh god, did I just say that out loud?

'I'm just getting Mum some flowers.'

She sensed his magnetic pull, tried to push back, but couldn't help herself. 'Oh, that's so sweet of you.' Her heart swelled at his gesture – he and his mum had always shared a close bond. 'Is it for a special occasion, or just because?'

'A very special occasion, it's her birthday.' He looked to the vase filled with yellow sunflowers. 'These beauties are her favourite, so I was hoping Suzie would have plenty in stock.'

'Well.' She took a couple of steps to his side. 'It looks like you're in luck.'

'Uh-huh, big time.' He plucked ten flowers out, and then turned back to her. 'Hey, I'm cooking her a birthday dinner tonight, and I know Mum would love to catch up with you, so why don't you come and join us?'

'Really?' Feeling put on the spot, she wasn't sure if the right thing was to accept or decline his nice offer.

'Yes, really, Mum's always had a soft spot for you.' He paused momentarily, as if for effect. 'And what better time to catch up than her birthday?' His expression was filled with hope.

She did like his mum, a lot, and it would be lovely to see her. 'Only if you're absolutely certain.'

'I'm positive.'

'Okay, sounds lovely, count me in.' Then she remembered Shea was cooking teriyaki salmon, but before she could say anything, Shea was right beside her. 'Hey Connor.'

'Howdy doo, Shea?'

'Yeah, really good thanks.' She glanced at Samantha. 'We can have the salmon tomorrow night, Sammie, so don't feel tied in to be with us tonight.'

'You sure?'

'Yup, go and be free.' She looked to Connor. 'It'll do her good to get out.'

Samantha guffawed. 'Geez, thanks, mate, it sounds like you're trying to get rid of me.'

'That's because I am.' Shea grinned good-naturedly at Samantha's playful chagrin. 'So go, and have some fun.'

'Awesome, I'll call by and pick you up at six then,' Connor chimed in.

'Oh, no, you don't have to do that, I've got a hire car.'

'I know I don't have to, but I want to.' His smile was ever so charming, and damn sexy to boot. 'That way you and Mum can enjoy a couple of glasses of wine without you worrying about driving back to Shea's.'

'Thanks, Connor, but what about you being able to enjoy a few drinks with us?'

'I'll just have a couple of light beers, so all good. The cook has to remain somewhat sober, or God knows what we'll be eating.' He lightheartedly grimaced.

Samantha and Shea chuckled at his spirited expression.

'Right, okay then, it's a date …' Samantha felt a rush of panic at her verbal diarrhoea. 'Well, not date date, but sort of, but not …'

Oh lord just kill me now!

'Relax, Sammie, I knew what you meant.' Connor's chuckle was sexily gravelly.

'Right, yes, of course you did.' Oh lordy, if her face got any hotter right now …

'I'll take these, thanks Suzie.' Connor gave her some grace by turning his attention to the florist. 'Catch you later, Sammie, and say g'day to that husband-to-be of yours, Shea.'

'I will, Connor, catch you mate,' Shea said, entwining her arm into Samantha's then basically helping her out the front door. 'That man has very clearly got something over you, my dear friend.'

'He does not.'

Shea rolled her eyes. 'Oh, pull the other one, Sammie, you go all gaga every time you're around him.'

'I do not,' Samantha definitively stated.

'Uh-huh,' was all Shea said, but her face told Samantha everything she didn't want to know.

Connor Gunn did have something over her. And she liked it. Way too much.

CHAPTER
10

True to his word, Connor turned up smack on six o'clock. Samantha had been ready and waiting since five-thirty, after changing three times and finally deciding on her first choice of a floaty turquoise sundress and tan sandals. The matching earrings and necklace Shea had loaned her added a nice boho vibe to the outfit; if only she felt inside the way she looked on the outside. The fluttering butterflies in her belly had grown bigger wings in that half an hour of toe-tapping, leg-jiggling waiting, much to Shea's amusement, making her as restless as a frog in a sock.

'You've got it bad for him, girlfriend,' Shea had said with a cheeky smirk.

'I do not,' was Samantha's way-too-quick, and slightly feisty, reply.

'Ha, you can't fool me, Sammie,' had been Shea's spirited response.

Samantha's retort had been to give her friend the finger as she'd bid her goodbye and scooted out the front door with Connor's mum's gift and a bottle of good cabernet merlot in hand. She just hoped she liked the perfume and bath salts she'd picked up from the chemist, along with a lavender-scented silk eye mask. And as she'd traipsed down the steps – towards where Connor was watching her from the driver's seat, his forearm resting on the windowsill and his arresting blue eyes glued to her every step – she had to ask herself: who in the heck was she kidding? She still had that thing for him, the one that made her insides tip and tumble, and that magnetic lure he'd possessed over her all those years ago was still there, stronger than ever. And she couldn't help but wonder, as she neared the purring grumble of the V8 four-wheel drive, whether she was feeling so attracted to him because Connor was so comfortingly familiar in her time of vulnerability, or was it because deep down, underneath all the weight of their past and the shine of her armour, she really hadn't ever stopped caring for him, possibly even loving him?

'Hey, Sammie Samsung, you look nice,' he said as he jumped out and dashed around to the passenger side door. 'Here, let me get that for you.'

'Thanks, Connor.' She smiled, and then slipped up and into the passenger seat. He passed her the seatbelt. 'Always the gentleman, aren't you?'

'I'm not sure about that, but I do my best.' He grinned as she snapped the seatbelt into place. 'But make sure you don't tell anyone about my chivalry, because I got me a hard reputation to uphold around these parts.'

Samantha smirked at his look of mock seriousness. 'Do you, now?'

'Yup.' He shut the door and hightailed it back into the driver's seat.

After loosening the constricting seatbelt, Samantha gestured towards the forest of fragrance trees hanging from the rear-vision mirror. 'Got enough air fresheners, Connor?'

'Ah, yeah, there's a story about that.' He put the gearshift into first then spun the LandCruiser around. 'I went and left the window down last week and a feral cat decided to climb in and add its touch of cologne.' Offering her a quick sideways glance, he grimaced and shook his head. 'After scrubbing from top to bottom, I didn't think I'd ever get rid of the stench, so the next best thing was to try and cover it up with a wad of those thingamajiggies.'

Looking around as if she were about to spot the offending cat, Samantha sniffed hard. 'Well, they're doing the trick because I can't smell anything but vanilla and strawberry.'

'That's good, mission completed.' He tapped the steering wheel, then after a few silent seconds smiled at her. 'So Mum's really excited you're joining us tonight.'

'Great, I'm looking forward to catching up with her after all this time.' She was a little nervous, too, given the fact the last time she'd seen her was at Angus's cremation. 'So what's on the menu?'

Connor tipped his head a little to the side. 'That's for me to know and you to find out, Miss Evans.'

'Hmm, a man of mystery, hey?'

'Always.'

Silence settled again, but this time it felt natural, comfortable. Connor turned the stereo up, and the fact that he had Garth Brooks on made Samantha wonder if that was on purpose or just a coincidence – it had been playing the last time she'd sat in here, all those years ago, on the very night everything had changed between them.

After a leisurely few kilometres of having a dirt road completely to themselves, Connor slowed and pulled through the gates right on dusk. Samantha dug her feet into the floor as they bounced over a succession of cattle grids. Gazing out and over the dusty pink landscape, she was shocked at how well she knew every rise and fall, every curve and stretch of flatness, as if she'd never left at all. Something inside her soul stretched and sighed as if waking from a dreamy sleep, as a weird sense of belonging here floated and settled inside of her, as if she was finally home after a long arduous journey. The intoxicating sensation had her taking a few slow breaths as she tried to make sense of it.

'Does it still look the same?' Connor's husky voice invaded her thoughts as his headlights swept over his property, igniting the silhouettes of cattle and horses for as far as the eye could see.

'Yes.' With a dreamy smile, Samantha turned, nodding. 'Other than all the new horse agistment paddocks, it's exactly as I remember it.'

The sprawling homestead now in her sights, she looked to the wrought-iron railings of the front verandah lined with potted plants, then up to the bedroom window facing the paddocks. That was where Angus had tried countless times to go all the way with her, but she'd remained steadfast on not having sex before marriage. The accident had gone and changed all of that – just like it had changed everything that had mattered to her back then.

'Are you okay, Sammie?' Connor's hand came to rest upon hers.

She blinked poignant memories away. 'Oh, yes, sorry, I was a million miles away.' Not having realised they'd pulled to a stop, and the engine was no longer running, she sucked in a breath, both from being startled and also from the beautifully warming feeling of Connor's reassuring touch.

'You sure?' He regarded her with all-knowing eyes.

The lump of emotion lodged in her throat finally dissipated. 'Uh-huh, all good in the hood, I am.'

'All good in the hood, hey? You're getting mighty hip there, Sammie.' Connor's smile was slow and sexy.

Shrugging off the melancholy caused by her past, she had to laugh at her old-school response. 'Good grief, being back here is certainly bringing out my teenage self.'

'Yeah, well, I reckon that's a great thing.' Shoving his door open with his boot, he offered her one last contemplative look filled with too much to fathom before jumping out. 'Now let's get inside so I can get back to cooking my Michelin-star meal while you and Mum catch up over some vino.'

She grabbed the gift bag with goodies and the bottle of wine from her feet, then climbed out and met Connor at the bonnet. 'You're talking yourself up there, don't you think, chef Gunn?'

'Trust me when I say, I'm gonna walk the walk with my menu tonight.' He almost stripped her soul naked with his penetrating glance.

A second longer caught in his gaze and she would have revealed everything she'd been none too aware of herself until this very heated instant. And as he hooked his arm into hers and led her towards the homestead, she breathed him in deeply, letting the beautiful familiarity of him fill up all the places that were void inside of her. She had to silently admit that his company soothed her frayed nerves so effortlessly and her tattered heart so movingly. Simply being in his presence covered her in a blanket of relief, and she mentally tugged it in nice and tight as they stepped into another of the houses that had helped shape the woman she was today.

* * *

In his element, Connor felt happier than he'd been in what felt like forever. His mum's favourite group, The Highwaymen, was playing from the stereo. Waylon, Willie and the boys' voices were compelling, and the candles he'd picked up were lit, creating a relaxing ambience. But watching the two most important women in the world to him from his posting at the stove, he was tumbling into memories he didn't want in his head. And as he turned the scallops in the foaming garlic butter ever so gently, he firmly told himself that even if she was single again, he wasn't going back to that place with her. It wouldn't be good for him, and it certainly wouldn't be fair on her – especially not with his health concerns. 'History repeated' wasn't going to be a phrase anyone could use when describing their newly reforming relationship. When she left town again, undoubtedly taking another piece of himself with her, he wanted to remain in contact this time round, to be able to check in with her from time to time and be welcome to visit her in London if the opportunity ever arose. They were friends, had always been despite their rift, and always would be from this moment forward. Being around her again showed him just how important it was to have her in his life. And besides, it was hard to know exactly what he was feeling, given the fact he'd had his emotions under lock and key for so damn long. At the same time, curiosity about where they would've gone, if things had been different, was driving him insane. So, self-control was everything right now.

Because if he'd thought her beautiful before, it was nothing compared to the stunning woman she was now. Another glance in her direction, as he carried the pan over to the plates to begin dishing up their entree of scallops on cauliflower puree with scatterings of micro herbs, reminded him of that fact. Although she'd tamed her wild hair, and dusted make-up over her adorable freckles, she couldn't fool him into believing that wild girl he'd roamed this countryside with when they were kids was gone. Nuh-uh, she was still there, hiding beneath her armour, just waiting to be reminded of how free and happy she could be, if she allowed herself to let go. And he was going to do his best to remind her, as subtly as possible – because he knew better than most that Samantha Evans needed to come to her own conclusions, and discover her own truths along the way.

Closing the distance between the breakfast bench and the dining table he'd set with the best china by the bay windows, he stopped and waited, plates in hand. They were so wrapped up in their laughter and conversation that neither his mum nor Samantha noticed him. He cleared his throat, and caught their attention, the wide smiles on their faces warming his heart no end.

'Oh, hey, love.' Placing her wine glass down, Joyce sat up straighter in readiness to receive her food.

'Sorry to interrupt, ladies, but here's the first course.' He placed the dishes down with pride, loving the way both his mum and Samantha looked at the decadent food with the wow factor he'd been aiming for.

'Connor, I take my hat off to you,' Samantha said with a gasp. 'Because by the looks of this, you've certainly walked the walk.'

'He has, hasn't he?' Joyce picked up her knife and fork. 'It smells divine, I can't wait to tuck in.'

His plate in hand, Connor joined them at the table. 'Well go on, tuck in then, and don't be backwards in coming forward with your thoughts.'

The groans from both Samantha and his mum were enough to let him know just how much they were enjoying their first course. Come time for the main course of beef cheek slow cooked in a homemade Thai red curry sauce, served with lime and coconut jasmine rice, both women were speechless. Chuffed with his culinary skills, he almost licked his plate clean but held back, wanting to uphold some manners at the table. All the while, he kept sneaking glances at Samantha as she rolled her eyes in foodie pleasure. With that flush on her cheeks, be it from the heat of the spicy curry, or his presence – *yeah, dream on Gunn* – damn, she looked sexy without even trying. Mind you, she'd always driven him wild.

'My gosh, Connor, if you weren't a diehard cattleman, I'd be encouraging you to become a chef.' Samantha rested back against her chair and rubbed her belly. 'I think I'm going to go into a food coma, I'm seriously full to the brim.'

'So does that mean you want to skip dessert, then?' His hand rubbing the five o'clock shadow across his jaw, Connor eyed her interrogatingly.

'Would you like to ask for legal representation before answering that, Sammie?' Joyce chuckled, shaking her head. 'I don't think she'll be able to say no to your homemade apple and mulberry pie, son.'

'Yes, you're correct, Joyce. I've got this.' Sucking in an almighty breath, Samantha leant forward and placed her hands on the table. 'Let's see this irresistible dessert you've made, Gunn.'

'Right you are,' he replied, in the worst but best English accent he could muster, sending both women into cackling laughter again.

An hour later, with his mum now settled on the sofa with a mug of hot chocolate watching her favourite movie, *When Harry Met Sally*, Connor was enjoying his Frangelico-spiked hot chocolate on the back verandah along with Samantha. It was a lot quieter now they were on their own, and he was enjoying the silence of surrounding bushlands and her mesmerising company. Just out of his reach, standing tall as she looked out over the moonlit landscape with her arms wrapped around herself, she was clearly resolved to keep a safe distance from him. And that was probably a good thing because the attraction between them was undeniable. Like a bee to a honey pot, he was drawn to her more and more each and every time he was with her, and he liked to believe she felt the same way. Stolen glances across the dining table, when both of them had thought the other wasn't looking, but in fact was, had been frequent. Over a decade ago, she'd run for the bright lights of London. Yet, here they were, with that same old familiar feeling between them.

If the gossip was true, and she was a single woman again, maybe he should do something about whatever this was, before he went and lost her to another man again because something was telling him he'd need his head read if he denied the chemistry between them.

But what was he meant to say?

If anything at all?

Maybe keeping his mouth shut was the best option?

'Do you ever think about what could have been, with us, I mean, Sammie?' Shocked at his own audacity, Connor had to look away from her wide-eyed glance. 'Damn, did I just say that out loud?' He grimaced as the sound of the crickets chirping from the down pipe seemed louder than ever.

Samantha's intake of breath was audible, as was her heavy sigh. 'That was another lifetime, Connor.' Her chuckle was short, and maybe even a little cynical, but without being able to see her face, he couldn't be completely sure. 'We were just messed-up kids back then, with no idea about the world.'

'Messed up, yeah, but I don't agree with the latter half.' His hurt at her flippancy was evident in his tone, but he couldn't help it. 'We'd been dealt so many blows I reckon we knew much more about the world than most kids our age, to be fair.'

She seemed to think about this for a few lengthy moments, and then shrugged. 'Yeah, I see where you're coming from, but I still think we were very young and naive in a lot of ways, too.' Then she did what she always did when she was feeling out of her depth, and bit her bottom lip as if stopping herself from speaking her truth.

Connor wished to god she'd say whatever it was trapped behind those oh-so-kissable lips of hers, but he wasn't about to force her – maybe he should take a leaf from her book and stop re-reading old pages. 'Sorry to put you on the spot like that, it's just, you know me, I like to say it how it is, and I couldn't help but wonder if you ever thought about what would've happened between us if you hadn't left here.'

She nodded, but remained silent, and Connor knew that was enough of this conversation.

She yawned, but it looked and sounded forced. 'Gee whizz, I'm tired, I think it's home time for me.'

'Yeah, righto, it is getting on a bit.' He glanced at his watch and noted it was almost ten-thirty. 'Just let me grab my keys while you say bye to Mum, and I'll drop you back.'

'Okay, thanks.' She followed him back inside, where they found Joyce fast asleep on the couch.

'I won't wake her,' Samantha whispered.

'Cool, I'll let her know you said goodnight,' Connor replied quietly before switching the television off.

They both tiptoed back outside, and climbed into the LandCruiser. With the energy feeling a little weird, Connor flicked the radio on and turned it up just enough to make any silence somewhat more comfortable. The drive back to Shea and Jack's place was nothing like the trip they'd had earlier. The energy between them had undeniably shifted, and it felt uncomfortable. And he hated the fact that it was he who'd made it this way. As the four-wheel drive ate up the white lines of the highway, he beat himself up the entire way for being such a fool in bringing up a past that should have been left where it was. But it was too late now – he would have to just do his best to shovel the pile of memories he'd verbally dumped at her feet to the wayside.

Pulling to a stop outside the homestead, he shifted in his seat to watch Samantha clamber out. 'I'll catch you sometime over the next couple of days,' he said to her back.

After shutting the door, she turned and cleared her throat. 'Yes, okay.' She could barely meet his eye. 'And we can go over the last of the details before the big day, just to make sure we're both on the same wavelength.'

'Yup, sounds like a plan,' he replied, all the while wondering if there was an underlying meaning behind her words.

'Thanks for a beautiful dinner, Connor, and please remember to let your mum know I said goodbye.' She paused. 'I mean, goodnight.'

'Will do, night.' Before he had to sit and watch her walk away, he waited until she was safely out of the way, then headed back in the direction of home. A little miffed that the night, which had started so great, had ended so awkwardly – even though it was mainly his fault – he thought it was high time she was the one to watch him go.

Getting back to his safe haven, he felt her recent presence lingering, as though she'd left a sprinkling of her spirit there to taunt him. He kicked off his boots and headed inside to find his mum gone from the lounge room. His hands running along the railings of the staircase, he took the steps two at a time just to make sure she was safely tucked up in bed. The light spilling out from beneath the door let him know she was and, not wanting to bother her, he turned near the top and made his way back down the stairs and outside. He needed a cold shower. Now. Then he would hit the hay and spend most of the night staring at the ceiling, wondering why he'd said what he did, when his instincts told him the outcome wasn't going to be a favourable one. Was it his hurt, climbing to the surface and finally fighting back, or was it because he wanted to stir up her feelings, to see if they had an inkling of a chance? Whatever the divide had been between them while she had been away, thanks to his foot-in-mouth moment, it was hinting at its presence again. Hell, if she was separated from Benjamin, he'd swim through sharks to get to her, to make her see what was still there, but was he going to tear himself to pieces trying to do it?

CHAPTER 11

After climbing into bed at midnight, Samantha had slept well, all things considered. It had been a shock, being put on the spot about their past, but what had she expected? Of course he'd wondered, just as much as she had, about where they might have gone if she'd had the courage to stay in Gum Tree Gully all those years ago, but she wasn't about to let him know that. It would do them no favours, none at all, to be pining over what could have been. No, they needed to focus on the here and now, and that meant turning all their attention to their positions as maid of honour and best man. Shea and Jack deserved the most splendid of days, and it was her job, and Connor's, to make sure that happened. So, from here on in, that's what their conversations were going to be all about, if she had her way. Which she was quietly determined to do.

Her hands tucked behind her head, and her morning meditation coming to an end, she plucked her AirPods from her ears and popped them back into the case. Taking a moment to breathe deeply, she allowed her mind to settle into the day ahead. Lost in peaceful solitude, with nowhere to be and no deadline to meet, she actually found herself humming as she rose from her bed and swept the curtains open to reveal the twinkling brightness of the brand-new day. A kookaburra sitting on the Hills hoist caught her attention, its song one of raucous laughter. The old wives' tale was that was sung when someone was newly pregnant. Ha, it certainly wasn't her with a yet-to-be discovered bun in the oven. It had been so long since she'd been in the throes of lovemaking that she was sure she'd forgotten how to, or what it felt like to be wanted, ravished, loved like that. And it would most likely be quite some time until she ever did again.

Although, if she wanted to have the children she so longed for …

She shook her contemplations off. It was time to get on with her day, instead of pondering her lack-ofs, because as the meditation had preached for twenty minutes to her, there was a lot for her to be grateful for, and gratitude brought a better attitude. So, after showering, then deciding on a pair of jeans and a pretty peasant top, she noted the little spring in her step as she bounced down the stairs and towards the scent of freshly brewed coffee.

Shea's sunshiny face met her. 'Good morning, lovely.'

Samantha grabbed a cup from the draining rack. 'It is a good morning, isn't it?'

'Geez, what's gotten into you?' Shea's expression was a picture of playfulness as she leant into Samantha's space. 'Ahh, let me rephrase that, who's gotten into you?'

'Shea, behave yourself.' Busying herself with whipping up her caffeine fix, she glanced over her shoulder to discover Shea watching her like a hawk. 'What?'

'Somethings different this morning, so come on, spill.'

'Dinner was a success, and that's it really.' She wasn't about to whinge about the moment Connor changed all of that.

'A success hey, well, from where I'm standing, it appears to have been a massive hit.' She wriggled her brows. 'Samantha and Connor sitting in a tree, K-I-S-S-I-NG.'

'Stop it.'

Shea folded her arms. 'What if I don't want to?'

Samantha plucked the wooden spoon from the utensils jar and pointed it in Shea's direction. 'Or else.'

'Ha, I'd like to see you try and use that.' Shea flashed a challenging grin. 'I remember my Mum threatening us kids with that all the time, but she never used it on anyone's backside, God love her.'

With the conversation moving on, Samantha breathed a silent sigh of relief. 'Uh-huh, she thought she was scary, but she was far from it.' Her spoon clanked against her mug as she stirred her coffee into a frenzy. 'Would you like me to take over dinner duties tonight, and give you a break?' She turned and took a sip, her hip resting up against the breakfast bench. 'I can't promise it'll be anywhere near as delectable as your cooking, but it will at least be edible, and healthy.'

'Thanks, but all good. I reckon we'll fire the barbecue up tonight, whack some steaks and sausages on. I'll give Connor a call, and see if he'd like to join.' She held a hand up to stop the words that were about to fly from Samantha's mouth. 'Because that's what would usually happen given the fact he and Jack are best mates.'

'Okay, all right, fair enough.' Shea had a good point. 'How about I whip up a potato salad, and something for dessert.'

'Yummy, sounds good to me.' She planted a kiss on Samantha's cheek. 'Thanks, again, for offering to watch Amaya today.'

Samantha glanced out the kitchen window, to where Amaya was riding her pushbike with training wheels in circles with Fudge loyally at her side. 'My pleasure,' Smiling from the heart, she turned back to Shea. 'And FYI, so you and Jack can totally forget about everything and relax at the day spa, I've got this babysitting thing in the bag.'

'I know you do, Little Miss Practical.' Hooking her handbag over her shoulder, Shea offered one last smile. 'I'll be seeing you this arvo, hopefully a totally new woman.'

'You will feel a million bucks afterwards, I'm sure.' She offered a wave. 'Ciao for now, brown cow.'

Shea chuckled. 'Oh my god, the things we used to say.' Her footsteps faded down the hallway, and the click of the front door sounded.

Happy to be contributing to dinner, and helping with Amaya, Samantha strapped Shea's apron on and got to work. With Johnny Cash serenading her from the stereo, she whisked, stirred and swayed around the kitchen. An hour and a half later, with a pit stop somewhere in the middle of it all to take Amaya a plate of gingernut cookies and a glass of milk, the golden syrup pudding was steaming away on the stove, and the potatoes were now boiled, and cooling in the strainer on the sink. Embracing the feeling of a successful morning, she was just about to head out and spend some time with Amaya in the garden when a crashing sound followed by wails had her racing to the back door, down the steps and across the lawn, to where Amaya now lay beneath her pushbike, with scraped knees and elbows.

'Oh, my poor darling.' Scooping her up, she cuddled a sobbing Amaya to her. 'Shh, you're okay.'

It took a few minutes of cooing and soothing before Amaya's cries had diminished to more of a sniffle. It was then that Samantha notice how she was lying in her lap, staring at her. 'What is it, sweetheart?' She wiped snotty locks of hair from Amaya's cheeks and tucked them behind her ears.

'You're berry pretty, Aunty Sammie.'

'Oh sweetheart, that's lovely of you to say.' She kissed her forehead. 'But I think you're the most beautifullest of all.'

'Nuh-uh, I think we're both princesses.' Pressing a kiss into Samantha's cheek, Amaya wrapped her arms around her neck. 'I love you, berry muchly.'

A rush of unfamiliar emotion filled Samantha, and tears prickled her eyes. 'I love you, too, sweetheart, berry, *berry, muchly.*' There was something so pure, so raw, so profound about a child's unconditional love – it was no wonder Amaya was Shea's world. One day, she hoped to be blessed with this kind of love from her own children. 'How about we get you cleaned up, and then for lunch we make ourselves a big banana split sundae with lots of whipped cream and sprinkles.'

'Really?'

'Yes, really?' She dared not think about the whopping number of calories, and besides, seeing Amaya's beaming smile was worth every drop of sweat she'd need to generate to work it off later.

Popping Amaya to her feet, she assessed her cuts and was relieved to see they only needed some antiseptic cream and a bandaid. Standing, she took Amaya's little hand in hers, and they wandered back inside, where they enjoyed an afternoon of ice-cream eating, a tea party, face painting, dress-ups and finally a little doze on the couch while watching *Happy Feet*.

It was just going on dusk when she watched Connor pull into his usual parking spot. With tongs in hand, Jack went to greet his mate, while she and Shea busied themselves laying the dishes and salads out on the verandah table. She could feel Connor wandering up behind her, before she heard his voice saying her name in greeting.

Planting a wide smile on her face, she tucked her fidgeting hands into her linen shorts pockets and turned to acknowledge him. 'Hey, Connor.'

'Wow, this looks bloody yummy.' Bringing his eyes from the decadent spread of food, he flashed her a daredevil glance, skittering tingles from her head to her toes.

She could only imagine what it would feel like if he really did touch her in that way she'd dreamt about last night, much to her frustration. 'It's not as flash as your dinner was last night, but it'll be yummy all the same.'

'I'm that hungry I reckon I'm going to inhale it.' He plucked a piece of potato out of the bowl, and as soon as it was in his mouth, groaned. 'Oh my gosh, Sammie, this is yum.'

'It's only potato salad.' She couldn't help but grin at his pleasure-filled expression.

'What is this nonsense you speak of? Only potato salad?' He sucked mayonnaise from his fingertip. 'That bowl of beauty right there is an Aussie classic at its absolute finest.'

'Like I said before, always the charmer.' She jerked her head away from his mesmerising stare – she didn't want to get caught up in his dazzling eyes and charismatic smile.

Not tonight.

'Oh hey, Connor.' Shea plonked down a plate of fresh-from-the-oven garlic bread, then brushed a g'day kiss on his cheek. 'Glad you made it.'

He held up a six-pack of ciders and a bottle of sparkling wine. 'Thought I'd bring something a little different tonight.'

Taking both from him, she nodded. 'Very nice, thanks.'

'No worries.' He stepped away and joined Jack at the billowing smoker barbecue.

Samantha was glad to go back into the kitchen with Shea for the last of the utensils and napkins. Connor had a way of stealing her breath, and she needed to steal it back.

'I know it's a taboo subject, Sammie, but you and Connor have this …' She looked to the ceiling as if searching for answers. '… certain thing.'

'A certain thing, hey.' Samantha chuckled. 'Now that's saying a heck of a lot.'

'Okay, smartarse.' Shea poked her tongue. 'I don't need to explain because you know it too.'

'Do not.'

'As my mum would have said in this given moment, I wasn't born yesterday, my dear.' She bustled past, cutlery in hand and a smug look on her pretty face. 'Now come on, Evans, I'm officially on strike now so let's go put our feet up and leave the men to serve up and then clean up tonight.'

'I really like the sounds of that,' Samantha said, following her, but she didn't think Shea was being serious.

A couple of hours later, feeling like a beached whale as they sat around the fire pit, Samantha felt like she'd been waited on hand and foot since pulling up her camp chair. Even though there was a little tension between her and Connor, she believed they'd covered it up well, and all in all, it had been a lovely night with easygoing conversation and lots of laughter. She startled a little when a loud yawn came from where Connor sat across from her, on the other side of the fire pit.

'Are we keeping you up, Gunn?' Jack said, with a chuckle then a loud yawn of his own.

It started all of them off, as they began yawning.

Conner stretched his arms high. 'I better get going soon, I have to be up at a sparrow's fart.'

'Me too,' Jack replied.

'We best get our beauty sleep then, mate.' Sculling the last of what would have been warm cider by now, Connor stood and stretched. 'Thanks for a great night, you lot.'

'You're very welcome,' Shea replied.

'Catch you on the flip side.' He leant over and gave Shea's cheek a friendly kiss, followed by a manly shake of Jack's hand. He turned to Samantha and hesitated. 'Night Sammie,' he said with a nod as he passed her.

'Night, Connor.' She watched him disappear into the darkness, then rested her head back again. 'That was a really nice night,' she said with a contented sigh, all the while wishing she could have enjoyed a goodnight kiss from him, but not in the same friendly way as Shea had.

In another life, another time …

Jack and Shea agreed about the lovely night with mumbled responses.

The deep grumble of Connor's LandCruiser being revved to life enticed them all from their chairs, into the house and to the comfort of their beds.

Samantha plugged her phone into the charger, switched the lamp off and fell back against her pillow. With the curtains softly swaying in the cool country breeze, she watched the moonbeams dance over the ceiling as she tried to collect her thoughts in a way that would send her off to dreamland quickly. But her thoughts weren't having a bar of her discipline. They took on a mind of their own, as she imagined Connor tall, strong and very naked, hungrily ripping every inch of clothing from her, and then dropping to his knees and kissing her in the place that was now aching with longing. Squeezing her legs together, she rolled over and hugged a pillow to her.

For goodness sake, Samantha, get a damn grip.

Pressing her eyes shut, she willed herself to sleep. It was late and she really needed to try and get some rest. A few minutes passed, then a few more, until it felt like she'd been laying there for almost an hour. Tossing the pillow she was clutching over her head, she groaned into it as she willed her wayward mind to visit the land of dreams. Maybe she should try meditating, or counting sheep.

Let go, let go, let go …

One sheep, two sheep, three sheep, four sheep ….

Five and a half hours later she woke at the crack of dawn. Desperate for a run before she weighed herself down with more pointless contemplations about a man whose name she wasn't even going to say – it would do her no favours – she quickly got dressed in her exercise gear and runners, and tugged her bed-hair into a messy bun. Feeling her way down the stairs, she cringed as they creaked beneath her feet. Pausing briefly, she listened for any sound of having woken Shea or Amaya, but thankfully silence met her. Then she tiptoed towards the back door and stepped outside just as the sun was beginning its ascent into the dusty pink-hued sky.

After stretching her limbs to life, she popped her AirPods into her ear, picked a high-energy Spotify list and then took off at a steady pace. She was unsure of which way she would end up going and how long she would jog for, but she wanted to allow her mood to take her on a whim. Reaching where the long winding driveway split into two, she decided to take the hardest way – mostly uphill, but the lookout at the top would make the extra effort worth her while, she was sure.

Losing herself to the sound of her music, her rhythmic footfalls and a countryside that never stopped taking her breath away, she found herself at the peak of the knoll before she knew it. A few more steps, and a patchwork of lush green fruit fields and earthy brown countryside rolled out before her eyes in the most mesmerising of ways. Stopping to catch her breath, she used the time to stretch again, all the while keeping her gaze towards the sunrise-soaked horizon. One of her favourite tunes started, and in a rare moment of impromptu excitement she felt an irresistible urge to have a little dance – and seeing as no one was watching, she let loose. Busting out some kick-arse moves with all her heart and soul, and singing the lyrics out loud, she almost jumped to the clouds when the tap of a finger upon her shoulder had her spinning around to see a very amused, and equally sweaty, Connor staring back at her. That was right about when she lost her footing and ungracefully stumbled smack-bang up against him.

OMG, could I be any more of a klutz?

Never had she felt so red-cheeked in all her life. 'Hey, you.' She plucked an AirPod out with one hand, and unthinkingly left the other hand against his chest to steady herself.

'Fancy running into you out here, Sammie.' His voice was a sexy drawl. 'And those dance moves were very nice.' His grin widened. 'Stellar, in fact.'

With his dimple-clad smile making her legs even weaker, she suddenly realised how close she still was to him and jerked her hand back from his, ahem, *very nice-feeling* chest. 'Sorry, you startled me.' Plucking her mobile out from her Lycra pocket, she stabbed *stop* on the song that driven her to embarrassing folly. 'I didn't know you jogged?'

'Yup, I do, whenever I get a chance.' He gestured to the phone clutched tightly in her hand. 'You really should get rid of that thing, or at least leave it behind when you head out and into the great outdoors.'

She held it up. 'This thing?'

'Yup, it's a pleasure spoiler.'

'Ha, okay, says the blind leading the blind.' She noted he wasn't laughing, and tipped her head in curiosity. 'Hang on a minute, don't you own a mobile phone?'

'Yeah, I do, but I don't have it glued to my hip like most people, and half the time I don't even know where it is.' He shrugged at her look of bewilderment. 'What? I like not being able to be contacted sometimes, it makes me feel free.'

'Fair enough.' Wanting to get out of his effortless bubble of magnetism, she glanced at her Fitbit. 'Anyhoos, I best get on with it.' She didn't wait for him to respond, just started off at a slow jog. 'Got to keep my heart rate up, to burn all the calories I ate last night, so I'll catch you later, Gunn,' she called over her shoulder.

'Righto, laters then, Evans,' he called back to her.

* * *

As the sun set on yet another productive day spent in the comfort of his leather office chair – his Australian stock saddle – Connor decided to call it a day and head home to his haven. He'd finally reached the bottom of his seemingly never-ending list of chores, and now grease splattered his shirt, dust was engrained in every pore and he felt drier than the Simpson Desert.

He couldn't wait to scull an icy-cold beer and stand beneath the stream of a hot shower until his aching muscles uncoiled. Maybe he might even do both at once. And why the heck not? You only live once. Which was the mantra Samantha seemed to have been embracing when he'd caught her in the act of boogying her cute little butt off early this morning. Just recalling her dancing like she didn't have a care in the world made him smile. Arms high and eyes closed, her face tipped to the bright blue sky and her feet tapping fast, she had appeared to be in a world of her own, and in that instant he'd wanted to join her in that place where she appeared to be at total peace. Since her return home he hadn't seen her so soft, relaxed and happy, and there was something about the sweetest of vulnerability that came with that, that made him want her all the more. He'd wanted to reach out and possess the woman she'd become, and the teenage girl that had once been his for those few magical hours, but he'd reined himself in. It had been mighty tough, with her hand upon his chest and her beautiful lips so close, not to lean in and kiss her like he damn well meant it, like he damn well craved to. But after stuffing up a few nights ago, he wasn't about to do anything else that would upset the friendship they'd reformed. Besides, for all he knew, she was still a married woman who just didn't wear her wedding ring.

Arriving at his back door, he kicked his boots off and stepped inside. Thoughts of Samantha remained with him as he flicked light switches, washed his hands, turned his stereo on and turned up George Strait's honky-tonk voice, grabbed a beer and headed straight for the shower, where he stripped off, cracked his longneck open and stepped beneath the spray of water with an audible *ahhhhh*. Ever since running into her, literally, he hadn't been able to shake her from his mind, and he didn't want to – he'd enjoyed many little smiles to himself today, all because of her. If only she knew just how much of an effect she had on him. If only she knew how he'd treat her like the most precious piece of art on this earth if she were his. If-onlys really did suck. And so did the maybes. Day by day, each time he got to spend exquisite time with her, he was finding himself more in tune with her than he cared to be. If only things could be different. If only she wasn't going away – again. Once upon a time, in a time and place far, far away, they'd had a chance for a possible happily ever after.

And they'd gone and blown it.

Royally.

Closing his eyes, he rested his head against the coolness of the tiles as the stream of hot water pummelled his lower back. And just like that, he was back there, with her, both of them heartbroken eighteen-year-olds. The image of her collapsing into his arms the night before his brother's cremation, sobbing hard against his shoulder as she'd clung to him tightly, was seared into his brain like a brand. In that poignant moment swirling with grief and loss and torturous regrets, she'd been all he'd ever known, and all he'd ever wanted. She'd been his best friend, his confidante, his everything. She'd been exposed, vulnerable, unguarded, yielding to his touch, hungry for a union with him, as if she'd been desiring it for as long and as much as he'd been. With her captivating aura of fire and air, and her glorious copper locks framing her perfectly freckle-dusted, creamy white cheeks, she'd pushed him back, climbed on top of him, and after he'd been ever so gentle with her, they'd made the sweetest, deepest of love all night long. Learning he was her first that night, he'd believed they were going to be together forever from that moment on. Yet, the very next morning, straight after Angus's funeral, she'd left town without a word, and he'd been left to mourn the loss of her, and of them, and now she was back and a whole different person. Seemingly strong and centred, and extremely womanly on the outside, he knew she was still that vulnerable, wild, carefree Sammie he knew all too well beneath her armour. The impact of the woman she'd become had at first shocked him, but now it made him want her more than he ever had as a teenager with a childhood crush.

Turning off the taps and stepping from the shower, he dried off as he tried to chase thoughts of Sammie from his mind. But it was an impossible task. So he gave up trying. His stomach growled, then growled again as he tugged on a pair of boxer shorts. Food was next on his agenda. And after a dinner of bacon and eggs, topped with lashing of baked beans, he took the contemplations of her to dreamland with him where they were living the life he daydreamed of having while awake.

The following morning, feeling as if he'd spent the night with Samantha after dreaming about her all night long, Connor found himself feeling a little coy as he pulled to a stop beneath the jacaranda tree, climbed out and strolled towards where she was sitting, seemingly enthralled by the goings-on in the round yard. In a world of her own, totally unaware he was approaching, she was a sight for him to behold. She was perched on the top rung of the timber fence, her long jean-clad legs dangling over the side, and with the sun straight in front of her the wide-brimmed hat didn't do much to shade her pretty face. With her freckles more pronounced than ever, he liked the fact that she hadn't covered them up with make-up today. The more natural Samantha Evans was, the more captivating he found her. And it wasn't just her outward beauty that mesmerised him; heck no, it was the way her head tipped a little to the side, and her lips pursed in concentration, as she watched the horse and its rider strutting about the round yard. She didn't hear him approach, nor did she feel his presence when he was only a metre from her, and her innocent obliviousness allowed him a few more precious heartbeats of drinking her beauty in deeply. And in the space of those few heart-pounding seconds, he felt a scorching, ferocious rush of sensations – desire, need, protectiveness, a boundless connection that couldn't be explained with words, it simply had to be felt, and he felt it deep down in his heart and soul right now. So much so, he wanted to reach for her, so he could pull her close and hold her safe and loved in his arms forever.

For F's sake, Connor, get a bloody grip, would you.

He took another step and leaves crunched beneath his boots. 'Howdy doody, Sammie.'

Startling, she spun to see him standing there, staring at her. 'Connor, hey, my goodness, I didn't even hear you pull up.' Her hand went to her chest. 'You seriously have to stop sneaking up on me like that, or you're going to give a girl a bloody heart attack.'

'Sorry 'bout that.' He gave the brim of his hat a tug. 'I didn't mean to give you a fright.' He quickly pulled together all the parts of himself that she so effortlessly affected, and flashed her a smile. 'How's she going?' Looking towards where Shea was giving the new mare cues, he joined Samantha at the railing, his boot heel on the bottom rung and his arms folded on the middle one.

'Yeah, really good, I think.' She offered him a smile warmer than the scorching rays hitting his back. 'Shea reckons she's coming along in leaps and bounds since you suggested changing her feed.'

'Awesome.' He nodded assertively – gratified he'd helped out with a simple suggestion that Shea had noted. 'That's real good to hear.'

They fell comfortably silent until Shea finished her training session and skilfully pulled the dutiful horse to a stop. Spotting him now, Shea offered Connor a wave and he mirrored her friendly gesture. 'Is Jack around the traps, Sammie?' He peered from left to right, noting Jack's ute was missing from its usual parking spot. 'I need a hand with something.'

'He's not, he had to duck into town for an appointment, but can I help?' She jumped to the ground, and as she looked up to him from beneath the shade of her hat, her meltingly soft gaze did unspeakable things to him.

'Thanks ...' He realised he'd chuckled a second too late and, wiping the smirk from his face, he quickly added, 'but I don't think it's something you can help me with.'

'Is that so?' She pulled a brash face and squared her shoulders. 'Are you saying I'm not capable, Gunn?'

'No, and yes.' He couldn't help the playful grin beginning to resurface. 'Sorry, but, yeah, I am saying that, sort of.' He grimaced at her sudden frown. 'Sorry,' he repeated.

'Okay, so tell me.' Smiling haughtily, she folded her arms tightly. 'Why is it, that you think I'm not capable?' She held her hand up to halt his reply. 'Does it have anything to do with me being a woman?'

She looked so determined, so rebellious, it was downright sexy. 'No, of course it doesn't.' The way he wanted her right now, *oh my god,* it made him feel like a savage. 'You're really, how do I put this? Citified, now.'

Heat rose to her cheeks and he couldn't tell whether it was because she was embarrassed, or really pissed off. Knowing Samantha Evans like he did, he suspected the latter.

Her chin jutted out, and she seemed to stand taller. 'Well, I beg to differ.'

'You do, do you?' He couldn't help but egg her on a little – she was hot when she was insubordinate.

'Damn straight I do.' Her hands flew to her hips, and clung there. 'So why not let me prove it to you?'

He shrugged, and nodded his head. 'Yeah, righto, why the hell not?'

A phone chimed and she plucked a mobile from her back pocket. Holding it up, she looked at the screen and a swear word mouthed on her kissable lips as her smile was swept away by a deep frown.

'Bugger off,' she grumbled as she stabbed a button, and then crammed the phone back into her jeans. Arriving back in the present moment, she smiled again, but this time it was forlornly. 'Sorry, what were we talking about?'

'You coming to give me a hand.' He gestured to where the phone had gone into her back pocket. 'Dare I ask who that was?'

'My ex's lawyer, very likely trying to get me to agree to the ludicrous offer he emailed to me yesterday.' Her steely gaze was now pinned on the far-flung distance.

So there he had it, from the horse's mouth … she was single!

Connor's heart both sank and buoyed. 'You mean that you and Benjamin have separated.'

'Yes, and no.' She finally turned back to him. 'It's more like we've completely split and are in the middle of signing divorce paperwork, and working out who gets what, which for the record, he's being very unfair about.'

'Oh shit, I'm so sorry, Sammie.' Her look of sadness was so grave that Connor felt nothing but heartbreak for her in that moment. 'Do you want to talk about it?'

Frowning even deeper, she shook her head. 'Nope.' Then she huffed. 'I'm determined to use the time here to try and move on, and hopefully come to a fair property separation agreement so I can put it all behind me.'

'Fair enough.' He sighed, nodding. 'I get wanting to do all of that.'

Shoving her hands into her pockets, she lifted her shoulders ever so slightly. 'I'm so tired of living in the past, Connor, I just want to somehow start afresh, you know, like a sunflower opening its heart to the sunshine for the very first time.' She tipped her head, her expression thoughtful. 'Does that make sense?'

'It sure does, and that's an awesome way to explain it.' It astounded him how she could look so sweetly innocent and wickedly smoking hot all at the same time, and that deep-thinking mind of hers – just, wow.

She replied to his compliment with a grateful smile.

She's single, Gunn …

With his mind going rampant with the possibility of them re-connecting in that intimate way, he firmly reminded himself that she was fragile. That she needed him to be a gentleman, and to respect their friendship, and to not cross any lines. That she needed him to be the kind of man that only wanted the very best for her in this quite often unfair world. He didn't want to do anything to break her. She'd been broken enough. Too many times. His job, as her long-time friend, was to help put her back together, as best he could in such a short amount of precious time.

'Right, well, come on then Sammie Samsung, time's a-wasting.' He needed to do something, anything other than stand here, wanting nothing more than to strip her naked so he could make the sweetest of unconditional love to her.

'Okay, let's do this.' She clapped her hands, and then, as if tripping on thin air, she lost her footing, stumbled, teetered and then tumbled.

A wave of protectiveness swept over him as he reached out and caught her. 'That's the second time in a matter of days you've fallen head over heels, Sammie.' He held her until she felt steady on her feet again, internally chastising himself for using a phrase that referred to falling for someone. 'Anyone would think you're doing it on purpose,' he added, laughing.

'Ha, you wish, Gunn.' She was laughing it off, too, but her cheeks were glowing red and there was that tender look in her eyes he'd witnessed all those years ago, when she'd thrown caution to the wind and kissed him.

Actually, I really do wish … he wanted to say. 'Whatever,' he said instead.

And as they traipsed towards where he'd parked, he couldn't help but contemplate how she fitted so perfectly into him, as if she belonged within his arms. In that moment of accidental intimacy, as he'd breathed her in, he couldn't help but notice how her hair smelt like it always had, of sunshine and wildflowers. The recollection had him missing her more than he'd ever believed possible after all this time apart, even though she was walking right beside him, all flesh and blood and bones, so real, so powerfully enthralling, so stunningly beautiful in every single way.

CHAPTER
12

Samantha couldn't believe her eyes when she saw what Connor had needed a hand with, especially as he'd thought she wasn't cut out for the job. Here she'd been, imagining a rogue bull had broken through a fence, or there'd be some heavy lifting or machinery involved, but no way, Jose, this didn't come close to any of that. Malarkey was what came to mind, as she tried to remain poker-faced. Watching from the sidelines as Connor tried his best to lure his mum's pet nanny goat back into its enclosure, with a handful of sunflower seeds of all things, Samantha did her best not to burst into uncontrollable laughter. With its stubby tail whisking about, and unblinking eyes wide with anticipation, it appeared as though the obstinate goat thought this was a game.

'Oh, bloody heck, I give up.' Clearly exasperated, Connor straightened, stomped his boot and huffed. 'I don't know why my mum loves you so much, you pig-headed brute.'

The goat tipped its head to one side, bleated loudly with tongue extended out, and then took a step backwards, away from where it should have been heading.

Tossing the sunflowers over his shoulder, Connor widened his stance and glared at the goat in a way that declared war. A Mexican stand-off at its finest. Samantha muffled a chuckle. She couldn't believe that this crazy goat had planted its feet and was refusing to budge an inch.

Seconds ticked by: one, two, three, four, five …

Connor's frown deepened.

Samantha actually found herself holding her breath.

Connor was the first to move, but in a split second the goat did too.

Taking off like a bull at a gate, with the bell around its neck clanging, it made a beeline for Joyce's vegetable patch.

'Nooooo, you don't.' Diving through mid-air, Connor landed with a thump as he grappled for the goat's lead, now dragging behind in the dirt. 'Bugger,' he bellowed as the tail end of the rope slipped from his fingers.

As if knowing it was out of reach, the goat skidded to a stop, spun around and bleated again. This time, it sounded as if it was laughing at Connor. And Samantha couldn't help but join the four-legged foe in her mirth. A man defeated, Connor rolled onto his back and swore out loud.

Pushing herself off the railings, she took steps towards the two. 'Why don't you let me have a go?' She grinned at his look of astonishment as he got to his feet. 'Maybe it just needs a woman's touch.'

'Okay, but if it rears up, you get out of the way, quick smart.' His thumbs hooking through his belt loops, he gave her a look of utmost seriousness. 'I've learnt the hard way how much a kick to the shins hurts, too many times.'

She nodded, trying but failing to match his seriousness. 'Trust me, I can move quickly if need be.' She hoped her lips weren't smirking.

'Okay, but I'm right here to help if things go pear-shaped.' He stepped out of the way. 'I got you,' he added, with an affirming nod.

'Thanks.' Amused, but trying to remain deadpan, she turned her back to him and faced the goat.

Approaching the defiant animal carefully while affirming she wasn't going to hurt it, she stopped a couple of metres short of the seemingly calm creature. Leaning down ever so slowly, she plucked the lead from the ground, and then stepped out of harm's way. Accomplishment filled her with absolute pride. This was further than Connor had gotten.

Go me!

'Come on then, you rascal, let's get you back home, huh.' She gave the lead a little tug.

The goat bleated but didn't budge.

Yanking the lead, she made a bleating noise back to it.

Connor's laughter echoed. 'What are you trying to do, Sammie?'

'I have no idea,' she called out while not taking her eyes off the goat for a second. 'But this bugger isn't going to get one over me, nope, no way.'

'Righto,' Connor replied. 'We'll see.'

A few minutes later and she was basically leaning backwards with the obstinate goat attached to the other end of the rope, doing the same. A game of tug-rope ensued. Her determination to see this through, and get the job done, was now overriding her common sense. After another minute of grunting and groaning, she basically turned into a drill sergeant as she barked everything she could at it, including a tongue-in-cheek threat of murder.

'Here, Sammie, I'll take over.' Connor arrived at her side, hands reaching for the lead rope.

'No, I've got this.' She tugged it out of his reach, jolting the goat into another bout of senseless heaving and hoeing.

Connor was smirking now. 'It kind of doesn't look that way from where I'm standing.'

'I said, I've got it.' She gave him a look that spoke of hell to pay if he challenged her.

He cocked his head and smiled at her. 'Are you sure about that?'

She growled beneath her breath. 'Yes, I'm absolutely one hundred and fifty percent sure.'

'Righto, if you say so.' Holding his hands up in surrender, he took a step back.

Clenching her teeth while ignoring the beads of sweat rolling from her forehead, she yanked the goat's lead harder, pulling with all her might, and that's right about when she realised she didn't have it at all. Not in the slightest. The collar sipped from its neck and the goat took off, straight through the gate they'd been trying to coax it towards. Arms flailing, she tumbled backwards, landing in a pile of fresh manure. A gate slammed shut near her – Connor had jumped in and secured the goat into the enclosure. The manure squelched between her fingers as she quickly tried to stand. A muffled chuckle caught her attention, and she glanced up to witness absolute mirth written all over Connor's face.

'Is something funny?'

'Nope.' His grin grew wider.

She threw him her best I'm-going-to-make-you-pay-for-this glare before bursting into laughter. And that gave Connor the freedom to join her. And just when she thought they'd stopped, he'd simply look at her and they'd burst into side-splitting laughter again. Once she felt as if she could stand up without being crippled by mirth, she held her manure-covered hands up. 'Are you going to be that gentleman you've been up until this very point in time, and help me up, or just stand there taking the piss?'

Connor screwed his face up at the sight of her dung-covered fingers. 'I think I'll choose the latter because your hands are gross, and besides, it's more fun taking the piss.'

'Fair enough.' Grabbing two handfuls of the still-warm manure, she flung it towards him. He ducked but wasn't quick enough. 'Oh my gosh, what an awesome shot!' she exclaimed after it smacked him fair in the face.

Grimacing and chuckling at the same time, he wiped a hand across his cheek, succeeding in nothing other than smearing the wad of manure even further.

She pointed at him. 'You've got a little something on your face, Gunn.' Now it was her turn to laugh like a hyena.

'I'm going to get you back when you least expect it, Evans, so keep your eyes well and truly peeled.' Every word was said in jest as he motioned to his eyes with forked fingers, then back at her.

She mimicked his actions, the pair of them laughing so hard they couldn't speak.

'Here,' he finally spluttered as he held out his hands. 'Let me help you out of your crappy predicament.'

'Oh hardy ha ha, Gunn.' She took his offer, unprepared for the electric jolt that arched through her. 'Don't give up your day job, will you.' Trying to hide what his touch had just done to her, she untangled her fingers from his and straightened to her full five-foot-nothing height. 'Cheers for that.'

'Cheers for getting that damn rogue back into his pen, a job well done, Sammie.' He gave her the thumbs up.

'Thanks, I told you I could do it.' She winkled her nose. 'I really stink.'

'Yeah, you really do.' He chuckled. 'Seeing as you helped me out, I reckon I might do the right thing, and offer you my shower.'

'I'm onto you, Gunn.' She eyed him sceptically. 'You just don't want me stinking up your LandCruiser when you give me a lift home.'

'Dang it.' His handsome face a picture of waywardness, he held his hands up in defeat. 'You got me.'

Side by side, they wandered up the dirt road and towards Connor's home, the place that had been one of their teenage hangouts all those years ago. As they closed the distance, Samantha quietly recalled the many times she, Angus, Connor, Shea, Jack and whoever else wanted to join, would spend the night holed up in the old farmhouse eating junk food, playing board games and then telling ghost stories until they fell asleep in their swags. Until now, she'd forgotten how special those memories were, and she mentally hugged them close.

'Here we are, home sweet home,' Connor announced.

Reaching the top of the gentle rise, Samantha gasped when the chocolate-box farmhouse came into full view. 'Wow,' she uttered, astonished by the transformation from a rundown old shack to this.

'She's a bit different now, huh?' Connor offered her a proud sideways glance.

'Damn straight she is.' She regarded him admiringly. 'Did you do all of this yourself?'

'I sure did. It took me almost eight months, and was a labour of absolute love.'

'I can see that, just from looking at the outside, Connor.' She graced him with a tender smile.

'Thanks, I can't wait for you to see the inside, too.' Pausing at a rustic timber fence, he opened the gate for her. 'Welcome to my humble abode, Sammie Samsung Evans.'

Stepping ahead of Connor now, Samantha looked to where little yellow and purple wildflowers rambled along the pebbled footpath and then at the sides of the four steps leading up to a wide verandah where jasmine bushes shared their sweet perfume. She noted how lush and colourful the gardens were, and how potted shrubs and a cosy outdoor setting graced the oiled timber floorboards of the verandah – Connor clearly took great pride in what he'd aptly named his Heavenly Haven.

Kicking his boots off at the welcome mat that read *LEAVE YOUR WORRIES BEHIND*, Connor opened the flyscreen door and waved her within. 'Ladies before gents.'

Following suit, she left her boots at the door and stepped inside to the lovely scent of caramel. Spotting the unlit candle on the coffee table that would have been responsible for the delicious smell, she then turned in a circle, checking his bachelor pad out.

'Wowsers, Connor, you keep the place super clean,' she said, removing her hat.

'You sound surprised.' He hung his hat on the hook by the door and then offered to do the same for her.

She tried to ruffle her flattened hat-hair into some kind of style. A quick glance at her reflection as she wandered past a mirror on the hall table was proof she'd done nothing but mess her hair up even more. Looking more bedraggled than ever, she shrugged at her reflection, instantly noting, and liking, the way she didn't feel the need for airs and graces in the company of Connor, who represented country hospitality at its finest.

With a spring in her step, she kept on meandering behind him as they passed through the very cosy-looking lounge room with a modular couch and Aztec designed cushions that matched the throw blanket over one of the armrests. A rustic timber coffee table made from an old wine barrel sat atop a cowskin rug, and tasteful framed pictures showcased Connor's love of land and livestock. Turning the corner, they wandered into a cute country-style kitchen with raw timber cupboards and creamy stone benchtops. Copper pans and pots hung above a well-used central butcher's block, and a you-beaut coffee machine and Thermomix sat proudly beside the standalone Aga stove. Everything in here screamed that the occupant could cook, which Connor had already proved at his mum's birthday dinner. His place was just like he was, so warm and inviting, and there was so much history in here, etched into the cracks in the walls and the creaks of the floorboards. The little yet commanding farmhouse almost inhaled and exhaled with life, making Samantha feel like she could breathe better in here, too.

'This place is mind-blowing, Connor, you've done an amazing job doing it up.' She smiled from the inside out.

'Cheers, Sammie, that means a lot, coming from you, especially seeing as you know what this place looked like before I got stuck into the renovations.' Leaning against the deep ceramic kitchen sink, he flashed her an appreciative smile. 'Would you like to have a cuppa, and a piece of my homemade orange and almond cake after your shower, before I drop you back home?'

'That sounds lovely, thanks.'

While Connor flicked the kettle on, then plonked two mugs onto the countertop, she paused at a floating shelf and picked up the photograph. A wistful smile tugged at her lips. Connor was just as she'd remembered him all these years, and he looked so young, so happy and so damn handsome.

'Do you remember that day?' he said over the sound of the tap running.

'Yes, how could I forget it?' Placing the framed memory back, she turned to him. 'That was the weekend we all went skiing at Lake Tinaroo, then camped overnight and got wet through to the skin when it bucketed down.'

'Exactamundo.' He gestured towards the doorway. 'I'll just go and grab you a towel, and rustle you up some clothes that might fit you, so you can have a rinse off, and I might do the same before we kick back on the verandah with some afternoon tea.'

'Plan, Stan,' she said, chuckling at the memory of them saying that to each other all the time when they were younger.

Minutes later, he reappeared with a white T-shirt, and a pair of sweatpants. 'You might have to roll the bottoms up.'

'Ahh, do you have anything that isn't see-through,' Samantha asked while stifling a grin.

Connor grimaced. 'Oh, crap, sorry, I didn't think of that.' A slow sexy smile slid across his mouth. 'Back in two shakes of a lamb's tail.'

And he was. This time round, he held out a black T-shirt. 'Better?'

She gratefully took it from him. 'Much, thank you.'

'Right, well, the bathroom is down the hallway, to the …'

'I remember where it is,' she said, cutting him off.

'Of course.' He thumbed over his shoulder. 'I'm going to use the outside shower, so I'll meet you back here.'

'Plan Stan,' she repeated, suddenly realising that being back here, revisiting a piece of the past where she'd always felt happy and carefree, was bringing back that happy-go-lucky girl she used to be, the one she'd all but forgotten about, until now.

'That's twice you've said that now.' As if reading her mind, Connor didn't budge, just stood there, his gaze locked onto hers, and his lips quirking in an all-knowing way. 'I like seeing you so comfortable here.'

Her pulse in her throat fluttered, and then her heart took off in a wild canter. 'Of course I'm comfortable here, this place is like another home to me.'

His smile turned soft and sexy. 'I like hearing you say that.'

Feeling that same old magnetic pull towards him, the one that had made her throw caution to the wind once before, she quickly took a step back. 'Okey dokey, I'm off to de-stink.' And off she trotted, hurriedly, towards the bathroom, before she could do what was on her mind, and take steps towards him so she could fall into those burly arms that had once held her so lovingly, so protectively.

They couldn't go there again.

Not now.

Not ever.

Almost two and a half hours later, after chatting about the upcoming wedding and the important roles they had to fulfil on the day and leading up to it, along with a casual chat about the day-to-day of their lives, they were making the most of kicking back on the outdoor settee with a little gap between them, their cuppas well and truly finished and their plates empty. Samantha had told Connor three times already just how delicious his cake was, and if she weren't so full after two slices, she would have devoured more. Boy oh boy, she was going to have some extra kilos to lose when she went back to London. Back to her life. Her very lonely, very messy, life.

The reminder that she wasn't here to stay jolted her.

The very thought of leaving Gum Tree Gully and returning to a place that now felt a million light years away left her soul aching and her heart heavy. She tried to ignore the weighty sensation as she focused on the ever-changing view and the wonderful company she was in. They had watched the blue sky being swallowed up by impending grey clouds, and the approaching sunset they'd been hoping to witness was now shrouded in darkness. As if Mother Nature was announcing her imminent show, a bright flash of lightning shot across the heavens, and then a booming crack of thunder sounded. Seconds later, crashing raindrops pummelled the tin roof and soon cascaded off the awnings of the verandah in a steady stream. For Samantha, the rhythmic rumble of the tap-tapping was the quintessential sound of the Australian bush.

Connor breathed in deeply. 'The fresh scent of rain is one of the most wonderful smells in the world, don't you reckon?'

'It is lovely, yes, but after living in a place where it rains almost every day of the year, I don't know about it being one of the best smells in the world.' Thoughts of warm baked bread, sun-baked earth and freshly ground coffee filled her mind.

'Try this, then.' He tossed her a sideways glance. 'Close your eyes, and really breathe it in, let Mother Nature's breath sit in your soul for a little bit, then exhale.'

Although she felt a little stupid, she did what he asked, and after a few inhalations and gentle sighs, found herself smiling as she joined him in sensory bliss. 'You're right, it is pretty amazing.' Flicking her eyes open, she turned to him, and the adoring expression on his face made something pitch inside of her, sending her heart racing.

He enthusiastically shifted in his seat, so he was facing her. 'Sometimes, we just have to stop and sit in the moment, and let it really sink into us, to appreciate it fully.'

'That's very deep, Gunn.'

'If you say so.' Smiling, he shrugged. 'Do you get much time to just stop and take a breath, back in London?'

'Hmm, well, with a city as electric as London is, and my office near Piccadilly Circle, not as often as I'd like to.'

'I thought as much.' He rested back. 'Seeing as you grew up in the country, doesn't that make you miss living here?'

'Not really.' A few weeks ago, she would have meant it, but saying it now felt like a lie, to him, and to herself. 'Or maybe it's more of a case of being so busy I don't really have time to think about here, let alone miss it.'

'I'm sorry to say, but,' he regarded her through gentle eyes, 'that's a really sad way to live, don't you think?'

'I'm not sure what you mean?'

'I guess I was trying to say that being so busy means that you don't have time to check in with yourself, which in turn makes you a cog in a massive machine that just keeps on turning, no matter how much you might want, or need, something.'

'Or someone.' Oh my god, did she just say that out loud?

'Yes, *or someone*,' he repeated in a tone that suggested he knew exactly who she was referring to.

Him.

Yes, that's right, Evans, you meant him.

Oh god, what was this feeling he was rousing, and where in the hell was he enticing it from? Feeling a bit like a deer in headlights, she wasn't sure what she was meant to do with it, or how she was meant to explain her sudden awkwardness away, so she clamped her mouth shut nice and tight. Sat up straighter. Fidgeted like she had ants in her pants. There was this almost irresistible urge to tell him she shouldn't have run from him all those years ago, to get down on her knees and tell him just how sorry she was for messing everything up, and beg him for a second chance. She had the sense that they were meant to be together all along, and she'd just lost her way, and now she was back on track, she was helplessly heading straight into all that was him at a hundred miles an hour in a speeding locomotive with no brakes.

What the F was going on?

'Are you okay, Sammie?' His hand came to her back.

Unable to speak, she nodded, blinking faster.

Feeling his unwavering attention on her, but not able to look him in the eyes, she scrabbled for something, anything, to say, to break the silence that was now pressing in on her. But her hands twisted in her lap as words got stuck in her throat. She swallowed down, hard, trying to rid herself of the growing lump of emotion.

She did her best to gather any scrap of willpower she could. And yet, the urge to tell him everything she was thinking was getting more powerful by the second. But there'd be no benefit from acting out on a whim. She'd done that once, and look where it had gotten her – over the other side of the world and married to a lie. She couldn't go and stuff their relationship up again. Connor didn't deserve it. She wouldn't be able to forgive herself if she hurt him. Again.

But this, him, the thought of there being a *them* was so beautiful, she wanted to reach out and touch the energy sparking between them, to somehow drag it into her heart and soul, bury it down deep in all the dark parts of her, because it was magical.

If only she could reach out and touch him.

All over.

Behave, Samantha ...

Knowing she had to get the heck away from the temptation of him, she glanced at her watch. 'Gosh, look at the time.' Unfurling her legs from beneath her, she shot to her feet. 'I reckon it's time I should be heading back. Shea will be wondering where I've gotten to.'

Connor didn't respond straight away, instead just looked at her in a way that told her he knew exactly what she was thinking. 'Shea knows you're here with me, but yup, all good, I'll drop you home.' He stood, his smile a little tight-lipped, and his casual air had all but disappeared. 'I'll just go and grab my keys.' He seemed to hesitate, and then leaning in, he kissed her cheek for one heartbeat, two heartbeats. And when he pulled back to look her in the eyes once more, there were flames flickering and flashing in his baby blues. 'I care for you, Sammie, deeply, always have and always will. No matter what. You don't have to feel awkward around me, okay? This is me, Connor. Remember that you're always safe with me.'

With overwhelming emotions momentarily taking away her ability to reply, she bit her bottom lip and nodded. But then, from somewhere unknown, she dragged her real self from the depths and unshackled her heart as she threw her arms around him. 'Thank you, for being you.'

'You don't need to thank me.' Connor's arms tightened around her, so lovingly, so protectively.

Samantha felt like she was right where she needed to be. 'I care for you, too, Connor, always have and always will, no matter what.'

There was a shudder in his breath. 'That means the world to me, Sammie.'

Not wanting to let him go, she rested her cheek against his chest. They stayed like this for a few moments, until she unravelled from him, and this time, dared to look him in the eyes. 'Other than Shea, you're the only person in this world who cares enough to know the real me, and I adore you for that.'

'We're connected, you and me, in ways many will never experience in their lifetime.' He smiled now, ridding her of any lingering unease. 'I'm so glad you came home for the wedding.'

'Yeah, me too.' She breathed a sigh.

'Let's get you home, hey.' But something in his gaze told her that was the last thing he wanted to do.

CHAPTER
13

Thanks to his racy dreams, Connor's first thought for the day had been how much he wanted to get his hands all over Sammie. The things he would do to her, and the heights he'd take her to ... Now, thirteen hours later, he just couldn't seem to shake the fantasies that stirred his inner longings. It had been a long hot day, slaving his guts out as he and a hired group of stockmen drove a herd of obstinate cattle from the far-reaching back paddock to their new pasture. Now, with the sun disappearing behind the mountain ranges, he was glad the day was done and dusted. He kicked his boots off at the back door, and the flyscreen slapped shut behind him as he strode into the welcoming coolness of the farmhouse. Tugging his hat off, he slung it onto the hook, then eased his neck out. His shirt and jeans were covered in dust, mud splatter and grass stains, and his body ached from where he'd thrown himself from his horse in a bid to literally grab the disobedient bull by the horns. Thank goodness he'd been able to get control over a situation that could have turned out very differently, had the bull gotten the upper hand. The stubborn bastard had certainly given him a run for his money. A shower was in order, but first he need to whip up some dinner because he was starving, and then, after he rinsed the day off, an early night was on the agenda. Tomorrow was going to be another big day.

Almost an hour later, swiping the mist from the mirror above the bathroom sink, Connor met his reflection as he pondered whether he could be bothered to shave. He'd pass as a thug, with the dark stubble giving him an unruly edge. But nah, he'd do it tomorrow. Wandering to his bedroom, then dropping the towel slung around his hips, he searched through the clothes basket for kicking-back attire. Then, donning his favourite boxer shorts and nothing else, he ran his fingers through his shower-damp hair – his way of combing it – as he made his way into the kitchen to rustle up a snack. The scent of his bacon and egg dinner still lingered, making him wish he'd cooked up more than one helping. He swung the fridge door open, grabbed the carton of milk out and, not bothering about getting a glass, sculled what was left of it. Heading to the pantry, he sung the lyrics to the Brad Paisley tune playing from the stereo in the lounge room and then plucked out a packet of Kingston biscuits, firmly telling himself not to polish off the entire packet in one sitting, the way he quite often would.

Two biscuits in, a knock at the front door had him rising from the stool at the breakfast bench, and wandering over to it. To his delight, he opened the door to the most beautiful of faces. 'Hey, Sammie.' Wearing a simple cream dress that swished at her ankles, with matching earrings and no make-up, she looked effortlessly stunning.

Her gaze flitted over him, and snagged on his chest, before coming back to meet his eyes. 'Oh, hey, sorry, I should have called first, but Jack said I needn't bother, and that calling in is what's done round here, so here I am.'

'He's right about that, so come on in.' He watched a rush of heat give rise to a blush on her cheeks. Knowing it was him who'd caused it, he smothered the grin that was fighting to surface. 'So what do I owe this impromptu visit to?'

'Seeing as we've only got a couple of days to go,' she said, slipping her sandals off and padding past him., 'I thought I should pop over, and organise a couple of things for the wedding.'

The tattoo on her left foot caught his gaze. 'I remember watching you get that.'

She lifted her foot a little, gazing at the eagle feather tattoo as if for the very first time. 'Oh this thing, yeah, it bloody hurt like hell.'

'I know, you were squeezing my hand so hard I thought my fingers were going to drop off from lack of circulation.'

'Ha, yeah, that's right, I'd forgotten about that.' The gold bracelets on her slender wrist jingled as she raised her hand to tuck loose tendrils of hair behind her ear.

Lost in all that was her, Connor momentarily found himself speechless.

Damn, what was she doing to him?

'Would you like something to drink?' he finally said.

'Yes please.'

He led her into the kitchen. 'Coffee, tea, or something stronger?'

'Something stronger sounds good to me.'

'Righto, what tickles your fancy?' Wandering over to his array of spirits on the bench, he motioned for her to choose one.

'Oh, yum.' She picked up the bottle of Baileys Irish Cream. 'How about a shot of this over some ice.'

'Great choice, I'll have one too, I reckon.' He pulled up a stool. 'Here, make yourself comfy while I go grab a T-shirt, and then I'll make us those drinks.'

She did. And he went and made himself a little more respectable, wishing to goodness he'd had that shave. Returning, then busying himself with grabbing two tumblers, then some ice from the freezer, he silently cursed as he tried to get his rising emotions under control. Never, ever had he felt so compelled to act upon his longings. But the country music playing in the background, her alluring perfume teasing his senses and the way she had her chin resting on her hand as she watched his every move, everything about this very moment was making him crave to stop what he was doing and take her into his arms, so he could kiss her like he wanted to.

Drinks made, he passed one to her, then motioned to clink glasses. They did, and in union brought each to their lips. He watched her take her tentative sip, and then sigh in pleasure, her eyes rolling to the ceiling.

'I gather you like it.' He smirked at her look of gratification.

'Uh-huh, I haven't had a Baileys on ice for years.'

'It's a nice night so do you want to enjoy our drinks out on the back verandah?'

'Sounds good to me.' She followed him outside. 'Isn't it a glorious evening?' she said, staring at the sky, her smile wistful.

'Isn't it always here?'

'Yeah,' she said and nodded, 'it pretty much is.'

They got settled, and she got to business chatting about a few details they needed to organise to help the wedding day run as smoothly as possible. His job was to make sure the cars arrived on time, that Jack was wearing his new Akubra and not his work one, and that he had the rings in his jacket pocket; hers was to make sure the make-up and hairdresser arrived on time, that Shea remained calm at all times and that the reception hall was decorated to perfection.

Now the business side of things was done, Connor was keen to learn all he could about her future plans. 'So, are you looking forward to getting back to the hustle and bustle of London?' He'd start off with the easy ones and work his way into the harder questions.

'In some ways, yes, and in others, not really.' She sighed weightily.

'Yeah, right, so what are the good and the bad of going back?'

'The good is I do love having everything at my fingertips, like my favourite cafés and restaurants, and endless clothing stores to choose from – oh, and the food markets, you'd seriously love them, seeing as you're such a great cook.' Her smile reached inside him, enticing his own smile wider. Then she frowned and tipped her head a little to the side. 'And then the bad is that I'll miss you and Shea and Jack and Amaya so much, and I have so much to sort out with Benjamin when I get back, too. He's already settled into his new life with his new partner, in what used to be our home, while I'm in the apartment until we finally agree on who gets what.'

'Geez, it didn't take him long to get back into a relationship.'

'Ha, yeah, well, unbeknown to me at the time, he was already in a relationship with this certain person before we broke up, and they were having sex in our marital bed for years.'

'Far out, he cheated on you with another woman in your house, in your bed, for years?' A weight settled in his chest. 'What a rotten son of a bitch.'

'A *lying* son of a bitch.' She shook her head. 'I can't stand people who condone lying, it's the lowest of the low, in my opinion, to deceive a person you're meant to love.' She breathed a wry laugh. 'And to top it all off, it wasn't with a woman.'

He tried to comprehend. 'What do you mean?' His eyes widened as he watched her press her lips together. 'Oh, damn, okay, now I get it.'

Her nod was exaggerated. 'Uh-huh.'

'Wow, he likes men, too.'

'Uh-huh.' She blinked faster, as though she was trying to keep tears at bay. 'Actually, FYI, he only likes men.' She prodded her chest. 'I was the guinea pig he used to figure out if he could be in a heterosexual relationship, which clearly he couldn't be.' She held her hands up in an exaggerated shrug. 'So here I am, almost thirty, childless and about to get divorced. What a shitshow.'

'I'm really sorry, Sammie, you don't deserve to be treated like this.' The hurt in her eyes spoke loudly of the heartbreak she had been through, and was still harbouring. If he could take it from her, and carry the pain of it, he would, in a heartbeat. 'And FYI, if you were mine, I'd treat you like the one in a bazillion kind of woman you are.' Hopefully, that helped her a little.

Samantha took a long moment to reply, all the while staring at him with an unreadable look on her pretty face. 'I know you would, Connor, because you're one of the rare, good ones left in this world full of selfish heartbreakers.'

He couldn't help the sense of pride that filled him. 'You really think so?'

She placed her hand on his. 'I know so.'

He offered her an appreciative smile. 'I wish there was something I could do to help you feel better about it all. But just know I'm here for you, anytime, okay.'

'Thanks, Connor, but it's my mess, and I'll clean it up.' She shrugged, but her shoulders didn't relax back into position. 'I'll be right in the end, I always am.' She sighed. 'Thanks for being such a great mate.'

Mate? He didn't want to be her mate. He wanted to be her boyfriend, her fiancé, her husband, all in quick succession, because he knew his feelings about her were forever. But he could never be the father of her children, and that was a massive boulder in their path, in their way of a happily ever after. She wanted children desperately, and he could never give her that. The reality of his shortfalls, in this poignant moment, hit him hard. As did the fact he was keeping something from her that he should have told her eleven years ago. A secret she might never be able to forgive him for. His thoughts were pulled back to that night eleven years ago, to the call he'd made that had changed everything. If only her father hadn't picked up the phone, maybe, possibly, Sammie's parents would still be alive, to love her, to share life with her.

'You okay, Connor?'

'Yeah, sorry, just tired after a big day.'

'Of course, you need to get some sleep.' She stood before he could tell her he would rather sit here all night long in her company.

'That wasn't me telling you to bugger off, you know,' he said lightheartedly, as he came to his bare feet.

'I know, but I should be getting back anyway.'

Holding her arm loosely, he walked across the verandah, down the steps and over to her hire car. 'Let me know that you got home safe, won't you?'

'I'm only just down the road.'

He tapped her windowsill. 'Doesn't matter.'

'Okay, will do. Night.' Her smile was honeyed, and at the same time oh so sexy.

'Night Sammie.' He stepped back so she could turn the car around. 'Dream sweet.'

'Thanks, I'll try to, you too.'

Oh, trust me if it's anything like the last couple of nights, I will.

'Yup, I'll try to,' he called back.

He waved her off, then waited until her taillights disappeared – just in case she might do what he longed for her to do, and turn around – before heading inside and to his bed, where he spent almost an hour tossing and turning before drifting into dreamland and meeting her there.

* * *

The best part of the day, the coolest part, was long gone. Pausing for a much-needed breather, Connor looked to the blindingly blue sky without a single cloud in sight. It was only mid-morning, and the day was already turning out to be another scorcher. Beads of sweat ran between his shoulder blades and soaked through his mud-splattered shirt. He dropped his tools, straightened to his towering height, and with a tug of his hat to ward off the blinding sunshine, studied his handiwork. The new line of fencing would hopefully keep his neighbour Charlie Harrison's rebellious cattle out, and his own herd in. He didn't want another episode like the last one a few weeks back. It had taken both him and Charlie an entire day, and half the night, to find their wayward cattle and get them back into their respective paddocks. Time was precious, and he didn't have the luxury of wasting any when it came to his heavy workload. With that workload in mind, he glanced at his watch and swore beneath his breath. In less than an hour he was meant to be meeting Jack for a counter lunch at the pub, so they could go over the last of the wedding plans. There was no way he could go in there, looking and smelling like a rubbish tip. A quick run through the dip was in order, so he needed to get a shift on if he didn't want to be running late. Quickly climbing aboard his four-wheeler motorbike, he revved it to life and then, spinning it around, sped back towards the farmhouse.

Twelve on the dot, by some miracle, he strode through the front doors of the pub, frazzled but proud as punch for being on time. He said g'day to a few familiar faces in passing, making sure not to stop for a chat; some of the old timers could talk the legs off an iron pot.

Jack sat waiting for him at the bar, a cold one in hand. 'Hey, Gunn, how goes it?'

'Yeah, good.' He shook Jack's outstretched hand. 'You?' He nodded to the barmaid, who asked him if he wanted his regular pot of mid-strength beer.

'I'm much better now I'm here, mate, the household has seriously gone crazy with wedding fever.' He pulled a grim face. 'I'm just glad most of the finer details are up to Shea and Sammie, because you and me would stuff it up for shizza.'

'Ha, I could only imagine, seeing it's only three days away.' He elbowed Jack. 'And speak for yourself about stuffing things up, buddy, I class myself as a professional planner.'

Jack chuckled. 'Yeah, you're better at it than me, I must admit.' He picked up the menu and scanned it. 'I'm bloody starving, you ready to order?'

'Yup, good to go.' After ordering his usual fall-off-the-bone ribs with a side of creamy garlic mash and salad, Connor turned back to Jack. 'Can I get you another beer, mate?'

'Thanks, that'd be great buddy, but just make it a middy. I'll go get us a table while you do that, hey.' He headed off towards the dining-room doorway.

Joining Jack with two icy-cold beers in hand, he placed the drinks down on the coasters, pulled a chair opposite his mate and sat.

Wrapping a hand around his glass, Jack held it up. 'Cheers to escaping the craziness of the women for a little bit.'

Clinking the rims of their glasses, Connor took a long guzzle. 'Huh, that bad, is it?'

'Oh bloody hell, don't get me started.' Jack lightheartedly rolled his eyes. 'If I have to hear about the colours of flowers, or where to sit who so there aren't any arguments, one more time, I'll seriously go nuts.'

'Yeah, but it'll all be worth it when you can officially call Shea your missus.'

'It sure will be.' Jack grinned like a man head over boots in love. 'Shea is the best thing that's ever happened to me.'

Connor knew precisely how his mate felt because that was exactly how he felt about Sammie. If only he could make her his wife; now wouldn't that be the best thing that had ever happened to him, and then some.

* * *

Sitting on her tousled bed, with her finger hovering above the button that had the possibility of changing her life forever, Samantha bit her bottom lip and hit send before she changed her mind. The email that agreed to a substantially smaller sum than she'd first wanted, giving Benjamin ownership of her apartment and the house, whooshed away into an inbox over the other side of the world. She hoped to God she'd made the right decision because there'd be no turning back now. Yes, she was going to have to pack up her apartment when she returned, and find herself a new place to call home, be it bought or a rental, but the six-digit figure in return would give her a very comfortable fresh start, wherever she chose for it to be. After being here the past few weeks, she'd learnt that peace of mind, and happiness, outweighed everything else. And that included any sum of money or material possessions. What mattered most was the love, support and companionship of her beautiful friends. Which she had. Always. Benjamin couldn't take that from her.

Blinking against the brightness of the screen, she breathed a sigh as she snapped her laptop shut and then stretched her arms high, leaning from side to side to ease her lower back out. Try as she might, she was finding it harder to ignore the strong sense of belonging that had been creeping beneath her skin and stroking her tortured heart since arriving here. And early this morning, before the sun had even had time to rise on the gift of the new day, she'd made a decision that had shocked her, and still did. But it was made now. She wasn't going to tell another soul what was on her mind until the wedding day had passed. She didn't want any focus on her and her messy problems, not when the next few days should be all about her friends and their wonderful lives together.

Hurried footfalls sounded in the hallway. 'Sammie, oh my god.' Shea tore into the bedroom and thrust a phone in her face. 'Can you believe this?'

Wincing, Samantha blinked faster. 'Back up girlfriend, it's all blurry.'

Shea took a few steps back. 'Better?'

Samantha nodded, then when she spotted what had been Shea's stunning white wedding dress, now torn and blackened, her eyes widened to the same size as Shea's. 'Holy crap.' She covered her gaping mouth. 'What happened?'

'Magda, the seamstress, just sent this to me. Apparently, she left the iron on, and it was near my dress and oh my god what am I going to do now.' She burst into tears. 'I can't believe that my dress is ruined two days before the wedding.'

Shooting to her feet, Samantha wrapped her arms around Shea. 'It's okay, we can fix this.'

'But how?' She sobbed against Samantha's shoulder.

'We have a way around this.' Pulling back a little while keeping her emotions in check, she held Shea's hands as well as her teary gaze. 'We can alter my mum's wedding dress to fit you.'

'Thank you, but I can't do that.' Shea looked at her as if she'd lost her mind. 'You kept that for your own wedding one day.'

'Yes, I did, but then I got married in a rush and didn't have time to get it sent over to me.' She drew in a breath, her smile tight-lipped. 'And who better to make use of it than you, my beautiful friend.'

Still looking at her incredulously, Shea laughed and cried at the same time. 'Are you sure about this?'

Samantha nodded affirmingly. 'I'm one hundred percent certain.'

Shea shook her head. 'I can't, Sammie, it's yours to wear.'

Her emotions bubbling to the surface, Samantha let her tears fall. 'There's no way I'm ever getting married again, so what better person than you, and your seamstress of course, to be the ones to bring it back to life.'

A glimmer of hope filled Shea's eyes. 'Do you really think we can pull this off?'

'Of course we can, now let's get cracking because time is ticking.' She took Shea's hand and led her from the bedroom, towards the loft. 'Now you don't have to worry about something old and something borrowed, because it's a double whammy with Mum's dress.'

Climbing the ladder into the roof of the house, they got to work, sorting through Samantha's boxes. An hour later, they'd found what they were looking for, as well as a couple of photo albums from their childhood years. Samantha couldn't believe the way the special packaging had preserved her mum's vintage lace wedding gown. It was stunningly beautiful.

Climbing back into the homestead, then pushing the ladder up and out of sight, Samantha brushed her hands off on her shorts. 'Shall we take a breather with a nice cup of tea and something sweet, before taking it to Magda this afternoon for the alterations?'

'Sounds like a perfect plan.'

'Great, you go and kick your feet up and give Magda a call so you can fill her in on our plan, and let me take care of you for a change.' Samantha held her hand up to stop Shea's rebuttal. 'You're always looking after everyone else, so go, be off with you. I'll meet you out on the verandah once I've rustled up our morning smoko.'

Stepping outside with two cups of Earl Grey and a packet of ginger nut biscuits tucked beneath her arm, Samantha placed everything down on the coffee table, then sunk into the chair alongside her friend. Leaning over, Shea grabbed a thick leather-bound photo album from the hardwood floor and plunked it into her lap.

Opening the packet of biscuits, Samantha passed a couple to Shea. 'Well, are you going to open it, or just sit there staring at it?' Dunking a ginger nut into her tea, she quickly brought the soggy treat to her mouth before it broke off in her cup, savouring the flavour.

'I'm warning you now, with how emotional I'm feeling today, there might be a few more tears.' Shea flicked the cover open, and the first page was of them as fifteen-year-olds.

'Wow, look at how young we are.' Samantha ran her fingertips over the glossy protective film.

'Weren't we ever,' Shea replied softly.

'There's part of me that would give anything to be that girl again, so that I could do things differently, but then there's another part of me, that would never want to go back there because I don't think I'd survive all the heartbreak a second time round.'

'You've been through way too much, my friend.' Shea offered her a sad smile. 'Let's hope from here on in, your life is filled to the brim with good things and happy memories, hey.'

Samantha swallowed down her impulse to tell Shea what she'd gone and done, agreeing to Benjamin's under-par offer, but she kept her news to herself. 'Trust me when I say I'm going to do my best to make that so.'

'I'm so very glad to hear it, Sammie.'

As Shea continued to flip page after page – some photos enticing laughter while other brought out tears – poignant nostalgia wrapped around Samantha's heart, the comforting sensation of sharing all of this with her dearest friend somehow making her feel stronger, happier and safer. Towards the back of the album, they were now seventeen years old, both with womanly bodies and boyfriends on their arms. Jack and Shea were a match made in heaven from the get-go. As for Samantha and Angus, she knew without a shadow of doubt from the hollowness in her eyes and the lacklustre smile on her face that they most certainly were not. For a few fleeting moments, she imagined him in heaven, alongside her mum and dad, the image bringing her peace. Nevertheless, the potency of how much she'd lost in the accident, and how much grief she'd had to endure, hit her hard. She tried to push it away, like she had countless times, but a defiant sob rose, bringing more from wherever it had surfaced from. Shea wrapped an arm around her and pulled her close. They clung to each other, both crying now. No words were needed, their mutual understanding of the deep cavern of losing loved ones enough to bring each other comfort. Then, both of them gathering themselves enough to continue their trek through the lens-captured past, Shea got back to turning the pages of the album. The very last page was a group photo, and it was in this one Samantha noted how closely Connor was standing to her, and how he was looking at her.

So did Shea, it seemed by the nodding of her head and the knowing look in her eyes as she came to meet Samantha's gaze. 'Tell me you can't see it here?'

'See what?' Ignorance could be bliss, or so she liked to tell herself.

Shea rolled her eyes. 'You know what.'

'Yes, I see it.' Nodding, she took a long deep breath, and then another. 'But that was eleven years ago, things are different between us now.'

Shea snorted. 'Oh, come on, Sammie, it's pretty obvious nothing's changed.' She leant forward on her elbows, her eyes sparkling with cheekiness. 'Surely you can tell that he's still extremely sweet on you?'

'He is not,' Samantha protested, while feeling a blush rising from the heat now swirling through her. 'We're just friends.'

'You really believe that?' Shea exclaimed, her eyebrows almost meeting with her hairline.

'Yes.' Why did she keep lying to Shea, and herself? Guardedness, fear, self-doubt, or all three?

Shea took a moment to respond. 'Connor Gunn has always had an eye for you, it's just that he never did anything about his feelings, out of respect for his brother.'

'Okay.' It was all she could say. Feeling the guilt from never having told Shea what she and Connor had done that night before Angus's funeral, Samantha chose ignorance, again, as she turned her gaze down the long dusty drive where a heat haze hovered. 'Don't you reckon it's hotter today?'

'Don't try and change the subject, Evans.'

Rolling her eyes skywards, she groaned. 'You're not going to leave this be, are you?'

'No, not until you accept the truth, and decide what to do with that.'

'Right, let's say you're on the money, and Connor has always felt a certain way about me, that's all good and well, but as for me, with the mess my life is in right now, getting involved with him is the last thing I, or he, needs.'

Shea huffed. 'You two have known each other forever, so stop analysing the risks of everything, and for once in the past eleven years of your controlled life, go back to being that young carefree girl and throw caution to the wind.'

'That girl is long gone, dead and buried, in fact, so I don't think that's possible.'

'Anything is possible.' Shea smirked. 'You just need to relax a little and you'll see that I'm right.'

'What do you mean? I *am* relaxed.'

'Hmmm.' Shea regarded her pensively. 'If you say so.'

'I know so.'

'Do you?'

Samantha waved a dismissive hand through the air. 'Enough chatter about me, let's get you into Mum's dress.'

'Distraction is your frenemy, Sammie.' Shea sighed frustratedly. 'All you'd have to do is let him know you're ready for whatever this is between you to come to life, and I know he'd take care of the rest, and you, for that matter.'

'You, dress, to Magda's, now.' And Samantha meant business.

An hour later, standing behind Shea and Magda, Samantha was fighting off another bout of tears as she watched Magda, with a measuring tape clamped between her lips, lace the back of the dress up. 'You can open your eyes now, Shea.'

Her eyelids flickering, Shea took a breath before coming to meet her reflection in the full-length mirror of the sewing room with Samantha's chin resting on her shoulder. She blinked faster as her hands ran over the vintage lace.

'It fits like it was made for you,' Samantha said softly.

'It does, doesn't it.' Turning to face her, Shea threw her arms around her. 'Thank you, Sammie, for being the most selfless person I've ever met.'

Samantha hugged Shea tight, feeling the essence of her mum within the stiches of the gown. 'Right back at you, my darling friend.'

CHAPTER 14

Connor woke with the first peek of sunrise over the mountain ranges and headed downstairs and into the kitchen, keen to grab his first cup of coffee for the day along with a bite to eat. Heading out for a day's hard yakka on an empty stomach was becoming a bad habit that needed changing. Being hungry made him tetchy. It didn't take him long to whip up a strong hit of caffeine along with a piece of wholegrain toast slathered with crunchy peanut butter. Steaming mug in hand, he padded down the hallway, and out onto the verandah to his usual vantage point. Soon, the sky would be a haze of blue, ignited by the blaze of the North Queensland sunshine. Bite by bite, he washed his breakfast down with gulps of coffee. Then, with his morning ritual savoured, he tugged his boots and hat on and headed off to work, optimistic it was going to be a good day.

That optimism changed within seconds of meeting up with Oyster.

'Damn it,' Connor huffed. 'I can't believe the bastard has gone and done it again.' He kicked at the tyre of the quad bike. 'Now my whole day is going to be eaten up with dealing with that.'

'Don't shoot the messenger,' Oyster groused.

'Sorry buddy, just sick of that damn bull.'

'Yeah, me too boss. He needs to go.' His rollie hung from his bottom lip as if glued there. 'You wanna hand finding the bugger?'

'Yeah, thanks, I'd appreciate the help.'

'Right, well, let's go get him.'

Flying along on his four-wheeler motorbike, Connor was hell-bent on seeking out, and capturing, the rogue bull that was having a wow of a time destroying his fences. Choosing to go on horseback, Oyster had gone in the opposite direction with the walkie-talkie shoved in his back pocket. With plenty of bushland for the one-tonne beast to hide in, the first few hours were frustratingly fruitless. As time ticked by, Connor's patience began wearing paper thin. The heat of the day pushed down upon him, making the job even more frustrating, as the deafening call of cicadas pressed in on him from all sides. Now riding against the blinding glare of the mid-morning sunshine, he finally spotted the brute. Saddling the quad bike, he gritted his teeth as he came to a sliding stop in front of another gaping hole in his fence line. Eyes narrowing, he let loose an entire sentence of cuss words. What in the actual F was this bull's problem? He'd saved him from the meatworks, but now he was seriously rethinking that decision. Oyster was right in saying the bull had to go.

He grabbed his walkie-talkie from the basket strapped to the front of the bike. 'Hey, Oyster, I found the son of a bitch near the east side paddock, over on Charlie's land, and another bloody gaping hole in the fence too.'

'All the way up yonder, well, I'll be buggered.' Oyster's voice crackled through the speaker. 'There must be some fine heifer somewhere there to lure him that far away.'

'Yeah, most likely.'

'I'll head on up there now, boss.'

'Righto, I'm just going to head back to the shed to grab some tools.'

'Roger that.'

Over the other side of what should have been his ten-acre pen, with all four hoofs firmly planted on the neighbour's land and his horned head challengingly lowered, Connor's nemesis glared back at him. Snorting, it then stomped its front foot. Unperturbed by the beast's show of muscle, Connor growled back at him. He'd reached his limit. There were no more free passes. The good-for-nothing rogue had done his final dash. When he got his hands on him, the feral brute was going to be heading off on the first possible truckload to the local saleyards, which was in a couple of days' time. What happened after that wasn't his concern. Earning a livelihood from livestock wasn't for the faint-hearted. He couldn't have cattle that constantly added unnecessarily to his already heavy workload. Hard-heartedness didn't come naturally to him but had been bred into him by his cattleman father, God rest his soul. There was a time and place for a soft heart, like when he was in the mesmerising company of Samantha, but not here, and not now.

Revving the bike, he spun it around and, like a man on a mission, headed towards the outbuildings. Leaving the motorbike in neutral, he left the motor running and jumped off. With determined steps he strode into the shed, where his boot heels clomping on the concrete floor echoed. Heading towards the switches, he flicked them on, and the shed ignited with florescent light. Grabbing his toolbox from the workbench, he stomped back outside and, climbing back on his quad, headed off to fix the fence. But before he could do that, he knew he was going to spend a good part of an hour trying to get the blasted bull back on his property. He didn't want it wreaking havoc with old Charlie Harrison's heifers. His neighbour wouldn't be pleased if that happened.

Before Connor knew it – after shedding blood when the tip of the bull's horn caught his forearm, sweating his butt off while tending to the agisted horses and holding back frustrated tears as he wrestled to get everything done in dwindling daylight – it was thankfully the end of yet another day, and by some miracle all his jobs had been completed. Well, all but one. He still wanted to head over to see Sammie and was chuffed she'd accepted his invitation to catch up over a couple of beers while they ironed out a few last details. She'd even offered for him to stay for dinner. He was using the excuse of touching base on the last of the wedding plans, but in truth, he just wanted to be near her. Stripping off his shirt, he dunked his head beneath the cold water of the laundry sink, wondering if he was suddenly hot from wandering into the farmhouse, or because he was thinking about her. Something told him it was the latter. Far out, at this rate he was going to have to leave the water running cold for his shower if he wanted to avoid arriving at her door on fire.

Right on the dot, dressed casually but attentively, with an easygoing smile planted on his face, he knocked on the front door of the homestead, and couldn't help the frenzied beat of his heart when she tugged it open. 'Hey, Connor. On time, as always.'

'Howdy, Sammie.' He shoved his free hand into his pocket in a bid to stop himself from grabbing hold of her, and … *Stop it, Gunn.* 'Yup, can't help it, I'm a stickler for,' *you*, 'punctuality.'

'Me too, and I have to say, in my experience, not many people are.' She regarded him thoughtfully. 'It says a lot about a person, being punctual.'

'It does, hey.' If only he could tell her exactly what he was thinking.

As if a pause button had been pressed, they just stood there, staring at each other. Seconds ticked by, but it felt as if time was standing still.

'So, can I come in?' His tone was lighthearted.

'Crap, sorry.' She seemed to snap to. 'Of course, you can.' She stepped aside. 'It's not like you're a stranger.'

'I'm far from it.' His gaze drifted over her face, then for a fleeting second, lingered on her glossy lips. Memories of having his mouth pressed up against hers all those years ago had him all hot under the collar of his Ariat polo shirt. 'Here you go, I brought the good stuff.' He passed her the six-pack of locally made tropical ale.

'Oh, wow, I'd forgotten all about this brewery.' She looked at him with amazement. 'I can't believe you remembered how much I like this stuff.'

'Of course I do.'

For a long silent moment, she just stared at him again, then whispered, 'Thank you for being so thoughtful.'

'My pleasure.' The house was oddly quiet, and he swore his swooping heart was beating as loud as drumbeats. 'Are Jack and Shea about?'

'Oh, no, they went into town to catch up with her aunty for dinner.'

Something inside of him cartwheeled. 'So, looks we're home alone.'

'Yes, something like that.' She held the six-pack of beer up. 'Let's go and crack open one of these each, shall we.'

'Yup.' He fell into step beside her as they headed into the kitchen. 'Something smells bloody good.'

She smiled appreciatively. 'I made us a chicken, bacon and leek casserole, with creamy garlic and spring onion mash.'

'For real?'

'Yes.' She smirked at his look of wonder. 'I *can* cook, you know.'

'I believe you can, I've just never had you cook for me, that's all.'

'Hey yeah, I haven't ever cooked for you, have I?' She chuckled. 'Well, there's a first time for everything, as they say.'

He took steps towards the red Dutch oven sitting atop a trivet and lifted the lid with a nearby tea towel. 'Damn, it looks just as awesome as it smells.'

'It should, I put a lot of love into it.' Reaching up on her tippy toes, she endeavoured to pluck bowls from the overhead cupboard.

Connor liked the fact that he was going to eat food with her love in it. Yum. 'Here, let me.' He came in behind her and, reaching with ease, plucked two bowls out.

She turned to find herself flush up against him, and the look in her beautiful green eyes ….

Danger, Will Robinson ....

With the *Lost in Space* catchphrase ringing loudly in his head, Connor knew he should've stepped back, away from the only woman who'd ever made him feel so *much*, but something rid him of the ability to do it. And then she did that sensual thing, where the corner of her bottom lip slipped between her teeth, and she coyly looked up at him beneath long dark lashes. The need to possess her sparked, fired and scorched his insides. Oh god help him. Time screeched to a grinding halt, and the entire world faded away. There was nothing to concern himself with, nothing to explain, nothing to do except be present with her. It was just him and her, the real them, held captive in this intensely profound moment. His heart was beating like boxers' fists against his rib cage, as if trying to break free, so it could finally get to hers. Oh, how he wanted to tell her everything – how he felt about her, how he wanted her, how it was his fault her parents were on the road that night, about how he couldn't give her all that she wanted, so she could make her own mind up about him, with all the knowledge she was entitled to, to be able to make an informed decision. And by god he was just about to do all of that, and more, when he was literally saved from making a complete fool of himself by the bell.

The echoing chime sounded from the direction of the oven.

Their bubble burst.

She pointed to it. 'I better go grab the dinner rolls out before they burn.'

He cleared his throat. 'Mm-hmm' was all he could muster.

With a tiny coy smile, she ducked beneath his arm, and he watched her sashay away from him. Out of his reach. Thank god. For her sake, and his. Because he didn't have very much self-control left when it came to her.

Almost none.

And that was dangerous.

'Do you want me to help with anything?' he asked, all the while thinking about how badly he wanted to tear her clothes off so he could make love to her until the sun came up, and then some.

'No, all good, Gunn, you just pull a chair up and I'll bring your bowl over.' She didn't look at him as she spoke, was instead busy dishing up, but the slight tremor in her voice told him she was feeling some of the heat that he sure was.

Hopefully, every single one of the flames firing from his heart right now was warming her skin in the most arousing, irresistible of ways. He wanted her to feel him, deep down inside, where she'd buried the memories of them long ago, along with how she'd felt about him that night. Because that, right there, in his strong opinion, was the sexiest caress of all. Heart to heart. Soul to soul. Without a single brush of skin on skin. That was the depth of a true deep and meaningful connection without even uttering a word.

Although he was wrapped up in her, nice and tight, Connor was glad for the small reprieve from her all-pervading gaze, so he could pull himself into some sort of line. He was a respectful man, with a raw hunger, yes, but an honourable man all the same. Nothing was going to happen tonight or the next night, or the night after that. Nor would it while she was here all alone, for almost a week, while Jack and Shea were off on their honeymoon. She'd made it very clear she was going back to London. He was acutely aware that he was staying here. If he tasted her sweetness again, if he heard her honeyed whispers and her husky cries of pleasure, if he had her in his arms, her soft skin silky against his, he wouldn't be able to go without her ever again.

So that was that.

He needed to get a grip on the reality of the situation before someone got hurt.

And it was over his dead body that he'd ever hurt her.

CHAPTER
15

While slowly serving their dinner onto the good dinnerware Shea had insisted they make use of as she'd walked out the door with Amaya on her hip – the dinnerware that had brought her so hazardously near to Connor, so close she could see his quickened pulse beat in the thick of his neck and could feel the strong beat of his hastened heart against her hand – Samantha took quiet deep breaths in a bid to slow her own racing heart. Standing there, pressed up against him with nowhere to go, with his eyes possessing hers and nothing else in the world mattering for those few beautiful, shared breaths, it was as if the dark clouds that had been shrouding her tortured heart had pulled back, bowing out to the brightest blue sky she had ever seen with far-reaching horizons that allowed her to breath all of him into her. Swept up by the force of him, before she'd even had time to stop herself, her buoyed soul had drifted oh so effortlessly into his. And in that enthralling moment, between reality and fantasy, between her in breath and out breath, she'd felt the reunion of two hearts, two minds, two bodies that had for one magical night, so long ago, beat and burnt as one. She knew in that breath-held second that she needed to get away from him, before she went to a place that they'd never return unscathed from.

Her life, and his, were different, separate, thousands of miles apart.

She needed to let go of the fantasy of there ever being a them.

When she turned with their plates in hand, somewhat recomposed, he wasn't sitting at the table like she'd suggested. Instead, he was standing, staring off into the distance through the bay windows, his arms crossed and his stance wide. She couldn't help but wonder what he was thinking about, what he was feeling after their fleeting reconnection, what he would have done if she'd reached up on her tippy toes and kissed him in that shared, sequestered moment.

'Here we are,' she said as brightly as she could while placing the bowls down. 'Dinner is served.' She plastered a painted-on smile to his over-the-shoulder regard of her, before going back to grab the bowl of warm, buttered bread rolls.

'Wow, Sammie, this looks delicious, you've truly gone and outdone yourself.' The scraping of his chair sounded. 'And I'm absolutely starving.'

So am I, for you, she thought while feeling a little risqué.

'I wouldn't say I've outdone myself, but thanks,' she said, pulling the chair out beside him, then sitting. 'It's an easy meal to whack together.'

Forking some chicken and mashed potato, then dunking it into the creamy sauce, he took his first mouthful. 'Oh, my good god,' he garbled. 'This is absolute heaven.'

'I'm glad you think so.' She tucked in, too, gobsmacked at how delicious it was. 'Mmm.' It was an involuntary sound, which Connor mirrored. Thank goodness for Shea's endless array of cookbooks, and her friend's easy directions as she waded her way through ingredients and method.

Taking a swig from his beer, Connor eyed her over the top of the bottle. 'How's the alterations going with your mum's dress?'

'Yeah, really good, Magda's almost finished.' Her fork paused in mid-air, she smiled. 'Shea looks absolutely stunning in it.'

His forearms came to rest on the table. 'It was really noble of you, to give it to Shea to wear, Sammie, because we all know how precious that dress is to you.'

'It is, but then again I did have the opportunity to wear it, and didn't, because I married in a hot minute and didn't have time to get it sent over to me.' Guilt flooded her. Holding her emotions at bay, she shrugged. 'I'm not going to get to wear it now, so Shea might as well put it to good use.'

'Like I said, selfless.'

She thanked him with a small smile, and then they ate in a companionable silence, all the while with Connor occasionally looking at her as though he was contemplating something deep. She didn't dare ask what it was, for fear of allowing him a glimpse into her own inner thoughts about him and her, living a happy life together in another time and place.

Gathering up his last forkful, Connor paused and regarded her kind-heartedly. 'You really think you'll never marry again.'

And there it was, what was on his mind. 'After going through an unpleasant divorce, no, not in the foreseeable future, and maybe never.'

'Oh, Sammie, don't let a mistake take away your right to be everlastingly happy with your person.'

Connor had hit a sore point, and she jumped to her own defence. 'I can be happy without being married, you know,' she snapped, regretting it straight away.

Offering an understanding glance, he nodded. 'Yeah, I suppose you can be, but life is so much better when you get to share it with someone special, don't you think?'

She grimaced, nodded, and then shook her head. 'Yes, and no.'

'Ha, you and your yes and no answers, Evans, talk about being elusive.'

She grinned at his cheeky hint of a smirk. 'Kind of like the Aussie "yeah nah" that makes other countries confused.'

He pointed his fork at her. 'Yes, exactly.' He placed it into his empty bowl. 'Now that, Sammie Samsung, was bloody amazing.'

'Why, thankya, kind sir.' She wiped her lips with her napkin and pushed her bowl a little away from her. Then she rested her head back, turned her cheek and gazed at the starry sky out the bay windows. 'It's such a beautiful night. I reckon we should head outside and stargaze.'

'Yes, we should.' He shot to his feet and gathered the plates before she could stop him.

'Leave it, Connor, I'll do it later.'

'No, you won't do anything of the sort.' Having piled everything up, he carried it over to the sink. 'I'm going to clean up, seeing as you cooked. It'll only take me a couple of minutes, unlike how it would've taken you hours to make that delicious meal.'

'Okay, fair point.' How could she not adore the man he was, stacking the dishwasher so sexily.

Fifteen minutes later they were stretched out on a picnic blanket beneath a sparkling blanket of stars. With only a few inches between them, and Connor's hands tucked beneath his head, Samantha lay on her belly, her chin propped up on her hands and her eyes looking up to the wonder of the country night sky. A sneaky glance here and there in Connor's direction affirmed he was loving this just as much as she was, if the dreamy smile on his handsome face was anything to go by. She liked how neither of them felt the need to fill the sweet silence with useless chatter. It was so nice to just *be* with another, just because they wanted to *be*. There was no agenda, no expectations, no timeframe. No matter what they were doing, she noted how she always felt at peace within his company. There was a lot to be said for such security. Time spent with him was easygoing, natural, effortless, just like it had always been when they were kids. It was heartening to know some things really did stay the same in what was usually a very fast-paced world spinning beneath her feet.

Gazing at the bright, silvery glow of the full moon, then to the graceful silhouettes of the horses grazing languidly beneath it, their tails swinging casually, she breathed a serene sigh. There was so much to appreciate in this landscape filled with so few man-made monstrosities and so much untainted countryside. She was really starting to love the slower pace here, where everything revolved around Mother Nature. If only she didn't have to go back to a life she wasn't sure she wanted to exist in anymore. If only it was as easy as packing her things up and coming back here.

If only ... She whispered to herself, unaware that her utterance had travelled to the man beside her.

'If only what, Sammie?'

She drew in a breath. 'If only I hadn't left here all those years ago.' She bit her tongue, not wanting to let the cat out of the bag.

'Yes.' He rolled onto his side and propped his head up on his hand. 'Keep going.'

She took her time to summon an explanation. 'I do wonder where I'd be now, you know, what I'd be doing, if I'd be married with kids, and all of that.'

If I'd have married you, she thought.

Glancing to the sky, he blew a weighty breath, then bringing his gaze back to hers, smiled slowly, sexily. 'I'm most certain you'd have been snapped up by a very lucky man if you'd stayed here, Sammie.'

'Snapped up hey, with how many kids?' This conversation was going into uncharted territory, and she liked it, way too much.

His shoulder lifted ever so slightly, and something unfathomable crossed his face. 'You would have a tribe of kids, if you could, I'm sure.'

Bit of an odd answer, she thought, but mentally shrugged the niggle of it off. 'Yeah, I would've liked to have had one or two ankle-biters by now, and maybe another on the way,' she huffed. 'But here I am, divorced and childless, so forget Samsung Sammie, you'll have to start calling me Spinster Sammie.' Emotions rose and almost overwhelmed her, but she sniffed them back, blinking faster.

Connor sat up and his hand came to her back. 'Oh Sammie, you're going to find your happy place, and the person to share it with.' His voice was deeply compassionate and his smile so heartwarmingly sincere.

'I don't know about that.' The burn of tears threatened, and her throat tightened. 'But thanks for the vote of confidence.' She tried to laugh but sounded like a strangled chicken. She sat up and wiped at her watery eyes. 'God I'm being a sook, I'm so sorry.'

'Don't you dare apologise.' He took her hands in his. 'Benjamin did love you in his own way, I'm sure, I mean, how could he not? As you know now, though, he just isn't marriage material, not in the heterosexual sense anyway.'

She smiled sadly. 'Yeah, well, he had a funny way of showing he loved me if he ever did.'

His thumb was still rubbing against the back of her hands. 'I can't say that I'd disagree with that.'

'Anyway, enough about me and my pathetic life.' She gave his hands a grateful squeeze, then tucked hers back into her lap. 'I want to know more about you, like why aren't you shacked up with some amazing woman with a brood of kids?'

'I suppose I haven't met the one.' He half-shrugged. 'And to be honest, I don't think I'm cut out to be a father.'

She was shocked to hear him say such a ludicrous thing. 'Oh, come on, Connor, you'd make the best dad ever.'

With his Adam's apple bobbing, he remained silent.

'I'm sorry if I've hit a nerve, Connor.' She noted how his jaw tensed. Resting a hand on his arm, she offered him a compassionate smile. 'You're a good bloke, and you'd make a woman very happy, as well as rocking the dad thing.'

He darted a glance her way and the look in his eyes tore at her heart. 'Shit, Connor, are you okay?

His posture stiffened even more. 'Yup, I'm good.' He smiled but it was tight-lipped.

There was something he wasn't telling her, but it wasn't her business to prod, and she didn't want to make him any more upset than he clearly already was, so she let it be. 'I'm here if you ever need to talk about anything, anything at all, okay?'

He cleared his throat. 'I'm good, Sammie, don't you worry about me.' He ran a hand roughly through his hair. 'I best be getting home soon, and letting you get some shut-eye.'

'Yeah, it is getting late.' She looked to where the family four-wheel drive was usually parked. 'Shea and Jack should be home soon, too.'

Connor stood and held out a hand to help her up. She obliged, gathering up the blanket, and they wandered side by side towards the house when an ear-piercing screeching noise, way too close for comfort, caught her attention. Halting mid-step, she glanced upwards and sets of beady eyes stared back at her. Flapping ensued. There was a swoop. She swore. Three times. The overhead branches swayed wildly in a flurry of wings as startled fruit bats flew in every direction. Arms flailing, she screamed blue murder. Connor was laughing somewhere beside her, and just when she thought all was lost, his arms came around her protectively, picked her up from the ground and carried her over to the foot of the steps that led up to the homestead's back door. To safety.

'Thank you, for saving me from near death.' She grinned.

'I think it's pretty safe to say that they were more terrified of you than you were of them.'

'Yes,' she said, her grin wider. 'Well, regardless, thank you for coming to my rescue.'

'My pleasure.' Leaning in, his kissed her cheek. 'Thanks for an awesome night again, Sammie.'

'Ditto, Gunn.'

He shoved his hands into his pockets. 'Night then.'

'Night.' She watched him walk over to his LandCruiser, jump behind the wheel, then turn the four-wheel drive around, offering her a wave and a gentle smile as he drove past her and into the night.

* * *

Tink. Tink. Pitter Patter. A faintly familiar noise had Samantha putting her book down on her chest, and then looking towards the ceiling. The sound quickly intensified into more of a drumbeat. It had been a very long time since she'd heard heavy rain on an Australian tin roof. The scent of renewal and promise floated upon the cool breeze now blowing the curtains aside at the bay windows. Cosying further into the lounge chair, she liked the fact she now had an excuse to lie there for longer. Just a few more pages and she would go and make herself the cuppa she'd been thinking about having for ages but hadn't made yet because she hadn't been able to pull herself away from her riveting book.

Almost an hour passed before she finally dragged herself to the kitchen, her nose still in her novel of loss and love and happily ever afters as she blindly wandered. The kettle whistled from the stovetop, making her jump. It was time she placed the book down, for safety's sake. Carefully grabbing the wooden handle, she carried the kettle over to her mug. As soon as the boiling water touched the tea-leaves, the herby scent of Earl Grey tea rose. She added two sugars and a splash of milk, and headed out of the kitchen. Stepping outside, she padded across the verandah, and leant against the balustrades. The pelting rain had eased to a light shower, and off in the distance mist shrouded the mountaintops. Everything looked clean, fresh, renewed. It was a stunningly beautiful sight.

Her mother's sweet singsong voice fluttered in from the past. *Live freely, stand strong, be you no matter what, because life is startlingly short, and that, my darling child, is the best advice I can give you ....*

She couldn't help but smile at the recollection of words she'd long ago forgotten, as a tiny flutter in her soul gave rise to goosebumps. Having always been on the move, she'd finally found the courage to stop, and she liked the sensation of it, a heck of a lot. She could hear herself think. She could take a decent breath, filled with the invigorating scents of the countryside. She could be herself, at any given moment. It almost felt as if she could start over here. Like there was a new story building inside her, just waiting to be told. If she sold her business, she could ...

'Hey, you, what you are doing out here?' Shea padded towards her.

'I'm not doing much at all, and I love it.'

Sliding an arm around her, Shea rested her head against Samantha's shoulder. 'Do you want to know what I think?'

'If I said no, you'd tell me anyways.'

'Ha, you know me well, my darling friend,' she said. 'I think you need to learn how to dream again, Sammie.'

Speechless, Samantha drew in a breath and nodded.

'I'm here to help you remember that spirited young woman you were before you left.'

'I know you are, and thank you for that, Shea.' She sighed softly. 'I love you heaps.'

'I love you too, Sammie.' Shea kissed her cheek. 'You may not be blood, but you are my sis, always have been, and forever will be.'

There was so much love in that shared moment, so much kindness, so much tenderness, from the only woman walking this earth that loved her unconditionally, that Samantha almost burst into tears.

CHAPTER 16

Connor shifted up gears and tilted the brim of his hat to ward off the blinding sunshine pouring through his dusty windscreen while Johnny Cash crooned from the speakers. Tapping the steering wheel in time to the fun tune, he sang the lyrics to 'A Boy Named Sue' out loud. With his forearm resting on the open window, and the balmy breeze whipping his shaggy hair around his face, he was doing everything he could to keep his focus on the here and now. But it was proving a feat when his illusory thoughts had been at odds with reality all damn day. Having woken with the image of Samantha Evans in his heart ever since she'd been back on home soil, he'd used the humdrum jobs of each day to try and push his yearning for her to the back of his mind, but now, with night closing in, and nothing significant to keep his mind busy, all he could think of was her.

Once again.

It had been another long day spent thinking about what could have been with Samantha if she hadn't run for the hills all those years ago. He'd only come to the conclusion that regrets were futile and hindsight was doing him no favours. He'd then got to thinking about where they both were now, and the fact that even if she was here to stay, that he didn't stand a hope in hell with her, not when he couldn't give her the family she so wanted. The family she deserved to have. The family she needed to have, given the fact that she'd so cruelly lost her own. Add in the detail that he was still keeping the secret that had weighed him down for almost half his life from her, and they'd be doomed right from the start. And yet, in the grand scheme of things, all of this didn't change the fact that they were good friends, and he cared about her, one heck of a lot. There was no way in hell he was going to let his feelings get in the way of their friendship a second time round. Or was he just trying to fool himself into believing he had control over what was endlessly deep love for her?

By the time he turned onto the highway, the sinking sun had finally met with the horizon, sending pink and purple shooting across the blue. It was a mesmerising sight that held him captive as he wound his window up and cranked the air-conditioning. Unwittingly inching over the speed limit, he cursed out loud when he saw the flash of blue and caught sight of a police car coming up his rear. Slowing, he pulled to the side of the road. The copper drew in behind him. Money was tight enough, the last thing he needed was a speeding fine.

He pushed the button to wind his window back down. 'Howdy, Officer Lund.'

Carl Lund gripped the windowsill. 'You in a rush to get somewhere, Gunn?'

'No, not at all.' He met the copper's eye, hoping for him to see honesty written in his. 'I'm really sorry, it was a lapse of my senses.'

'I see.' He nodded, sucked in a slow measured breath as if weighing up what to do next. 'Seeing as your mum's a good friend, as was your dad, I'll let you off this time, but slow down buddy, okay.'

'Thanks, I will, you can take my word for it.'

The officer slapped his windowsill. 'I am, so don't let me down.'

'Righto, I won't, thanks again.' He made sure to pull out sensibly.

As he passed over the rickety old bridge, the bitumen of the highway once again hummed beneath the four-wheel drive's tyres as he eventually slowed to take a corner. He was glad to be making his way over to Jack and Shea's for their last catch-up dinner before the big day; not only would he get to hang out with his best mate, it also meant he could lay his eyes on Samantha again. After keeping his love for her at bay all these years, he was shocked by the intensity of his feelings for her now she was back. In just twelve days, she'd climbed beneath his skin, into his bones, and deep into every dark crevice of his heart and soul, igniting the blackness he'd thought he'd have to just get used to with her infectious light. She made him feel alive, made him want to live more than ever, made him *him*. The woman she'd become mesmerised him beyond anything he'd ever imagined possible.

In just over a week's time, he was about to lose her a second time round.

It was the story of his life, with fate being one cruel bastard all over again.

He wished he could persuade her to stay a little longer. So he had more precious time to help her see the love they shared for one another was eternal. If only she could let go of her life back in London, something deep inside of him knew she'd be much happier here. He innately knew it was selfish of him to want her when he couldn't give her what she so deeply desired, what she essentially required, and he was struggling with the torturous guilt his secret brought him, but there was also this uncontrollable urge to make her his, so he could wake up every single day to her sunshiny face. So he could love her like she'd never been loved before.

Two hours later, having been kicked out so Shea and Jack could clean up the kitchen, sitting on the top step of the back verandah with his third, and last, light beer in hand, Connor couldn't ignore how quiet Samantha had been all the way through dinner, and dessert, any longer. 'I don't mean to barrel into those thoughts you seem deep within, but are you okay?'

Taking a sip from her glass of red wine, she half-shrugged then turned her gaze to him. 'I suppose.'

'What kind of an answer is that?' He sucked in a breath. 'I wish you'd talk to me, it might help, you know.'

'Okay, here goes ...' Using the sleeve of her silky blouse, she wiped beneath her eyes. 'Sometimes, actually, most of the time, I honestly don't know who I am anymore.'

'Well, I can answer that one for you.' He knew the workings of her almost as well as he knew the lines on his palm. 'You're Sammie Samsung to your core.'

'Trust you to say something like that.' She graced him with the softest yet sweetest of smiles. 'I adore how you strip everything back to the bare bones, because it reminds me how simple life can be if I allow it.'

'I'm glad I could help.' On total impulse, he placed a kiss on her cheek.

She did that thing that drove him wild, and chewed on her bottom lip.

He couldn't sit here and not kiss her, so he did what he had to and shot to his feet. 'I suppose I should get going.'

'No, please don't.' She rose, and placed a gentle hand on his arm. 'Not yet.' Then she held his wrist, as if to stop him walking away from her.

'Sammie, what's going on with you?'

She looked down. Closed her eyes. Opened them. Looked as if she wanted to speak. But then she seemed to have swallowed her words as she shook her head and took a breath.

So, to encourage her, he took her hands into his. 'Sammie, please, I need to know what's happening.' She looked so vulnerable, so torn, so … was that love he could see in her teary gaze?

She blinked faster, turned her head away from him.

Seconds passed, then a full minute. So long that when she turned back to him, she appeared to have recovered. 'I should let you go.'

He almost swore in sheer frustration but held it back. 'Okay, but only as long as you can promise me you're all good?'

'Uh-huh, I'm good.' She smiled. 'I'll let you go and say bye to Shea and Jack.'

And so he did as she asked, all the while tearing himself to shreds trying to figure out what she was about to say to him, then didn't.

* * *

As she flew to and fro, the rusty chains gripped in her hands squeaking with age and her tippy toes appearing to touch the blueness of the sky, the old wooden swing seemed to be working a treat as a soothing calmness came over Samantha. Having gone to bed with a heavy heart, and a quiet determination to overcome it, she'd thankfully woken with a clearer head. She knew what she had to do if she were to find her mislaid happiness. She just didn't know how she was going to do it. Or if she'd even have the courage to. But at least there was a little clarity within the cloudy uncertainty of her life. Which meant there was hope. And where there was hope, there was life, or so Anne Frank had written. At the very least, she had a teensy bit of direction, or maybe it was more of a bearing. What would come from her inner rousing, she hadn't a clue, she just knew she had to go with the flow, if her analytical mind would allow it.

The ringing of her phone jolted her from her musings. Plucking it from her pocket, she couldn't help her giddy smile as she slowed the swing, then stabbed the answer button just in the nick of time. 'Hey Connor.'

'Hey, Sammie, I was just wondering if you'd like to come and have dinner with my granny and me tonight?'

A flash of the headstrong, caring, country woman his grandmother was flashed through her mind. 'Oh my gosh, I would love that.'

'Great, I'll call past and grab you at five-thirty, if that's okay. Granny likes to eat by six.'

'Sure, yup, sounds good, see you then.' Ending the call, she applauded herself for grabbing hold of an opportunity with both hands instead of weighing it up for so long that it began feeling too heavy.

She rose and made her way towards the back door. The timber floorboards were hot beneath her bare feet – she wasn't sure if her hurried steps were because of the burning, or because she had a spring in her step because she knew she was seeing Connor later.

Shea's head popped out the door of the laundry. 'You still keen to head into town for some brunch before we go to our nail appointment?'

'I sure am, I'll just nip to the loo, and grab my bag and shoes, and I'm all yours.'

'Awesome, I'll just go over to the shed to drop some things off to Jack, and then I'll meet you out at the Prado.'

She gave her the thumbs up. 'Plan, Stan.'

By the time they got into town, Samantha was so hungry she could've almost chewed her own arm off – talk about regaining a healthy appetite since she'd been back. Slipping into the coolness of air-conditioning, she felt her skin prickle with relief. The café buzzed with idle chatter, and the mouth-watering scent of sizzling bacon wafted. Taking a seat opposite Shea, she grabbed the menu and ran her gaze over it. They both ordered the house Caesar salad with the salt and pepper calamari topper along with a bottle of sparkling water to share and an espresso martini to toast the upcoming nuptials.

The drinks arrived in record time, and Samantha held her cocktail up to Shea's. 'To becoming an honest woman real soon.'

'I know, right.' Shea couldn't smile any wider if she tried. 'I seriously can't believe I'm going to be a married chickee in two sleeps' time.'

Nodding, Samantha moaned in foodie pleasure when she took her first sip of what could be one of the yummiest espresso martinis she'd ever had – who'd have thought it would be in

Gum Tree Gully of all the places. 'And FYI, I think it's about time, too.'

'Yeah, tell me about it.' Shea rolled her eyes.

'Ha, I am.'

'You're so funny, Sammie, not.' Shea winked, then chuckled. 'But seriously, I hear you. It was just between building up the business, then having an unplanned baby, which I wouldn't change for the world, mind you, then with Mum getting sick, well …' She sniffled, as if holding emotions at bay. 'Life has had a way of stalling us at every possibility.'

'It's been a big few years, hey.' Reaching across the table, Samantha took Shea's hand and gave it a tender squeeze; the guilt she felt every time she saw Shea upset about her mum's passing pressed in on her from all sides. 'I honestly don't know two other people worthy enough of tying the knot than you and Jack, and I can't wait to be right beside you when you do,' she added, with a wobbly smile.

'I do.'

'You're not meant to say that yet.' Samantha chuckled, and sat back. 'Especially not to me,' she added playfully.

'No, you crazy loon, I meant I know two other people who should be tying the knot, but aren't.'

Samantha was instantly curious. 'Who?' She darted her eyes around the café, expecting Shea to subtly point someone out.

'You and Connor.' Solemnity filled Shea's regard of her.

'Oh, Shea, stop it, that's just silly talk.'

'Seriously, Sammie.' Shea sat forward. 'It's about time you faced up to the truth of who you are, of where your soul wants to be, and who your heart is held by.'

'That's a heck of a lot I need to sort out, don't you think?' Her reply was curt, clipped, majorly defensive, she knew, but Shea had hit a bewildering sore point.

'I'm sorry, Sammie, but sometimes caring is via tough love, and I know that's what I'm doing right now, and it's hard for me to be so blatantly honest, but I love you, and I only want what's best for you.'

Softening her tone, because she knew Shea was coming from a good place, and was right about needing to find her core, Samantha chose to speak from her heart for once, instead of her head. 'I do need to do all the things you mentioned, to find my peace, and my true happiness, but it's really hard when I've been fundamentally running from myself all these years.'

'I know, and I get it.' Shea stole a moment, and took a breath. 'The best way around it is to start with the obvious.'

'Which is?'

'To acknowledge you may have gone and dated the wrong brother all those years ago.' Shea grimaced.

Samantha had to agree. 'Touché.'

'Oh my gosh, you've honestly thought that, too?'

'Since I've been back here, and spent time with Connor, yes, I have.' Man, it felt good being honest.

'Well, in that case.' Shea raised both hands in the air. 'Why not do something about it, my friend, and go on a proper date with Connor, huh?'

'No.'

Shea's nod was exaggerated. 'Yes.'

And so was Samantha's shake of her head. 'No.'

'And why not?'

The thought of doing so made Samantha's heart skitter, but she quickly pulled it into line. 'Because I'm going back to London at the end of next week, and whether I like it or not, for the foreseeable future, that's where my life is.'

'You could just pack up and move back here.'

'It's not that simple, Shea.'

'Oh yes, it is,' Shea replied with another nod.

'I have a very successful business there.' Feeling somewhat defeated, Samantha shrugged off Shea's look of *so what*.

'I know you have a successful business, Sammie, but that also means you can easily sell it. And in the long run, what's more important, a lucrative business that keeps you in a place that you may not want to be, or being able to be free so you can live in joy every day of your life?'

'Both are equally important.' Their salads arrived and although they looked amazing, Samantha had somewhat lost her appetite.

'Choose.' Daring glinted in Shea's brown eyes, made bigger by her glasses.

'I can't.' Samantha heaved a weighty breath. '*If* I decided to move back here, it's not just a click of the fingers affair. I'd have to find an agent, then list my business, then wade through the red tape of selling it.'

'Okay, alright, I get it.' Shea paused for a breath with her gaze gently devoted to Samantha's. 'I know it's not going to be easy, *if* you ever decide to come back, but nothing worth having in life ever is. So please, for the love of god, stop making excuses if coming back here is something you may want, that's all I'm trying to say.'

'I'll think about it.' Grabbing her fork, Samantha stabbed a piece of lettuce, and shoved it into her mouth. 'Holy moly, this dressing is divine,' she garbled.

'I know, right?' Shea followed suit, and for a few minutes they were silent as they enjoyed their meals.

Having a few moments to gather her thoughts, and place them back into order, Samantha finished crunching on a crouton and then gave her friend a smile. 'Thank you, for having the courage to tell me what you think is best for me.'

'Ever since you married Benjamin, and seemed so happy in London with him, I've tried to stay out of your business as much as I can, but having you back here, and seeing how happy it makes you being around the people who love you, well, I just couldn't hold my tongue any longer.'

'Well, just for the record, I'm so glad you didn't.'

Shea's expression was hopeful. 'You are?'

'Yes, and no,' Samantha chuckled. 'But mainly yes.'

'I like the sounds of that, Sammie.' As she finished the last of her salad, Shea's look of glee spoke a thousand words. 'We better get a move on, our nail appointment is in ten minutes.'

'Yes, let's skedaddle.' Samantha had almost licked her bowl clean, the salad was so lip-smackingly delicious. Taking her wallet from her handbag, she grabbed a couple of notes. 'This is my shout, and I don't want to hear any protests, okay.' She playfully flashed Shea a stern look as she stood.

'Geez, okay.' Shea gathered her things and came to Samantha's side. 'Thank you for a yummy lunch.'

The street was a hive of activity when they stepped back outside – Friday mornings were always busy in Gum Tree Gully, given the fact not much opened on a weekend, apart from the pubs and servo.

Samantha threw her handbag over her shoulder and hooked her arm into Shea's. 'Now let's go get snazzied up for your big day.'

Falling into step beside her, Shea grinned. 'Yes, let's.'

* * *

From across the other side of his granny's dining table, Connor subtly gestured to the clock above the mantelpiece with a flick of his eyes. Following his gaze, Samantha realised it was smack on six, and not a minute later. She grinned back at him. Although it would be overbearing, living in such an orderly manner, she couldn't help but adore Granny's need for schedules and punctuality. She'd had always been the same – some things never changed. And then a realisation slapped her hard and sharp in the face. Oh god, was she going to end up like Granny, divorced young, never remarried, living all alone, existing through each day as if it was Groundhog Day?

'Sammie, is everything alright?' His plate now piled high, Connor flashed her a charming smile.

'Oh, yes, sorry, I just remembered I forgot to make an important call.' She began helping herself to the mountain of food at the centre of the table. 'Everything looks so delicious.'

'I show my love through my cooking, my dear.' Granny's poise was regal, as was her smile. 'Shall we say grace, before we tuck in?' She reached a hand to either side of her.

Samantha dropped her fork like it was a hot branding iron. 'Yes, we shall.'

Connor offered her a secretive grin. 'I'll take the honours, tonight, Granny.'

'That would be lovely, Connor.'

They joined hands. Closing her eyes, Samantha relished the sound of Connor's voice as the heat of his touch sent sparks and shivers through her.

'Dear Lord, thank you for moving mountains to bring us all back together tonight, because family, and friendship, is everything. Also, thank you for the food we are about to eat, and the farmers who put it upon Granny's table.'

'Amen,' Granny said.

Begrudgingly taking her hand from his, Samantha placed her hands together and said 'amen' too.

'So, dear, how's your business going in London?'

Savouring her mouthful of the creamiest mashed potato ever, Samantha nodded. 'Really good.'

'That's good to hear.' Granny took a sip from her wine glass filled with sparkling water. 'How long is it before you head back?'

Beside her, Connor grabbed himself another spoonful of the rich beef stew, along with two dumplings. 'Too soon,' he replied before she got a chance to.

'In a week,' Samantha added.

Granny chewed her forkful of food slowly, thoughtfully. 'Would you ever think about moving back here, especially now you're a single woman again?'

'Granny,' Conner breathed. 'Mum shouldn't have told you that.'

'Well, she is my daughter-in-law, and we tell each other everything.' Granny huffed and rolled her eyes. 'Besides, what's wrong with me wanting my only granddaughter back here, where she belongs?'

'Well, for one, she's not your granddaughter,' Conner said, a little tightly.

'Maybe not in blood, but I will always see her as such, and I think that living all the way over the other side of the world is silly.'

Not wanting the pair to knock heads over her, Samantha jumped back into the conversation. 'Thank you, Granny, for caring so much.'

Granny simply nodded.

Connor offered Samantha a look of apology. 'So, Granny, how's your mah-jong team going? Are you still at the top of the leaders' board?'

'Oh yes, we are.'

Samantha noted his quick change of subject, and she appreciated that she was no longer the topic. In between reminiscences, laughter and a very yummy dessert of creamed rice and stewed cinnamon apples, the rest of the evening went smoothly, and by the end of it she was sad to say goodbye to Granny. Given that she was almost eighty-five, Samantha was aware that she might not get another chance to spend such precious time with her.

They hugged tightly, and Granny gave her a kiss on the cheek. 'Now don't stay away so long this time around, Samantha.'

'I promise I won't.' And she meant it.

Climbing into the LandCruiser, they waved goodbye. Waylon Jennings' honky-tonk voice was their comfortable company as they headed out of town and back towards Shea and Jack's place.

After pulling up out the front of the homestead, in the shadows of the towering paperbark tree, Connor turned to her. 'I'm sorry about Granny asking you about moving back here, she means well, she just hasn't got the gift of the gab.'

'Don't apologise.' Unclipping her seatbelt, Samantha bent and gathered her things from the floor. 'I understand where she's coming from, and I adore her for it.'

'You really are so lovely, Samantha Evans.'

Straightening, she smiled at his warm regard of her. 'Why, thank you, Connor Gunn, you're not too bad of a person yourself.'

'Cheers.' He smiled, and the moment stretched, and lingered, then stretched some more. 'Well, night, then.'

'Night, then,' she repeated, finding herself ensnared by his pensive contemplation of her.

In the space between one heartbeat and the next, time seemed to stop. Then there was a strange sensation of gravity giving way, as she watched him edge towards her, and her to him. The compelling need to feel her lips pressed up against his was almost impossible to ignore.

Almost.

She abruptly pulled back, and mentally slapped herself. 'Right, well, I'll catch you tomorrow.' She couldn't get out of the LandCruiser quick enough. 'Thanks for dinner,' she said as she waved, then sped off down the pathway with her handbag clutched to her chest.

It wasn't until she'd reached the front door that Connor revved the four-wheel drive back to life, slowing to wave at her as he passed, before disappearing down the driveway.

Only then, once she'd had time to catch her breath and rid the jelly-like feeling from her legs, did she head inside to a thankfully dark house, climb up the stairs and tiptoe off to bed.

CHAPTER 17

Desiring him to take the lead, but not wanting to leave his side for a second, Samantha kept her horse slightly behind Connor's, just enough for him to know, and feel, that he was leading the way. The sight of him in his happy place, rocking gently in his saddle, his strong chiselled jaw relaxed and his handsome face shaded by his hat, she couldn't help but feel the magnetic pull dragging her heart that little bit closer to his. Even though it was a lifetime ago, she still remembered what it had felt like, with his mouth pressed up against hers while his hands caressed her skin so possessively, so seductively – it did things to her insides that made her stupidly believe that they, them, he and her, had possibilities that wouldn't have been conceivable to her until she arrived back in Gum Tree Gully. Even so, with the glimmer of hope between them, she had to firmly remind herself that this was the present, *not* the past. She didn't need to go and overthink everything. As if sensing her gaze, and reading her mind, he turned his head and smiled at her. Her heart fluttered. She wanted to hold onto this memory, and onto him, forever.

As the horses' hooves clip-clopped along the cobblestone path, she found herself staring into his striking eyes as he studied her. 'What are you thinking about, Mr Gunn?'

Even though there was hullabaloo all around them, his smile drew her in closer, making her feel like it was only her, and him, amid thousands of people. 'I'm wondering why you don't just move home with me.'

'Because it's not that simple.' Her horse startled as a black taxi came out of nowhere, blocking their path. 'I have a life, and a very successful business here.'

'You have a life in Gum Tree Gully, too, Sammie, with me.'

And that was right when the dream abruptly ended.

Forcing her eyes open against the glittering sunshine pouring through the curtains, Samantha sat up. Pushing the covers back before she'd even had time to rub the sleep from her eyes, she slipped from the bed and stumbled over her pile of clothing that she'd dropped there the night before. But try as she might to pretend it didn't happen, it all came rushing back to her, and she had to plonk herself on the edge of the tousled bed. Rubbing her face, she groaned against the twist of her stomach. Connor had almost kissed her. And she'd almost kissed him. They'd come so close. Too close. Things were getting way out of hand. She needed to get a grip, on herself and the situation. Connor wasn't going to be some holiday fling for her. He was worthy of way more than that. More than she could give him. What in the heck had they been thinking? Good grief, she couldn't even blame it on being a little drunk, as they hadn't touched a drop of alcohol at Granny's.

The chime of her phone mercifully startled her from her thoughts, and she threw herself across the bed to grab it before it went to her message bank. 'Hey, Shea.'

'Howdy doody. I'm too lazy to walk upstairs. Do you want some scrambled eggs?'

'Oh, you're far from lazy, Shea, and yes please.'

'Right, well, you best get your butt downstairs, my friend.'

'Okay, I'll be there in a jiffy.'

After a trip to the loo, then the bathroom to wash her hands and splash some water on her face, the aroma of freshly brewed coffee perked her up and had her almost racing towards the kitchen. The space was white and bright, the glass sun catcher dangling in front of the window reflecting rainbows over the countertops. She momentarily found herself lost in the kaleidoscope of colours, her analytical brain taking a back seat to her dreamy one that said life could be magical, and miraculous, if she just allowed herself to see it.

Shea plonked a cup of black coffee in front of her. 'Enchanting, isn't it.'

'Yes, it sure is.' Samantha took a grateful sip. 'Ahh, you're a lifesaver, thank you.'

'No worries.' Shea floated back to the oven, where she clutched the handle of a pan and carried it over to the folded tea towel on the bench. 'The sun catchers are my reminder, every bright sunny morning, that the day can be filled with beauty, and magic, if I want it to be.'

'I really wish I could see the world more often like you do, Shea.'

'You can, if you choose to.' She tucked an arm into Samantha's. 'After we eat breakfast, I want you to get your riding gear on so I can show you more enchantment.'

Less than an hour later and the double hit of caffeine had kicked in nicely. Surefooted and calm, Samantha's mare was a dream. For almost two hours she and Shea rode through the countryside that had once been her backyard, their conversation comfortably sparse in the presence of Mother Nature. Dappled sunlight made the path ahead appear bejewelled, and all around them birds sang sweet melodies. She knew exactly what Shea was doing – allowing her to see what she was missing, to feel what she had left behind, and she revelled in her restraint. And in that moment of serendipity, images of the one night she'd spent with Connor filtered through her mind. It was as if fate was trying to make her see what, up until now, she'd refused to.

Their night of passion hadn't been a mistake, and neither had coming here – fate had played a hand at every turn, every step, at every bend and curve in her journey to this point in time. She just had to trust in the process. As scary as it was, she had to let her tight grip on the reins of her life go, a little. And with that revelation, despite the cooling breeze, she felt heat rising through her. She needed to step into her new future and to do that she had to face her fears. She had to go back to the cemetery. But not yet. This afternoon they were heading away from Gum Tree Gully, and to the coast. Because tomorrow Shea and Jack would be married. Only after that would she do what she needed to do to get her life on the right path.

* * *

Her make-up and hair done, Samantha left the hustle and bustle of the lounge room and wandered into the main bedroom of the ocean-view apartment at the Cairns Crystalbrook five-star resort. She needed to catch her breath before slipping back into her maid of honour duties. Running her fingers over the lace material of what was now Shea's gown, Samantha had to use every bit of resolve not to break into uncontrollable tears. She wanted Shea to be wearing this dress today, but she felt guilty about not being the one to follow through on her mother's wishes. Would the ache of her parents' loss, the one that still squeezed her heart enough to make her fear vulnerability, ever diminish, or would it remain in the place where she filed the feelings she didn't want to endure, or face?

Sinking down on the corner of the hotel bed, she reminisced about another time, another dress. The day she'd married Benjamin she'd been so happy, so hopeful for a future filled with the sense of finally belonging, and unconditional love, and her very own children to cherish. When the truth was, she was in fact a naïve, broken young woman who'd been led to believe that she'd found the one, and was walking into her forever. Benjamin had played his cards well. He'd played *her* well. Little had she known that her make-believe world was going to be yanked out from beneath her feet. It made her livid to think back over it with fresh eyes. But if she was going to once again become the optimist Shea was encouraging her to be, she had to focus on the fact that Benjamin had been a lesson, and in some way an escape from her world of heartbreak, if only for a little while. In the end he hadn't been meant for her. And she hadn't been meant for him. It went both ways. That also meant acknowledging the man who was meant for her, the man she was inevitably meant for, and that was both scary and overwhelming, and seemingly impossible, given the thousands of miles that separated their daily lives.

Shaking away her melancholy, Samantha stood, straightened her shoulders and focused on the day ahead. It was her best friend's wedding, and Shea deserved for it to be all about her and Jack. She was going to do her damnedest to make that so. Sliding off her robe, she eased the silken forest green bridesmaid dress up her legs and shimmed into it. The zip was a little hard to do on her own, but with a bit of ungraceful twisting, she got there. The brand spanking new cowgirl boots Shea had chosen were next. The first one took a little bit of grunting and groaning to get on. Mission accomplished, she heaved a breath. One down, one to go. Going to pull the next one on, she stopped short. There was a note inside. Plucking it out, she expected to see Shea's handwriting, but it was Connor's cursive scrawl. Her heart stopped, and she covered her mouth – whatever did he have to say?

Hi Sammie,

I just wanted to let you know how special you are to me. I'm sorry things between us have been a little, let's say, awkward at times, or possibly even confusing? I think I'm safe to say that we both know there's something unique lingering between us. There always has been, and forever will be. What it is, we may never get the chance to fully understand, and that's okay. Sometimes, sadly, life just doesn't work out the way we plan, as we both know. The most important thing to me is that you don't leave here and become a stranger to me again. I want you in my life, however that may be.

Here for you, always,

Connor xx

'Oh Connor', she whispered, clutching the letter to her chest, 'you're such a sweetheart.'

Blinking fast, she looked to the ceiling, then to the floor, then stood and paced with one boot on. Fanning her face as if that would somehow ward off her overwhelming emotions, she fought back her tears. After an hour and a half in the make-up hot seat, she wasn't about to ruin the beautiful job the artist had done. But boy oh boy, the feelings Connor was enticing: tenderness, gratitude, vulnerability, fear, euphoria, exhilaration and, she had to confess, love. It made her feel a little crazy, in both a good and a bad way. She just didn't know what she was meant to do with such raw sentiments yet.

Hobbling to the French doors, she stepped out and onto the verandah, and then looked to the heavens for fortitude. 'Mum, Dad, if you are up there, looking down on me, please give me the strength to make the right decision about my messy life, whatever that may be.'

'Sammie, are you in here?' Shea's voice carried outside.

'Yes, I'm coming.' Her self-control in check, she stepped back inside.

'Oh wow, Sammie, you look absolutely stunning.'

'Thank you.' Watching Shea doing the same face-fanning that she'd just tried, Samantha waggled a finger at her dear friend. 'Don't you dare cry, because your make-up is gorgeous.'

'I'm trying not to,' Shea half laughed, half whimpered as she fanned faster.

Samantha placed a comforting hand on her shoulder. 'Are you ready for me to help you into your gown?'

'I am.' Shea looked to where it was hanging, then back at Samantha. 'Are you okay?'

'Yes, of course I am.' Samantha swallowed down her lump of emotion and flashed Shea a wide smile. 'Now come on, let's get you sorted so you can go and marry that wonderful man of yours.'

Tying the silk straps of the bodice, Samantha stole a moment to admire how perfectly the dress fitted. 'You look incredible, Shea.'

'I still can't believe you let me wear it.' She spun and threw her arms around Samantha. 'Thank you, again, for being so generous.'

'Of course.' Samantha held her close. 'I love you.'

'Love you, too, Sammie.'

Amaya skipped in, bring with her an air of sweet innocence. 'Oh Mummy, you look like a princess.'

'Thank you, sweetheart, and you, my girl, are the prettiest flower girl I've ever seen.' Crouching down, Shea shared a kiss and cuddle with her daughter. 'Are you ready to watch Mummy and Daddy get married?'

'Am I ever!' Amaya said, spinning in a circle, sending her dress spiralling around her knees.

Hand in hand, the three of them left the room behind.

After making sure the train of Shea's dress was perfectly spread out behind her, then popping Amaya just in front of her with her basket of rose petals, Samantha took her place. The seated guests stood and turned towards them. The music started, and she gently ushered Amaya forward. Cute as a button, Amaya took measured steps, her little hand cascading petals as she made her way to the front. Sunlight streamed through the stained-glass windows of the church, casting bright colours over everything in sight and for an instant, the memory of the last time she'd walked down this very aisle, towards her parents' caskets, crashed down upon Samantha. Unfathomable grief gripped her for a breath, and then another, before she met Connor's steadfast gaze, and he silently helped her to find the courage to push through the sorrow. Forcing a smile, she moved towards him, feeling as if he was carrying the weight of her heavy heart with each of her steps perfectly timed to the music. Reaching the front, she took her place and turned to watch Shea and her father make their entrance. As strained as Shea and her dad's relationship could quite often be, she was glad he'd made the trip here from Tasmania for his daughter's special day. And the look on Jack's face, as he watched his bride-to-be walk down the aisle – aww, it was priceless. As she watched Shea take hold of Jack's hands, Samantha couldn't deny the truth staring her right in the face – she wanted, craved and longed for their kind of love: eternal, unconditional, profound, the same kind of love her parents had shared for one another. Emotions threatening to overcome her, she kept her gaze away from anyone else as the priest began the proceedings, especially Connor, because if she made eye contact with anyone right now, especially him, she'd so easily fall to pieces.

There were love-filled verses, heart-moving vows, the exchanging of rings and then the priest pronounced Jack and Shea husband and wife. The guests cheered as Jack bent Shea backwards, planting a kiss on her pouted lips. Then, after an hour of photographs, in many of which she found herself closely pressed up against Connor, in what felt like the blink of an eye, Samantha found herself at the reception, with plate in hand, ready to pick out what she wanted for dinner. The buffet table was lavish and as she moved along, she did her best not to fill her plate to the brim – she didn't want to overdo it, with her eyes bigger than her belly.

'Hey there.' Connor's deep voice carried over her shoulder. 'I have to say you're looking incredible in that dress.'

'Thank you.' Glancing back at him, she turned and ran her gaze up and down his six-foot suit-clad body. 'You've scrubbed up mighty fine yourself, too, Mr Gunn.'

'Why thankya, Miss Evans.' He struck a pose akin to James Bond, grinning that smile that would win any woman over in a split second.

She had to silently admit, even though she'd fought him off at every turn, that knee-buckling smile had won her over, too. 'Thank you for my letter,' she said, softly, as he stepped back in beside her.

There was a short pause. 'Did you like it?'

'No.' She had to bite her lip to add a dramatic pause. 'I loved it.'

'You did?' was his happy, husky response.

'Uh-huh.' She shifted her gaze from his and across the grandiose room, filled with cheerful people. 'It's been the perfect day, hasn't it?'

'It sure has.'

She looked to his piled-high plate. 'My gosh, are you going to eat all that?'

'I'm going to give it a good shot.'

'I'm going to hold you to that.'

'You do that, Sammie.' His smile widened. 'Now let's go and eat, so I can give this mountain of food time to settle before we have to get up and dance.'

'Good idea,' she replied, following him back to their designated bridal table.

And just like that, dinner was done, Shea and Jack had shared their first dance, and she and Connor weaved their way through the tables. Now, finally, she could be in the very place she'd been longing to be, wrapped up in Connor's arms. His tender, reassuring touch put her at ease as they waltzed around the glittering dance floor. Halfway through Dean Martin's 'That's Amore', she dared a glance up at him and was giddy in an instant. Heat seeped into her veins, the potency of it pumping her heart harder, faster. Leaning into him a little more, she steadied herself, drawing in a surreptitious breath as she bent her head downwards, her focal point now his broad tanned chest, hinted at from the open button of his shirt.

For goodness sake, was there any part of this man she didn't find attractive?

'We feel good together, you and me.' His voice was dangerously alluring, as too was his breath against her ear.

All she could do in that dreamlike instant was tip her head to him and smile. No words were needed. And in that raw, authentic, eye-opening second, she wanted to throw her arms around him and never let him go. Because when all was said and done, he and Shea were the only two people in this world that knew the real her, the broken messy her, the best her, and all the bits in between, and they still loved her regardless. So she savoured the next few minutes, when it was okay for her to be so dangerously, yet beautifully, close to him. If she could click her fingers right now, and have her life back here, with him, she would.

But life just didn't work like that.

And when the next song finished, so did their intimate time together, when Shea's cousin burst in between them and dragged Connor away to dance with her. Samantha didn't have a second to catch the breath he'd stolen from her before hands grabbed her and swayed her in the opposite direction. The next few hours rushed by, and she found herself in the middle of the dance floor with Shea, having the time of her life with the remaining guests. The dance floor gleamed beneath the glowing fairy lights strung from the ceiling of the grandiose ballroom and the multicoloured party lights sent scatterings of colour over happy faces. In the middle of busting out the moves to 'Nutbush City Limits', she caught sight of Connor, watching her. Her stomach somersaulted for what felt like the hundredth time that day. There was something in his intense regard of her, which spoke of everything he was aching to know. And she ached to tell him, to put his mind at ease. She knew he wasn't much of a read-between-the-lines kind of man. She understood he wanted her to just lay it all out on the table. If only she had the courage to. If only there was a way he could climb inside her head, so she didn't have to spell it out. So she didn't have to worry about saying it the wrong way. So she didn't have to make herself so vulnerable.

The song changed to another old classic, 'I Was Made for Lovin' You' by Kiss. Samantha squealed, as did Shea. The amount of times they'd all danced to this as teenagers, how could she forget the fun they'd had? Placing his beer down, Connor clearly remembered, too, as he took long hurried strides towards her. Then reaching her, he took her into his arms, and spun her in dizzying circles as they both sang the lyrics out loud. Jack joined in, too, and the four of them lost all the years that had come between them and were right back where they used to be as carefree teenagers. They bopped and boogied together, spinning and swaying. And when the song came to an end, and Connor let go of her hands, she couldn't work out whether the ground spinning beneath her feet was because of the champagne, or him. Then there was a sudden change of tempo and Phil Collins' voice rang out as 'A Groovy Kind of Love' echoed across the dance floor. Samantha didn't know whether to risk staying there, with the man who now held her heart within his hands, or make a run for it. Either way, the decision was out of her control because her feet wouldn't move.

As if reading her thoughts, Connor brought his finger to her chin and gently guided her gaze to his. 'You good?'

'I think so.' Her eyes filled with tears that she quickly blinked back.

'I got you, Sammie,' he replied, before pulling her nice and close. 'I've always got you,' he repeated, a lot more softly this time.

And he did get her, in every single way. More than any other man ever had, and much more than any other man ever would. She knew that. Without a doubt. Losing herself to this moment, and to him, she nestled against his chest, his touch making her feel safe, home, loved.

CHAPTER 18

Her bare feet sinking into the ground that she'd walked over many times before, Samantha inhaled the balmy air as she wandered back up the driveway, the mail she'd just collected from the old milk urn in hand. It was weird being here without Shea, Jack and Amaya around, but it was also giving her the precious time that she needed to think. About where she'd been, and which way she was going to go from here. But first, regardless of any decision, she needed to get back to London, to pack up her apartment and tend to her business, and hopefully, then, everything would just fall into place.

Overhead, the blooming jacaranda trees offered the colourful parrots perches, and a dappled canopy for her. She admired how their gnarled branches stretched across the trail, as if reaching for their significant other on the opposite side, almost embracing overhead. Wow. Even in nature, there was a need for union, for touch. Admiring the bright purple flowers adorning the

Australian natives and the blanket of purple beneath each, she smiled softly as she considered just how deep their roots would be embedded within this earth that she, too, stood upon. This land, that had once been her home, was the trees' foundation, and the blazing tropical sun way up high was their life force. Oh how she wished she had such strength and fortitude when standing still. A year ago, she'd believed she knew who she was and where she was going, and that had been far away from here, with Benjamin, but now she was questioning everything she'd laid her roots into. There was no depth, no heart, no room for growth for her back in London. There was nothing significant for her to grab hold of. No close friends to draw comfort from. Not even a cat, or dog, to go home to at the end of each day. But was she just daydreaming, in believing it was all here, waiting for her, if she moved back? Her heart was telling her one thing, and her mind was telling her another. Hopefully, things would reveal themselves, in time.

Shrugging her shoulders in a deliberate attempt to try and shake the contemplations off, she ran her fingers through her sweat-damp hair and pulled it up and into a messy bun before heading back into the homestead. The scent of frying bacon, eggs and mushrooms met her, enticing a growl from her stomach.

With her tastebuds luring her towards the kitchen, when she eyed the chef she got that same sparkly feeling in her stomach she always did when she was in the same room as him. 'My god, Connor, something smells really good.'

'Yeah, that's just my natural scent.' Plucking a tray of perfectly grilled tomatoes and crispy-looking bacon from the depths of the oven, he placed it onto the sink. 'I've just got to poach the eggs, and Bob's your mother's brother.'

'You're spoiling me.' Tossing the mail onto the bench, she edged in beside him. 'You don't have to come over here and cook for me, you know, I can fend for myself.'

'Yeah, I know, but a random day off calls for a good old cook-up and a decent cuppa, all of which to be enjoyed out on the back verandah.'

'You are so Aussie, Gunn.' She snatched a piece of bacon and jumped just out of his reach to devour it.

'Damn straight I am.' Connor wandered past her and offered a playful glance. 'That good, huh?'

'Oh my gosh, yes, what did you do to it?'

'A little drizzle of maple syrup, and a whole lotta love.'

'Nice combo.' She licked the remnants from her fingertips. 'Would you like me to get cracking with some toast?'

Stirring a hefty dollop of butter into the sizzling mushrooms, he nodded. 'Yeah, that'd be great, cheers.'

She manned the toaster, all the while unable to keep her eyes off the way his back muscles pulled his polo shirt taut, or how nice his butt looked in his board shorts. Startled when the toast popped up, she turned to see one of the pieces was jammed. After flicking the switch off at the wall, she used her fingertip to try and edge it out.

'Ouch, bugger.' She raced to the tap and turned it on, sticking her finger beneath the stream of water.

'Crap, Sammie, are you okay?' Tossing his tea towel, Connor came to her aid.

'Yeah, all good, I got attacked by the toaster.'

Taking her hand, he assessed the red skin as if it was made of the most delicate glass. 'You're going to have a whopper of a blister.' He looked at her, way more concerned than a slightly scalded finger warranted. 'Do you know if there is any aloe vera in the garden?'

Chuckling, she placed her hand against his chest. 'Bless your sweet heart, Connor Gunn.' Her smile was soft. 'But honestly, I'll be fine.'

'You sure?'

'Yes.'

She got to work buttering the toast, after he'd retrieved the offending piece, while Connor dished up their feast. Cosied up on the verandah, they devoured it like a pair of hungry teenagers and then kicked back, with their feet up on the railings of the front verandah, and enjoyed their cups of tea that Samantha had made.

'I suppose I better head home and get some jobs done.' Connor looked to her, his woeful expression telling her just how much he didn't want to go. 'I could stay here and happily hang out with you all day, but the agisted horses won't feed themselves.'

'I can come and help, if you like,' she said, a little too hastily.

'Yeah, actually.' His face lit up. 'I'd love that.'

'Great, I'll go grab my boots and meet you at the LandCruiser.'

'Righto, I'll take this lot and dump it in the dishwasher.' He collected the dirty plates, cutlery and cups from the coffee table.

'Leave it, Connor, I can fix it up when I get back.'

'All good, it'll only take me a sec.' He gestured to the door with a tip of his head. 'You go sort yourself out.'

'Okay, thanks.' Samantha couldn't help but fall for him that little bit more, with his kind, simple gesture.

An hour later and they'd loaded his ute up with feed. Climbing behind the wheel, Connor took a glug from his water bottle and then revved the engine, turned around and they headed down the bumpy track. He pulled up at the start of the agistment paddocks.

'If you want to swap, Sammie, you can drive, and I'll do the heavy work up back.'

'Actually, do you mind if I do it?'

'You sure?'

She nodded, eager to get her hands dirty. 'Positive.'

Jumping out and then up on the tray, she got to work, heaving the bales of hay to the edge and over the fence to the waiting horses. Connor rolled from one paddock to the next, each time checking in to make sure she didn't want to swap. Which she didn't. She loved the hard yakka. Had missed it, actually. They reached the last paddock that housed Connor's horse, Banjo, and pulling to a stop, Connor jumped out. Tail high in the air, the gelding gave a loud snort, then pig-rooted all the way over to them. Skidding to a stop just shy of the timber fence, he flicked his head and whinnied cheekily, his teeth bared in a horsey grin.

'I think he's showing off in front of you, Sammie.'

'Is he now?' Samantha pushed the last bail out and over the fence, and then laughed at Banjo's flamboyant arrival. 'I think he's a bit like his owner.'

Connor's sideways glance was sexy as hell. 'Fair play, Evans.'

She offered him a sassy smile in response. 'Ha, you love it.'

'You got me, I do, love it, that is.'

Her boots thudded on the ground beside him, and he held a hand up to steady her. She couldn't help but notice how he took care of her, always. And it made her feel warm and fuzzy all over, as if the sun belting down upon her back was reaching inside her, its rays caressing her heart and soul.

'Right, my awesome sidekick.' Conner turned his attention from Banjo to her. 'Time's a-ticking, and next up, we have a calf to feed.'

'Oh my gosh, really?' She jiggled on the spot. 'Can I feed it?'

'Yeah, of course you can.'

'Yay.' She clapped. She couldn't get to the stables quick enough.

After mixing it up, Connor passed her the bottle of milk. 'Here's his dinner.'

Grabbing a nearby bucket, she turned it upside down, and sat. 'Here you go, buddy.' The calf drank greedily from the bottle, so much so she had to tighten her grip. 'Holy heck, this little cutie has a death grip on this thing.'

'Yeah, he's a bit of a guts.' Connor ran his hand over the calf's russet-coloured head. 'I can already tell that he's going to be a tough nut, this one.'

Samantha pulled the bottle back to check if there was any milk left in it. Bleating, then poking his head through the gaps in the railings, the calf craned his neck, trying to grab hold of the teat again.

'I'm sorry, buddy.' Samantha chuckled as she wiped her hands on her jeans. 'It's all finished.'

'You'll get more tomorrow, my friend.' Connor gave its head another loving ruffle.

The calf bleated a few times in response.

Samantha reached over the railing and gave the calf a loving pat. 'Bye, cutie pie.'

'That's what his name is going to be,' Connor said as they headed back towards the LandCruiser.

'What, cutie pie?' She guffawed. 'Get out, as if you're going to holler "cutie pie" when you want him to come to you.'

'Why not?' Connor gave her a look that spoke of earnestness. 'I'm going to have to, if that's his name.'

Samantha was silently chuffed Connor had done such a sweet thing. Oh, her heart, how much more could it melt for this amazing man?

'Would you like a cold one, before I drop you back?'

'Would I ever.' She didn't want to leave him, not for a second.

After kicking their boots off at the farmhouse's back door, they washed off in the laundry before traipsing into the kitchen in search of icy-cold beers. With two retrieved from the depths of the fridge, they headed back outside and cosied up on the settee. There was something to be said about a country sky at sunset. Peachy orange hues turned what had been a bright blue, cloudless sky to a bronzed ochre, as if the heavens had caught a golden tan from the warmth of the day. It was so spectacular, Samantha couldn't drag her eyes from it.

'Beautiful, isn't it, Sammie?'

'It sure is.' Smothering a yawn, she rested her head against his shoulder.

And they remained like that as they witnessed the setting of the sun, comfortable in each other's company, and in silence. Somehow, someway, being back in the place that had been her home longer than London ever had, around the people who loved her completely, had given her a sense of peace she hadn't ever felt before. And it was so nice to have arrived back to a comfortable place with Connor, too. Yes, a lot was left unsaid between them, but that's the way it needed to be, because declarations were going to do them no favours. She needed to get her life in order first and foremost, before she stepped into any new chapters of her life. And then she wondered how Shea and

Jack's honeymoon was going, and whether Amaya was enjoying time with her grandad in Tasmania.

'I'm in love with you, Sammy.' Connor's voice seemed to come out of nowhere.

'Pardon?' Her exclamation was more a whooshed breath than a word as she sat up rod-straight.

'You heard me.' His smile was soft and warm, like a hot chocolate on a cold winter's night.

But she felt more like she'd just had a triple shot of coffee. Needing to move, she shot to her feet, nailing him to the spot with her stare. 'I did, but I don't know what you're expecting me to do with such a blatant declaration.'

'Whatever you like.' Sighing, he momentarily looked to the floor, then back to her. 'I'm so tired of keeping how I feel to myself, Sammie, and I suppose I just wanted you to know before you go back to London, because I do love you, always have and forever will.' He cleared his throat and then shrugged. 'Is that such an awful thing to make you aware of?'

That look in his eyes, so sincere, so tender, how could she be on the defensive? Yes, she was terrified, but … 'I don't know how we're going to work, Connor, given the fact I'm literally tied to London with my business being there, for the time being.' She gave him an apologetic look. 'And I have no idea when, or if, that's going to change.'

'I get that, but tell me, do you feel anything more than friendship between us, Sammie, and please, before you answer, be honest, with me, and yourself.'

He was the epitome of perfection, so why couldn't she tell him the absolute truth? What in the hell was wrong with her? 'Not enough to say I'm *in* love with you.'

'But you do, love me, that is?'

'Of course I do, Connor, we're long-time friends.'

He drew in a breath, but remained silent, his gaze searching hers for any sign that she wasn't telling him everything. Which she wasn't. And with the uncanny ability he had, of getting to those parts of herself she kept under lock and key, well, she wasn't going to risk him discovering her deepest feelings.

'Sammie, please, talk to me.'

With anxiety filling her, her mood nosedived. 'I already have.' She turned away and looked to the star-studded sky before he witnessed the tears building in her eyes. 'I think it's time you dropped me back home.'

'I'll go get my keys.' He heaved a huff, and then his footfalls began to make distance between them.

The slap of the screen door jolted her, and she used the few moments to gather what she could of herself before their journey back to the homestead. She really needed to stop spending so much time with him. She was giving him hope, where there was none. And she loved him way too much to do that to him. Tomorrow, it was time to stop running from her past, and to face it, head on.

CHAPTER
19

Looking to the sunny blue sky, Samantha questioned how it could be so bright and beautiful at a time such as this. Stinging tears threatened and a lump rose in her throat as she stood out the front of the Gum Tree Gully cemetery, very alone, very apprehensive, but also very determined. More so than she'd ever been. She wasn't certain she was ready to cross the boundary she'd mentally created between her parents' life and death, but would she ever be ready to revisit the grave of the two people who had meant the absolute world to her? The very two people who should have been at her side throughout every trial and triumph? Grief and anger choked her chest, and she almost turned around, but the drive to finally do what she feared the most out of anything in this world overcame her. Her parents were dead. Forever gone. She needed to see that and find a way to finally accept it. Then, and only then, she might be able to move into the life she was meant to be living, instead of constantly running away from Gum Tree Gully and living a lie.

Exhaling her held breath, she took that step, the one that would lead her down this proverbial trail. A few metres along, she met with the front gate. It looked tired and weather-beaten. She gave it a little nudge with her foot, but it didn't move an inch. Griping it tightly, she yanked hard and it finally gave, as if acknowledging her fortitude. Head held high and shoulders back, she strode through. The iron gate clanged closed behind her, as if announcing her arrival to the dead. Running her fingertips along the weathered grey tops of the timber picket fence line, she travelled down the path on autopilot. She walked past old graves graced with tall headstones and the occasional statue. She walked past children's graves, some cornered off with ornate fencing and little gates. She couldn't help but wonder if it was to keep their innocent spirits in, or the evil spirits out?

Trailing a bend, she reached a ridgeline and the wind whipped up and over the rocky outcrop, feathering wisps of hair across her cheeks. Ghost gums began to crowd either side of the path, the landscape in this part of the cemetery older, more established. She tried to shake the eerie feeling of the dead all around her. Thankfully emerging from the dappled shade of the towering trees, she took a few more steps over a pebbled track, then stopped in her tracks as she came face to face with her parents' graves. A shuddering breath resonated throughout her. Her heartbeat pounded in her ears. She gripped the strap of her handbag tightly. Tears threatened and momentarily blurred her vision, but she squared her shoulders once again and blinked faster. Their headstones sat proud and tall, just like her father had always been. Yet there were weeds trying to outrun his final stance of pride. Dropping to her knees on the grass, she snatched at the weeds with anger, and then plucking a packet of wet wipes from her handbag, she began cleaning each of the headstones. When that was done, she sat back on her haunches and read the verse that had been inscribed on both headstones.

> *Do not stand upon my grave and weep*
> *Instead rejoice the many happy memories you keep*
> *Live not a day, encumbered by sorrow*
> *Instead rejoice my life, and look forward to every tomorrow*

What was she meant to do? Rejoice in their deaths?

'Why did you have to take them from me?' she shouted skywards.

Folding forward, she brought her hands to the ground, one on her father's grave and the other on her mother's. It was then, in this hard-hitting, earth-shattering, moment, that the walls she'd been building for eleven long years, brick by brick, finally cracked and crumbled, and for a long while she sobbed her broken heart out, her tears soaking the earth her mother and father now called home. She wasn't sure how long it was before she eventually turned over and lay on her back, arms splayed. The day was getting on, but she didn't want to leave, not yet. Looking to the lacy white clouds drifting across the cornflower-blue sky, she watched each fleetingly shadow the sun, momentarily darkening the world around her, before the cottony softness floated onwards, and the harsh glare of the sun hit her again with force, as if slapping her cheeks in a bid to tell her to snap out of her lie, so she could see the life she could have – god willing.

And there it was.

The realisation she'd asked her parents for on the verandah of Shea's hotel room.

Sitting up, she grabbed her phone and stabbed her message before she changed her mind.

* * *

For some strange reason, even after the way he and Samantha had parted on shaky ground, Connor had woken with the feeling that today was going to be a game changer. And then all day long, the hunch had remained deep down in his bones, and he hadn't been able to shake the sensation. While still trying to make sense of it, all the while deciding if he should push the line further, seeing as he'd already stepped over the boundaries of their relationship, her text message had flashed up on his phone …

Connor, everything's fine, and there's nothing to worry about, but I need to see you ASAP.

So he'd dropped everything he was doing to get to her as quickly as he could. But he'd been out the back paddocks, fixing a broken water line, so it was almost an hour since he'd responded with *See you at the homestead as soon as I can. Xx*

In the past fifteen minutes, the sky had heaved with rolling black clouds and thunder had boomed. Just as he'd gotten into his LandCruiser a luminous snap of lightning had shot across the sky, and the heavens had opened up in wild monsoonal fashion. His windscreen wipers now swished back and forth on top speed, sweeping the pounding rain from his view. The droplets were heavy in his headlights, warning him to be wary, so he did his best not to drive like a bat out of hell to get to her. But by Christ he was hankering to see her, so he could find out if she was as desperate as he was to lay everything on the table.

Or was she about to tell him something he didn't want to hear?

God knew, he was about to do that to her.

Her text message spun like a broken record in his head. And drove him nuts. How cryptic could she be? If only everything was fine. But it wasn't fine. Not in the slightest. Far from it. He wasn't about to let her leave Gum Tree Gully without coming clean and telling her way more than how he was madly in love with her. He wanted to know whether, in a perfect world, she could bring herself to forgive him for playing a hand in her parents' accident, as well as accepting they would never be able to have children together, if she could leave her life behind in London and stay here, with him, so they could make the life together like they should have all those years ago.

Turning into the gates, he imagined how he was going to say it all without mucking it up. But when he pulled up out the front of the homestead, and saw her standing there, on the verandah, her arms wrapped around herself, and the sheets of rain blowing against her, whipping her hair around her face, he lost all sense of rhyme or reason. All he wanted to do in the very second was run to her, and take her into his arms, so she felt his love, so she felt him shielding her from any more heartbreak. So she knew, without a doubt, that if she gave her beautiful heart to him, that he would hold it preciously. Always and forevermore. Never in his wildest dreams could he ever intentionally upset her.

If someone had hurt her, so help him god ...

Leaping out of the driver's seat to do what his heart willed him to do, he took hurried steps towards her. But before he'd gotten the chance to reach the front gates of the white picket fencing, she cleared the steps two at a time and ran to him, tears and rain streaming down her face. Meeting, he took her with open arms, and held her against him. And she continued to weep, hard, her sobs wracking against his chest with her fingers gripping the back of his shirt. Hating seeing her so distraught, he held his own emotions at bay as he stroked her wet hair, while telling her over and over that he was here for her, that he had her, that she was safe with him. It was only when her sobs subsided to a whimper that he pulled back just enough to look into her eyes, to ask if she was okay.

She nodded and said 'Mm-hmm', but her hushed reply clashed with the tortured look in her red-rimmed, puffy eyes.

'Everything doesn't seem fine.' Worry tearing at his heart, he tucked locks of hair from her cheeks. 'Sammie, please tell me what's happened?'

She sucked in a shuddering breath. 'I went to their graves, Connor.'

She was shivering – he wanted to get her out of the rain. 'You did?' Wrapping an arm around her waist, he led her towards the steps and up to the swing chair.

'Yes, and it helped me to see things clearer.' She sat with his aid, and after wrapping the blanket slung over the back of the chair around her shoulders, he settled down beside her.

'What's become clearer, exactly?'

'Their deaths, being here.' She smiled through her tears. 'Everything, really.'

'Has it helped you, in moving forwards?' Oh god, how he wanted her to tell him she wanted to share the rest of her life with him.

'I believe it has.' She looked to where she was twisting her rain-damp shirt in her fingers.

'And?'

'And, I …' She sucked in a breath, and then looked to the rain, her bottom lip clamped between her teeth.

Anxiety settled in the pit of his stomach as he waited for her hesitating response.

She cleared her throat, and turned to him. 'I care for you, Connor, so very much, and I …' She paused again, sucked in another shuddering breath. 'But, I …' She paused again.

Connor was suddenly desperate to fill the silence, because if he didn't spill the workings of his heart to her now, right this very second, she might say something to stop him, and then he might live to regret it forever.

'Samantha.' Her name rolled from his lips, lips that were aching to meet with hers.

The fairy lights dangling from the balustrades reflected in her eyes, making the green even more dazzling. 'You called me Samantha, now that's a first.'

'Yeah, I did.' Even though the intensity of the moment was pressing down upon him, he managed a little chuckle. 'There's always a first for everything.'

'Yes, there sure is.' Placing a hand on his bouncing knee, she searched his gaze and drew in an almighty breath. 'Mind body and soul, I'm in love with you, Connor Gunn.'

And just like that, she rid him of the ability to speak, so he did all he could, and went to show her just how much her loved her, too, with actions rather than words, because as they say, actions are always way louder.

* * *

The marvel in Connor's eyes, as she declared her love for him, was like fireworks exploding. And then he was inching towards her, and she felt the same old rising panic in her chest, but she could also feel her heart reaching for his, as if trying to find its way home. And then he was so close she could feel his breath against her cheek. Time didn't exist as she tumbled into the calming abyss of his piercing blue eyes. Together, united, as they always had been, they were teetering from one heartbeat to the next. It was as if he was waiting for her to meet him, to give him the invitation to revive the flames that were smouldering in their hearts. If she even tried to resist him, would she be able to? And why did she even want to? The great divide she'd worked so hard to create no longer needed to be there.

Should I kiss him?

Her head and heart were having a battle of wills. He made her feel so beautiful, inside and out, and always had. She was never going to find the strength to go back to London and just get on with her life, as though nothing else mattered. Because what mattered was being here with him, and all those that cared about her.

Kiss him, Samantha …

With a soft, quivering sigh, she let go, and tumbled off the cliff she'd been so desperately trying to balance upon. And he caught her, in the most evocative of ways, as his arms slipped around her waist and he bent his head, making his intentions unmistakable. But he didn't push any further past the boundary that had been between them since she'd arrived home.

Home. She liked the sound the word made circling her mind.

With his mouth hovering enticingly near hers, her arms slipped around his neck and her lips parted in invitation, to him, to this, to there being a possibility of *them*. Longing, hope and promise danced, pirouetting and swaying her heart as she felt the sensation of his heart irrevocably catching hers. And even though she'd sensed it all along, now she knew without a shadow of doubt that he was a man who would always be there for her. No matter what. No matter the circumstances. And that's right when she realised that she'd never, ever felt like this before. The explosion in her chest, this, that, he was her love. Connor Gunn was the one and only love of her life. Never had she possessed a raw need to own another, like she wanted to own him right this very second. Reality could take a back seat because for now, in this mesmerising moment, she wanted to show him just how deeply she loved him.

But then, just as she was about to climb onto his lap, so she could be even closer to him still, he stopped, pulled back just a little and smiled in a way that told her he knew exactly what she was thinking. And that drove her wilder still. Not only could this man scorch her skin with a single glance, a single touch, he also held a flame to her soul. He knew her, like no other, from the inside out. And he loved her for all that she was, all that she had been and all she was yet to be. And she, terrifyingly, excitingly, exhilaratingly, felt the same about him.

But you have so much to sort out, back in London, it could be months before you see each other again, and in that time you could drift apart, or he could meet someone else, someone better than you, or ...

Sensing her hesitation, Connor brushed his lips over to her ear and whispered. 'Don't think, Sammie, just feel.' Trailing his fingers up her back, he sent quivers to places she didn't even know existed.

A shuddering sigh escaped her as she recognised she needed him just as much as she needed to breathe. And her silence was all he required. As he trailed his mouth down her neck, goosebumps rose as he gently tipped her head back and covered her throat with feathering kisses. Her pulse skittered, then pounded, then skittered again. His hot touch branded her skin as she melted against him, freefalling into the dizzying rush of sensation his slow, warm kisses were giving her. His fingers tangled into her hair, pulling her closer still. Gripping his shirt, she straddled his lap and her hunger for him became ravenous. She wanted him. All of him. Now. Always. Forever. She felt all the pieces of herself she'd pushed to the depths, and they rose, and bloomed like a sunflower turning towards the bright sunshine. All that mattered was this moment. And them. He took control of the kiss, as though he'd been starving for her all these years. And with the way he was touching her, kissing her, loving her, she believed wholeheartedly that he had been. Rising with her wrapped up in his arms, he carried her towards the doorway. She dropped her legs, and as her feet hit the floor, they stumbled backwards until her back came up against the wall.

His breath was ragged. 'I'm sorry, Sammie, I should stop this now, before ...'

'No, please, don't stop.' Samantha felt as if she was about to burst into flames. She didn't want this to end, not ever. She reached for him. 'Please, Connor, I want you, and I want this.'

'But what is this?'

She cupped his cheeks. 'I don't know.'

Connor slowly shook his head. 'I can't, we can't.' He turned away. 'Trust me, it's better if we don't take this any further, at least not until we talk about some important things, and how it would all work after that.'

'Yes, I suppose you're right.' A vice tightened around her heart.

He shoved a hand through his hair. 'I'm sorry, Sammie, I shouldn't have made a move like that.'

Fraught, wanting to fix things so there wasn't a weird feeling between them, she tried to chuckle. 'Ha, yeah, we should have learnt better from the first time, hey?' She didn't want him regretting kissing her, and making light of it was all she could think to do right now.

But the look on his face was evident he didn't find the comment funny, in the slightest. 'Sammie, come on, we don't need to go back there.'

Shame and embarrassment at her lack of tact made her cheeks hot. Then her voice of reason stormed to the forefront, firmly reminding her that she knew better than to act like some lovesick fool. Being reckless always got her into trouble and inevitably led to her being badly hurt. Angry with herself for not being the one to apply the brakes, she turned her back to him and bit back a sudden onslaught of tears. No matter how much she told herself she shouldn't feel this way about him, she couldn't help herself. And if she were being honest with herself, she still wanted him, more than ever. And she loathed herself for feeling so strongly, when she knew he was right. They needed to have some hard conversations before they took things any further.

'Sammie, let's not let this ruin the bond we've rebuilt, hey.' Connor came to her side, his gaze beseeching as he brought his hand to her cheek. 'You mean too much to me for us to part ways like we did the last time you left.'

Unable to form words in her tight throat, she nodded.

He opened his arms and she didn't resist his kind-heartedness. She pressed her cheek to his chest as his arms came around her, remarkably protectively and a little possessively. If only she could stay. If only he could leave and come with her. If only they could meet in the middle. But it wasn't that easy, they were no longer footloose and fancy-free teenagers with endless opportunities before them. His life was here, and hers wasn't for the time being.

CHAPTER 20

The next day, after a sleepless night, Samantha tried to keep herself busy by doing chores. Grabbing the last of her clothes from the drier and then carrying the beautifully warm mountain through to the lounge room, she dropped the pile onto the couch. But before she folded everything, she did what she'd been craving to do since flicking her eyes open at dawn and grabbed her phone. It was time to set things straight. Heading outside and onto the sun-soaked verandah, she settled herself on the daybed. She was nervous to press Connor's number, but like him, she didn't want anything coming between them before she headed back to London. She craved to hold onto the hope that they might still stand a chance, if she could get her life sorted out. She wanted to have the conversations they needed to have, and what better way than to ask if he wanted to spend the day with her, so they could talk everything through when the right moment arose.

The ringing of her mobile as she was curling her legs up beneath her made her jump. She couldn't help the smile when she spotted who it was. 'Hey, you, I was just about to call you.'

'Morning Sammie, great minds think alike.'

'They sure do.'

'So.' His tone was a light and playful. 'Why were you going to call me?'

'No.' She tipped her head. 'You rang me, so you go first.'

'Okay. I was wondering if you'd like to come over for a scoot around in the chopper, followed by that swim we've been talking about, but haven't got around to yet?'

The hope she was barely holding onto flourished. 'I'd love to.'

'Awesome, I can come get you, if you like?'

'No, all good, I've got my hire car.'

'Right, well, see you when you get here then.'

She nodded, even though Connor couldn't see her. 'Yes, okay, I'll see you in about an hour, if that's okay?'

'Great, I have a couple of odd jobs to get done, so that's perfect.'

It was almost an hour and a half before Samantha pulled up at Connor's place. She'd been so keen to look cute, but not too cute, it had taken her four outfits to come to the conclusion that she'd reached her goal. Her bedroom looked like a bomb had hit it, but with no time to clean it up, she'd left it for later, along with the pile of folding. She didn't want to waste another second that she could be spending with the man who possessed her every thought.

Wearing a floaty yellow dress, with her black bikini just visible beneath the thin cotton material, she stepped from her car and into Connor's magnetic energy. 'Sorry I'm late.'

'Fashionably, by the looks.' His gaze drank her in appreciatively. 'Yellow suits you, big time, very beachy, Sammie.'

Her heart fluttered, and she playfully curtsied. 'Thanks.' She eyed his attire of a singlet and board shorts, and stark white bare feet. 'And FYI, the beachside look suits you, too.'

'As you can see by the tanned sock marks.' He looked down and wriggled his toes. 'I don't get to dress like this much seeing as I'm pretty much always on the clock, but, today,' he brought his eyes back to hers, 'I thought why the hell not pretend it's a once-in-a-blue-moon kind of holiday.'

'I reckon that's a perfect way to look at today.' She handed him the basket of goodies she'd packed at a hundred miles an hour.

'What's all this?' He peered within as they made their way towards the farmhouse.

'Nothing special, just a little bit of this and that for our lunch, or smoko, or whenever it is we want to eat.' She smiled. 'I don't know about you, but swimming always makes me hungry.'

'Ditto, Sammie.' He held up the packet of Tim Tams. 'Oh lord help me, because I can never stop at one of these bad boys.'

'Ha, me neither.' Kicking her sandals off at the back door, she patted her belly. 'Mind you, I've put on a few kilos since coming back here.'

'I don't know where.' His gaze travelled over her. 'Because you still look fit as.'

'Aw, thanks, with Shea's amazing cooking, I feel like all I've basically done is eat.' She stepped into the coolness of the little farmhouse, loving the way it smelt of wood and spice and all things Connor.

'Too right, she's an awesome cook, hey.'

'Yes, and so are you,' she said, leaning against the butcher's block at the centre of the kitchen.

'Aw, thanks, Sammie.' Conner grinned spiritedly as he brought a finger to his lips. 'Shhh, don't tell anyone, though, or I'll have the whole town knocking at my door, wanting to taste my food.' Plunking the basket on the kitchen countertop, he then grabbed a few beers and a couple of bottles of water from the fridge and popped them into an esky on the sink. 'You good with beer and water?'

'Sure am.' She tapped the countertop, and then straightened. 'You've really done such a nice job on this place, Connor, you should be proud of yourself.'

He turned, and followed her gaze. 'Thanks, Sammie, I love it here.'

For a fleeting moment, Sammie imagined herself living here with him, and the thought filled her with joy.

If only …

'Right, you good to go?'

'Am I ever!' She clapped her hands together. 'I'm super excited to go up in the chopper with you. It's been forever since I've seen Gum Tree Gully from the sky.'

'It'll be the first flight with me at the helm, instead of Dad.'

'Yes, and I'm sure you'll make me feel as safe and secure as he always did.' She gave his arm a squeeze.

Reaching where the chopper was parked, he helped her up and into the passenger seat, and then raced around the front and jumped in beside her.

'I love the days I get to have this as my office window.' He passed her a headset.

'I bet, and why wouldn't you?' She slipped it on and positioned the microphone.

'Let's get this show on the road, shall we?' Popping his headset on, he began flicking switches.

Vibrations pulsed through her as the rotors whirred to life. The deep whop-whop echoed all around them, stirring up a cloud of dust. Pressing her feet into the floor, she felt her stomach lurch as they quickly rose into the sapphire blue sky. The landing pad dropped swiftly away, as did her stomach.

'You good?' Connor's husky voice crackled within the headphones.

She nodded. 'Right as rain.' No way was she going to admit her heart was racing like a startled horse.

As Connor achieved altitude and levelled off, Samantha found herself totally lost in the view. Up here, they were truly alone. At peace. Perspective really was everything. Swooping over the top of a mountain, Connor dipped a little closer to the ground. The lines of the creeks and fences, the slope and rise of the hills: Gum Tree Gully was like an open book from this height. Seeing the countryside from above put a whole new scope on the vastness of the land she'd once ridden wild and free on horseback. It was awe-inspiring and timeless; she wanted to reach out, craving to touch every square inch of it. She yearned to grab the dirt and bury it inside of her, so she'd remember the feel of the country she was eternally connected to beneath her skin when she landed back on UK ground. Then, before she knew it, way too soon they were landing and she was surprised to find herself wobbly-legged when Connor helped her out and her feet hit the ground.

'That was great fun, thanks.' She smiled broadly.

'Good, I'm glad you enjoyed it.' He brushed her windblown hair from her face and tucked it behind her ears. 'You ready for that swim now?'

'Mm-hmm, I sure am.' All she wanted to do right now was kiss the heck out of him.

Ten minutes later, and Connor was stripped down to his board shorts, and man oh man, she was having a mighty hard time keeping her eyes from his tanned, muscular chest, and instead on the gleaming dam.

'Race you, Evans,' he said, his expression challenging.

Stripping her dress off, she tossed it onto the picnic blanket. 'You're on, Gunn.'

After running a few steps, with her laughter catching on the breeze, Samantha dived into the cooling water right alongside Connor. They were almost always in sync. Arms stretched out, she dived deeper, her feelings for Connor doing the exact same thing. And after touching the bottom, she rose to the surface and met with his spirited, encompassing gaze. They shared a long moment of silent connection as she treaded water, then with a hint of a smile, he disappeared back beneath the surface, only to emerge a few metres away from her. Samantha couldn't help but keep sneaking glances in his direction. Even though he was heart-stoppingly good-looking, this feeling she had for him went way beyond the flesh. After last night, she knew parts of herself had retreated so she wasn't left vulnerable, but that didn't mean she didn't still feel as strongly for him. On the contrary, she loved him all the more for having the strength to put the brakes on, to do the right thing, to love her the way she should be loved. Needing a moment to herself with the contemplation, she breathed in deep, allowing the support of the water to offer her buoyancy. As she floated aimlessly, peacefully, contentedly, the sunshine warmed her front, as the water cooled her back.

Her eyes closing, she sighed – this was living. She could do this all day long. Lost in her thoughts, she jumped when Connor's fingertips brushed against hers. She willingly embraced the hint of intimacy. Their touch was so simple, yet it was a momentous gesture. She knew then and there that she was done for. That he'd won her over good and proper. Her place was here, in Gum Tree Gully, with him. She just had to find a way to make it so, sooner rather than later.

'You enjoying yourself, Sammie Samsung?'

Turning her cheek to him, she cleared her throat in a bid to free her voice, but he beat her to it.

'Because to me, it looks like you're having the time of your life.' His voice had deepened and his usual husky rasp was more pronounced.

'You know what,' she rolled over and started treading water again, 'I *am* having the time of my life.' His smile enticed more of an explanation. 'I didn't know just how much I wasn't living, and how unhappy I was, until coming …' She swallowed down a lump of emotion. 'Home.'

'Home, hey?' His all-encompassing smile was wickedly sexy.

'Yes, home.' She liked the way it sounded, and how her heart and soul felt at peace when she said it.

'Well, as they say, Sammie, home is where the heart is.'

'Indeed, it is.' She swam towards him, and pecked a kiss on his cheek in passing. 'I'm starving, how about you?'

'I could eat the arse out of a cow, so yeah, pretty much the same.'

'You and your descriptions,' she said, laughing. 'They seriously crack me up.'

'Good, because I like seeing you happy.' He climbed back onto dry land beside her.

Watching him, dripping with water, his hair shaggy and his arresting gaze glued to her, Samantha was sure her cheeks were as red hot as her libido as they made their way over to the blanket, got comfy and dug into the goodies basket.

Grabbing two beers from the esky, Connor twisted the lids off, then passed one to her. 'To happiness and living to our heart's content.' He clinked his longneck with hers.

'Cheers to that.' Thirsty after devouring half a packet of salt and vinegar chips, she took a big glug, and then unintentionally burped.

'Wow, that was a beauty.'

'Pardon.' Her hand still over her mouth, she laughed, and then burped again. 'Ha, oops, always the lady.'

'More like always the wild child.' His smile turned deep and meaningful. 'Which is exactly how I like you to be, Sammie – yourself.'

'I like how I can be myself around you, and Shea and Jack, too.'

'That's because we all love you, and you know you're safe with us.'

Biting her bottom lip, she nodded. 'Very true.'

Connor offered her a knowing smile. Her heart fluttered, then flew. And she wasn't sure how it happened, but she lost all self-control the second his lips met hers. An odd but welcome sensation rushed over her, as if the ground was tilting, as if everything was shifting at last. Surrendering to him, she returned his passionate kiss. Every single kiss, stroke and touch felt as if he were lighting wildfires beneath her skin. Hot surges of desire rippled through her, rendering her powerless to his magnetism. The loud voice of reason that had been arguing with her was rendered speechless. Tangling his fingers in her hair, he possessively brought her closer to him, pressing his lips into the place her pulse beat wildly in her throat. Then, trailing his mouth downwards, he paused at the swell of her breasts hidden beneath the thin cotton of her dress. Her nipples hardened and pressed into the fabric, and oh how she longed for him to caress each one with his mouth. But he then sought her lips once more, and they swirled tongues until she could take no more because he made her feel brave and that made her feel reckless. And she loved the sensation.

She needed him.

Wanted him.

Craved him.

'Connor, make me yours, please, now,' she begged. 'I can't wait any longer.'

Silently, he slowly ran his hands up her arms, then slipped the spaghetti straps of her dress from her shoulders. Her bikini was next to be off with his help, leaving her blissfully defenceless to him. She rose to her knees, enticing a low growl from him. Now, it was his turn. He slipped off his singlet, and the sight of his burly chest impulsively brought her hands to the hard planes of his flesh, then down to the waist of his board shorts. Together, they hurried to get him as naked as she was. His desire for her was evident. But he didn't rush to satiate it. With the back of his fingers, he trailed a path from her cheek, tenderly over the scar the accident had left her with, down her neck, over her collarbone and to her breasts. Her nipples were so hard she ached even more for his touch upon each one. Bending his head, he met her lips and kissed her long and slow. Then, he eased her onto her back, and trailed his hot mouth over her sweetest of spots. His tongue flicked and savoured, quickly sending her to the brink of euphoria. Rising shudders made it almost impossible to breathe as she gripped the back of his head and moaned in absolute pleasure.

'You taste so sweet.' His deep, raspy voice drove her wilder.

'I want you, now,' she cried out.

He slid over the top of her, gazing at her in that certain way that made her feel so very safe and so very loved. They fitted together so seamlessly, their bodies melting into one another's. He brought his mouth to her breasts, his lips trailing around each nipple, before meeting with the pertness. Every stroke of his tongue was like a match striking a flame. She arched into him, silently begging for him to suck harder, to bite to the point of pleasure and pain, where she could teeter within his dominance. He honoured her pleas, and as he did so skilfully, her sharp intake of breath pierced through birdsong all around them. And then, finally, he slowly slid inside her and it felt euphoric, finally being at one with him. He stopped deep inside her, and for a few drawn-out moments, held her as she caught her breath. Clasping her legs around him, she urged him to move inside her again. They built the crescendo together, matching each other's pace. Connor gave her exactly what he knew she needed from him. She could feel the waves building as she clung to him, then she felt herself freefalling off the euphoric ledge where he had her hovering, her gasps echoing as his hardness complimented her softness, in every single way.

'Now that, you, everything was so … ahh, I'm a very happy man right now.' Connor pulled her in close, and she rested her head on his chest as she caught her breath. 'I love you, Sammie.'

'I love you so much, Connor.' Her voice was exactly the way he made her feel – softly tender.

Relaxing on her side, with his heart drumming against her cheek, Samantha looked past the line of noisy galahs sitting on the fence line, and out and over the landscape now aglow beneath the setting sun. Eleven years ago, she used to spend her days immersed within the arms of Mother Nature's finest works, and now she had immersed herself in this amazing man surrounded by Mother Nature's untainted beauty. The wide-open spaces here permeated a sense of freedom she'd never gotten to experience anywhere else in the world, and she was happy for it to be the place where she and Connor had reconnected on the deepest of levels.

Just up the ridge, hulking forms of cattle moved slowly down the hillside, and horses whinnied to one another from their neighbouring paddocks, and behind it all, the sun was no longer high in the sky. Soon enough, too soon in fact, the day would come to an end, which meant she only had two more to go before heading back to London. And the thought of leaving Connor, after making such sweet love, made her heart squeeze painfully tight. As she nestled in as close as she could to him, an involuntary sigh escaped her.

'The simplicity out here is wonderful, hey?' Connor said dreamily.

'It sure is.' She turned towards him. 'I'm going to miss the hell out of this.'

He smiled sexily. 'I'm going to miss the hell out of you.'

Her chest constricted. 'I'll miss you, too, a lot.'

'Well, then.' His lips lifted at the corners. 'Why don't you stay a little longer?'

'I really wish I could, but I'm afraid I don't have that luxury.' Her longing to stay there was overwhelming, but she had to get back, to sort her life out.

'That sucks.' Sadness shadowed his eyes. 'I can't stand the thought of having to say goodbye to you.'

'It won't be goodbye, Connor, it'll be see you soon.'

He cupped her cheek. 'Can you promise me that?'

She placed a hand on his chest and propped herself up a little. 'I promise.'

'That's good to know, but I really need to get some stuff off my chest, Sammie, and leave the outcome of it to you.'

'What is it, that you feel we should talk about?' Anxiety filling her when she saw his look of apprehension, she sat up, and after tugging her dress back on, crossed her legs.

'Quiet a lot, actually, but I honestly don't know where to start.' The hush seemed endless as Connor followed suit and tugged his shorts on.

With them now sitting opposite each other, she drew in a breath. 'I want to make this work, Connor, so please, talk to me.'

'Me too, but I don't know how to say what I need to.' His next words caught and he cleared his throat. 'There's things you need to know about before you make promises of forever to me.'

'What in the hell are you saying, Connor?' She fought to hold back tears.

He dragged in a deep breath. 'I don't think you're going to want me, once you know the truth.'

Nausea swirled in her stomach. This couldn't be happening. Not after they'd just made beautiful, sweet, profound love. 'What aren't you telling me, Connor?'

He sucked in a sharp breath. 'Things that you're not going to like, one little bit.'

For a moment she was speechless, but then she gathered her frayed nerves and put what she did know into perspective – she loved him, he loved her, they could get through anything, surely? 'Right, well, now's your chance to come clean, or clear the air, or whatever it is you need to do, so we can hopefully move past this.'

Connor's lips pressed together, and closing his eyes, he slowly shook his head.

She felt exposed, and at the mercy of him, and she hated how vulnerable that made her feel. 'Well, come on then, please don't leave me hanging here like this.' She held her breath as she waited for his reply.

He wrung his hands together. 'I'm not so sure if I can be the man to give you what you want.'

'My god, that's not telling me a thing, Connor,' she huffed. 'We can't be together if you're keeping things from me, because that makes you a liar in my opinion, and liars are the lowest of the low, so please, talk to me.' Her tone was a mixture of frustration and anguish.

A mixture of emotions swept over his face – her scorn, fuelled by hurt, had reached her target. And she instantly regretted being so cranky. She went to speak again to somehow soothe him but stopped herself. Maybe, if she gave him a moment to catch his breath, he might then fill that silence and open up to her. Biting her trembling bottom lip, she tucked her shaky hands beneath her legs. And not long after, just as she'd hoped, her silence urged him on.

'Okay, here goes.' He heaved a weighty breath. 'There's no easy way to say this, so I'll just go ahead and say it straight.' His gaze was filled with anguish. 'I can't have children, Sammie.'

Shock slapped her. 'What do you mean?'

His Adam's apple bobbed as he took his time replying. 'I'm infertile.'

Thunder struck her heart, hard and brutal, and her stomach twisted into tighter knots. 'But, how?'

'I found out I had testicular cancer, and had to have both removed last month.' He dropped his head into his hands. 'I'm so sorry I never told you before now.'

Concerned for him, heartbroken for him, she squeezed past the sting of what felt like betrayal. 'But you're okay now, right?'

'I am, yes.' He sniffed, blinking faster.

'I'm so sorry that you've gone through something so terribly scary.' She took a moment to gather her thoughts – all she cared about right now was that he was going to live. And then a thought struck her, giving her hope. 'Don't they offer for you to freeze your sperm when you go through something like this?'

He nodded, inhaling sharply. 'They did, and I agreed to it at first, but I had a moment of recklessness … maybe spurred on by my rage at losing what made me a man, or at least that's what I thought at the time. So I went and signed forms to destroy my samples.' His voice broke and he roughly ran a hand through his hair. 'I was stupid, making a decision in anger, but there's nothing I can do about it now.'

Totally blindsided, Samantha had no idea how she felt about all this. 'I'm relieved to know you're going to be okay.'

'Thanks.' He paused. 'Does this change how you feel about me?'

'Honestly, I think I need a little time to let it settle.' She felt awful. 'Sorry, Connor, but I have to be honest with you.'

'I understand.' He gave her hand a squeeze. 'There are other ways to have kids, you know.'

'Yes, there are, but until now, I've never really thought about things like that. I've always just imagined having children with my husband, you know, the natural way.'

His expression was painfully sad. 'I get it, it's a lot to take in.'

She remained silent but offered him a sad smile in return. 'It doesn't change the fact that I love you, deeply, just so you know.'

'I admire you taking it like you have, Sammie, your kind heart is one of the many reasons I love you so much.' He paused, holding her gaze as he sucked in a shuddering breath. 'But that's not the only thing I need to talk with you about.'

'Oh my goodness, Connor, there's more?' Her quick reply was instinctive.

'Yes.' His forehead puckered, and for a few short moments, he closed his eyes. And when he unlocked the windows to his soul, and looked her way, there were tears building. 'I'm the reason your parents were on the road that night.'

'But how could you be?' Baffled, she shook her head. 'You were with me right up to when I got in the car with your brother.'

'Yes, I was, but then I called them as soon as you left and told them how you'd just gotten in the car with Angus, and that I – we, me and Shea and Jack – were concerned for your safety.'

'You did that.' It felt like someone had just kicked her in the stomach. 'And Jack and Shea know about this, too?'

He halted, as if not wanting to answer, and she held her hands up. 'Don't, just stop talking.' His browbeaten look told her everything she needed to know. 'I can't take much more.'

Liars, all of them!

Anger bubbled and rose from the murky depths of her heart, old anger, new anger, all of which felt shocking and red raw as she came back to earth with an almighty thump. She felt the sudden sting of tears, but quickly blinked them back.

'We were only doing what we thought was best, Sammie, and I was the one that eventually made the call. Shea was on the fence with it all, to be honest.' He was rushing his words now, his desperation evident. 'Your dad said he was going to go and find you, and take you home.' His voice broke, and tears ran down his cheeks. 'Please, try and understand I only did it because I loved you, and was worried for you, getting into a car with Angus in the state he was.' He reached out to her. 'Sammie, please.'

Bitterly hurt, and deeply disappointed, she jumped to her feet, well out of his reach. 'You've gone and done the one thing I told you is make or break for me; you've lied to me, and not only this trip home, but for years, Connor.' Her hands came to cover her quivering mouth. 'And to think that Shea and Jack knew this the entire time, and kept it from me too.'

'Sammie, no, please don't think of it like that.' He stood, took a step towards her, but when she took a step back, he stopped short. 'I was the one that made the call. Shea was trying to talk me out of it as I dialled your dad's number. And we, I, didn't tell you, because none of us thought it would offer any relief, and it certainly wasn't going to change anything.'

'You all kept it from me.' Stabbing her chest with her finger, she roared every word as the solid ground she'd been standing on with him gave way, and she once again felt adrift in a choppy sea. 'And no matter how you spin it, or turn it inside out, an omission is choosing to lie.' The waves of hurt intensified, crashing over her. 'I'm going to go, and don't you dare try to follow me.'

'But...' He reached for her.

'No, I don't want to hear any more.' Brushing past him, she headed down the pathway, towards the farmhouse, where she could get in her car and get the heck out of there.

'Sammie, please, wait.'

She ached to turn back to him, and run into his arms for the comfort she so needed, but how could he be the one to console her, when he was the one who'd just caused her heart to break in two? Sobs filled with anger and regret and heartbreak broke from her as she stormed away from him. The time between getting to the hire car and driving home was a haze. Arriving at the homestead, she ran for the safety of the house, needing, wanting, desperate to be locked away from this horrible world, this horrible place. Wrapping her arms around herself, she slid against the wall until she was sitting on the floor, her knees cuddled to her. Thank god Shea and Jack weren't here right now because she wouldn't be able to be in the same room as them. She was going to try and change her return ticket so she could leave as soon as possible, because she didn't want to see either of them before she left. This was going to take some time, and London would give her the time and space she needed to try and move past it. If she ever could. For now, she couldn't wait to leave Gum Tree Gully, and put as much distance between herself and Connor, Shea and Jack as she possibly could.

CHAPTER 21

Her eyes flying open, but unable to move, Samantha was left with the lingering sense of having been Connor Gunn's wife. She could smell the casserole in the oven, could hear their little girl singing as she painted at the breakfast bar, could feel his arms slipping around her waist as he came up behind her and placed his lips against her cheek. Then, in a heartbeat, she was making her way down a hallway, towards a bathroom. Thunder rumbled overhead, and the floorboards gave way beneath her bare feet. Freefalling, with arms flailing, she landed on hot, sun-baked earth. More thunder boomed, deafening this time, and a bright crack of lightning quickly followed, striking the ground way too close for her comfort. She started running as fast as she could, to get to safety before the storm hit, but there wasn't a building in sight. The surrounding trees shook branches at her, their gnarled limbs scratching and tearing at her skin. She tried to cry out, but the wild wind was whipping every word, every breath, from her lips. Then her left foot hit air, and so did her right. She frantically grappled for the edge of the ravine, her fingernails lifting as she clawed for her life. Heat scorched the soles of her feet. She dared a glance beneath her, her fear escalating to absolute terror as flames of a roaring bushfire grasped for her. The black billowing smoke suddenly engulfed her, and she tried to hold her breath but she was suffocating. And then her fingernails lifted, and she was falling, burning, screaming, dying.

Samantha woke drenched with sweat and kicking the sheets from her. Realising she'd been having a nightmare, she sat up and fought to drag in breath. The ceiling fan's blades were still and the hum of the air conditioner had ceased. The electricity was clearly on the blink. Fanning her face, she climbed from the tousled bed, taking a second to balance herself as the thump of a hangover arrived behind her temples. She needed to get outside, where she could breathe. Stumbling, she bent to pick up the two empty bottles of wine she'd dropped from the bed at some ungodly hour. Catching her reflection in the mirror, she grimaced. She looked like death warmed up, and then some. Burning the candle at both ends was proving she wasn't made of steel.

And all for what?

She'd worked her guts out to be as successful as she was, and done everything she could to build a life that had all gone to shit. And now, just as she'd thought she might have finally found her way, her life had blown up again. She should've known that her world was going to be upended by coming back here – putting it the right way up was going to be a near impossible task. But she was going to have to dig her heels in and brace herself for returning to London, because that was where her life was.

Whether she liked it or not.

But for now, she was stuck here. After calling the airlines she'd learnt she couldn't change her ticket. There were no seats left. She'd have to ride the storm out, until she could leave this godforsaken place. Maybe, tomorrow, she'd go to Cairns and stay in a hotel until her flight, so she didn't have to see anyone again. Not Connor. Not Shea. Not Jack. Yes, that's what she was going to do. But first, she needed to sober up, and make sure she was ready to drive the four hours back to the coast. After a quick glance out the window at the softly lit blue sky, she'd decided a ride might be just the thing to blow the remnants of Connor from her soul.

Undressing from her pyjamas, she grabbed clothes from the pile she was yet to fold, and tugged on a pair of jeans and a T-shirt. The house was unnervingly silent as she made her way down the steps and out the back door. After a sleepless night, filled with regrets and rage and heartache, her tears had done nothing to help ease the anguish of her loved ones' lies.

Twenty minutes later, Garth's hooves pounded the earth beneath her. It had seemed like a good idea at the time, riding him bareback through the scrublands, but with the weather changing its mood as ominous clouds ravenously swallowed up the blue sky she'd awoken to, and longed to be beneath in a bid to try and rid the deep ache from her heart, she began to question her hasty decision. Both she and Garth startled as a strike of lightning was followed by a crack of thunder. Then the heavens split, and rain poured down in sheets, the wild wind whipping each drop painfully against her exposed skin. Then something shot out of the bushland, and came straight for them, barely missing Garth's front hooves. She only caught a glimpse of the wild boar as it bolted. Seconds passed like minutes. Whinnying, Garth reared up in fright.

'Nooooo.' Her cry jarred as the horse thudded back to the ground, only to rear again.

Grabbing handfuls of mane, she fought to stay on Garth's back. But she couldn't hang on tight enough. Fear fired into the pit of her stomach. She was slipping. She had to jump, or risk being trodden under the horse's feet. A split second later and she was flailing through the air like a rag doll, with the ground rapidly approaching. Tensing for the fall, she felt the impact knock every bit of air from her lungs. Immediate fire tore along her back and burst into her legs. Hooves thudded dangerously close beside her. Gasping for her next breath, she tried to lift her head, but couldn't. Agony had her pinned to the ground, and unable to drag enough air into her dazed lungs. Excruciating pain shredded the edges of the dark mist engulfing her. Then the ground gave way beneath her, and she was falling, slipping, spinning sickeningly into a deep dark world.

* * *

Sitting at his desk, with his mind on one thing, and one thing only – the very woman who owned his heart, yet he'd gone and unintentionally broken hers – Connor ran his fingers through his ruffled hair and frowned at the computer screen. If only he could focus, but thoughts of Samantha and what happened the day before kept stealing his attention. With his head pounding, the figures were all starting to blur into one. Taking a moment, he rubbed his temples as he looked out the office window. Brooding dark clouds had rolled in thick and fast from the coast and had made true on their promise. After a week of blazing hot skies and ever-increasing humidity, Gum Tree Gully could do with the heavy shower of regenerating rain.

Behind him, the door creaked and a gust of hot air filled the air-conditioned room. Looking over his shoulder, he smiled. 'Hey, Mum, I didn't hear you pull up.'

'So I see.' Her smile was a little tight. 'If I was a thief, I would've gotten all the loot, and hightailed it out of here without you even knowing.'

'Ha, what loot?' He looked to the bunch of envelopes clutched in her hands. 'Thanks for grabbing the mail while you were in town.'

'Not a problem.' Walking straight over to his desk, she placed one in particular beside his empty coffee cup. 'This one's for you.'

He picked it up and looked at it. The front of the envelope was blank, as was the back. 'What is it?'

'Open it, and you'll find out.'

He noted the seal was opened. 'I see you've already read whatever it is.' He looked to her. 'Should I be worried?'

'Yes, and no, no and yes.'

'Bloody hell, Mum, now I *am* worried.'

She sunk to the arm of the single-seater couch, her strained expression a picture of concern. 'I should have told you about this before now, but I was afraid you'd be terribly angry with me, and I wanted to give you time to heal after your operation, you know, to get back on your feet and back to normal.'

'Okay.' Now he was positively terrified. 'Are you sick?'

'No, nothing like that, it's more to do with what happened between you and Sammie yesterday, which I appreciate you coming to me with, so you didn't have to deal with it all on your own.' She blinked quicker, folded her hands together and then took a slow, deep breath. 'You know how we filled the paperwork out before your operation?'

He shook his head. 'What paperwork?'

'The forms that were to arrange the termination of your sperm bank.'

'Yes.' He stopped breathing, hoping, praying, she was about to tell him what he wanted to hear. 'What did you do, Mum?'

She grimaced. 'I never posted it.'

'You what?' There was a god, and he'd answered his prayers.

'I'm so sorry, Connor, but I felt you were making a massive mistake, and I only did what I felt best at the time.' She took a breath and went to continue.

'You don't need to explain, Mum.' He leapt from the chair and dragged her into his arms. 'Thank you, for not listening to me.'

'Oh, son, I'm so happy you're not mad with me.' Crying with relief, she cupped his cheeks. 'Now, you go and beg that amazing woman for her understanding about the night of her parents' terrible accident, because she loves you, very much.'

Connor's buoyed heart sank. 'I'm not sure she's ever going to forgive me for keeping it from her, Mum.'

'Sammie's got a good heart, so I know she will, Connor. Just don't give up on her, and your relationship, too easily, okay.' She smiled though her tears. 'Sometimes you have to fight for what you want in this life, because the things that are worth the fight usually work out in the end.'

'You really think she and I can work through all of this?'

'I most certainly do, but if I'm wrong, and you can't work through this, you'll never work at marriage, because it's a tough gig and only the strong survive it. So even though this is an almighty challenge, it's a good sign of what's to come.'

'You always give great advice, Mum.' Buoyed by his mother's firm belief, he folded the forms and tucked them into his shirt pocket, then grabbed his hat from the chair and tugged it on. 'I'm going to head over to Shea and Jack's, so wish me luck.'

'You don't need it.' She waved him off. 'Now go, time's wasting.'

After driving like a bat out of hell and skidding to a stop at the front of the homestead, Connor was dismayed when his knocks on the front door weren't answered by Sammie. Grabbing his mobile, he tried calling her, five times, but every ring went unanswered. He could feel the paperwork in his top pocket, burning a hole right through his shirt, and his heart. He realised he should have called her straight away, but with his emotions running riot, he'd just wanted to get to her and speak to her face to face, heart to heart. Wandering around to the back of the house, he let himself in the back door.

'Sammie, are you here?'

Silence was his only response.

'Sammie!'

Nothing.

His stomach somersaulted – something wasn't right.

Racing up the stairs, he was met with a tousled bed and two empty wine bottles on her dresser. A pile of clothes was on the floor, and her pyjamas were strewn on the bedside table as if flung there. Had she gone for a run? A ride? She'd be in trouble with either, out in this wild weather. His heart in his throat, he raced back downstairs, outside, and noted her hire car was still there as he headed over to his LandCruiser. Back behind the wheel, he revved it to growling life and fishtailed as he took off down the gravel drive, towards the stables. A quick scan of the round yard and beyond confirmed that Shea's horse, Garth, was missing.

Oh god, please let her be safe.

A bumpy drive across the rain-swept paddock led him to the ridgeline, where he'd have the best view. There, he pulled to a stop, deciding whether to turn left or right, when Garth bolted past him. Saddleless.

Shit!

Turning in the direction the horse came from, he found Sammie at the top of the rise, face down, her limbs sprawled.

'Oh my god, Sammie.' He leapt from the four-wheel drive, ran towards her lifeless form and fell to his knees at her side. 'Sammie, please, stay with me.' His world spun. This couldn't be happening. He couldn't lose her now, not like this. 'Please, God, no.'

What if she'd broken her back, or her neck? What if she were …? He couldn't bear to think it.

Reluctant to touch her, for the fear of both not feeling her pulse or moving her when he shouldn't, he guardedly brought his fingers to where he prayed there was a beat, at the same time terrified he'd feel nothing but cold flesh beneath his fingertips. He held his breath as he sought her wrist out. Warmth met his touch, as did a slow, steady pulse. His heart leapt in response. Then her hand flinched. And her moans were muffled. She started making a gurgling noise. That's when he noticed the pool of blood beneath her matted hair.

'Don't move, Sammie.' He carefully brushed her hair from her cheek. 'I'm here, you're safe, I've got you, okay.' She couldn't die. He wouldn't allow it.

Taking his mobile from his back pocket, he dialled 000. 'My girlfriend, she's come off her horse, and she's hurt, real bad.'

The responder asked him questions, which he answered as quickly as he could. 'Please, hurry.' Resting a shaky hand against her cheek, he blinked back hot tears. If this were it for her, he'd never, ever, forgive himself.

* * *

He called me his girlfriend … It was Samantha's very first thought when she began to rise from the murky depths the painkillers had sent her to. Blinking, she wondered if the shimmery images were an angel. Had she died and gone to heaven?

'Sammie.' Connor's deep voice reverberated through her heart, enticing it to beat faster.

Her reply was muffled by something covering her nose and mouth. She wanted to reach out and touch him, but her arms wouldn't move.

Connor's hand came to her shoulder. 'Don't try to talk yet.' His touch soothed her. 'You've come off a horse, and you're in the hospital. But you're going to be okay.'

She was going to be okay? Was this their second chance?

The beeping of a heart monitor swam into her consciousness and became louder, crisper. When she finally got her heavy eyelids to open and her blurry gaze fell upon his handsome face, she knew without a doubt that she wanted to be way more than just a girlfriend to him. She didn't care that they couldn't have children. She didn't care that he hadn't told her about calling her father – it had been done with good intentions. She just wanted him. Them. Forever.

His blue eyes fastened on her and burnt right into her soul. 'Everything's going to be okay.'

With him by her side, she knew his words were true.

A nurse bustled beside the bed. 'Your vital signs are all looking good.' Her hand was cool on her forehead. 'I'm going to go and get the doctor now, back in a minute, okay?'

It felt like mere moments until the doctor arrived and after checking her over, the elderly physician smiled. 'You're a very lucky woman, Miss Evans.'

Thinking of how much worse her prognosis could have been, Samantha thanked the powers that be for saving her from such a fate.

'You're going to need complete bed rest for a week or two, which includes no flying back to London in the meantime, but then you can return to normal everyday activities.'

She found it hard to form any words, but Connor did it for her. 'Thank you, for everything, doctor.' His beautifully familiar voice was calming, soothing.

The doctor brought his hand to Conner's shoulder. 'Don't speak of it, Connor, all in a day's work.'

She steeled herself, while trying to gather the strength, and the courage, to say what she should have before all this had happened. 'I want to be with you, Connor, always.' Every word hurt physically, but she didn't care.

'You do?'

'Yes.' And she meant it, without a second of hesitation.

His look reached in and touched every fibre of her soul, placing all her broken pieces back together in a single breath. This was it. He was the man she'd been longing for, searching for, and he'd been right there, in her life, waiting for her to open her eyes and see him, all along. As contentment and calm filled her, she felt drug-fuelled sleep pulling her back under, and as much as she wanted to stay here, awake, with the love of her life, she simple didn't have the strength to fight it.

EPILOGUE

Two years later...

Watching the ultrasound screen, her breath held, Samantha clutched Connor's hand tightly. He offered her a silent look of encouragement, and she adored him for it. She knew, even though he hadn't said as much, that he was as nervous as she was, if not more so. This was their final try. There was nothing left in the bank. There was so much weighing on this very moment.

'Well.' The radiographer turned to them from where he had been squinting into the screen. 'It looks to me like you're having two healthy babies.'

Samantha gasped. 'Twins, are you serious?'

His smile widening, the man nodded. 'Yes, very.'

'Oh my god, Connor, did you hear that, we're having twins!'

'Yes!' Conner nodded. 'I didn't think you could make me any happier, but you just have.' Blinking teary eyes, he cupped her cheeks. 'I love you so much, Sammie.'

'I love you, too, with all my heart and soul.'

The sonographer stood, took off his gloves and tossed them into a bin. 'I'll let you get cleaned up and meet you out the front.'

'Thank you.' After gently wiping her belly with tissues, Connor helped her up. 'Come on, you three, let's get you all home.'

Samantha brought a hand to her belly, to their babies, and smiled. 'Us three, hey, I love that.' Could this man get any more sweet, any more loveable?

That afternoon, after telling Joyce the great news, and now squished up against Connor while leaning against the banister of their little farmhouse, Samantha gazed out and over their land. 'I honestly feel like the luckiest woman alive.'

'Ditto, except for the woman part.' Chuckling, Connor wrapped an arm around her. 'Tomorrow, we can go into town and get the paint for the nursery, and while we're out, we could call into Jack and Shea's and let them know they're going to be godparents, but for now, I just want to hold my fiancée real close.'

Samantha nodded. 'I like the sound of all of that, my love.'

Snuggling into him, she felt peace and joy and safety, and so much love she could have burst. All along, they'd been meant to find their way back to each other. And now she was home with him. Forever. With not only one, but two beautiful babies for them to love and raise in this majestic countryside they called home. She couldn't possibly be any happier.

ACKNOWLEDGEMENTS

A wholehearted cheers to my awesome team at HQ/HarperCollins Australia. I truly feel enormously blessed to be published by the wonderful group of creative souls you all are! To Rachael Donovan, you've led the way for me, guiding me, encouraging me, supporting me, I have so much to be grateful for when it comes to you. My career wouldn't be what it is, without you. To my meticulous editors, Rochelle and Kate, thank you! You've both helped me to make *Gum Tree Gully* the very best it can be. My marketing manager, Sarana, you're a superstar and such a pleasure to work with. And there are so many more of you who work passionately behind the scenes, and I appreciate everything you do for my books, from the bottom of my romance-loving heart.

To YOU, my cherished reader, thank you for being with me on my evolving writer's journey. To know I can touch your hearts, from the confines of my office, be it to make you laugh out loud, sigh with satisfaction, or dare I say it, make you cry along with my characters, means the absolute world to me. I hold dear the emails and messages I receive from you, telling me how I've given you time to yourselves, helped you through some tough times, or simply added some excitement to your days. Whether you have been with me for the past fifteen years, or jumped aboard the Mandy Magro train somewhere along the way, I appreciate each and every single one of you, for supporting me by delving into the pages of my books. ☺

Until my next book has you hiding from the kids, or sneaking in some reading at work, saying 'stuff it' to the housework, or whiling away a lazy day while you lose yourself in its pages, remember to kiss like you mean it, love like you've never been hurt, dance to your own beat, scatter kindness everywhere, do what makes you happy, and most importantly of all, keep smiling and dreaming, always.

Mandy xx

talk about it

Let's talk about books.

Join the conversation:

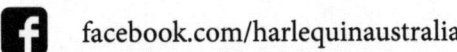 facebook.com/harlequinaustralia

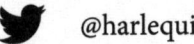 @harlequinaus

 @harlequinaus

harpercollins.com.au/hq

If you love reading and want to know about our authors and titles, then let's talk about it.